Chapters of Life

Tina K. Burton

CROOKED CAT

Printed for Crooked Cat by Createspace

First Green Line Edition, Crooked Cat Publishing Ltd. 2013

Discover us online:
www.crookedcatpublishing.com

Join us on facebook:
www.facebook.com/crookedcatpublishing

Tweet a photo of yourself holding
this book to **@crookedcatbooks**
and something nice will happen.

To Paul, with love, A&F

About the Author:

Tina started her working life as an assistant buyer in the purchasing department of a big television manufacturer, but then changed direction and trained as a youth counsellor. She has also worked with homeless people, and in the funeral profession, which she gave up eight years ago to write full time.

She feels that her previous jobs have given her an insight into people's emotions and she is able to draw on that for her characters. She writes short stories, articles, fillers and letters, which have been published in various magazines and newspapers in the UK and overseas.

Chapters of Life is her first novel. She is currently working on the sequel, Pieces of Cake, as well as a thriller, Born to Love Me, and has ideas for a romcom set around a dating agency.

She lives close to her family in Devon with her husband, Paul, where she likes to go for walks across Dartmoor.

Acknowledgments:

Thank you to my husband, Paul, for your support love and patience, and your unwavering belief that I had what it takes.

Chapters of Life

Chapter One

As Jo put the tarot cards she'd been using back into their silk lined box, her best friend Clare, who was also her boss, entered the bookshop annexe with a cup of tea for her.

"Another satisfied customer?" Clare asked, putting the drink on the table.

"Mm," Jo replied, "the cards she chose signified emotions and feelings. She's meant to be getting engaged soon, but likes someone else and isn't sure what to do about it. She said the cards have helped her make a decision now."

"Well done. That's the third reading this week, isn't it?"

"Yeah, and I have another one booked for tomorrow."

Jo had been reading the cards for years, but was still amazed at their accuracy. People often asked her how they worked, but she had no idea really, she just knew they did.

"Is it busy out there?" she asked, nodding towards the main area of the shop.

"Not too bad, quiet enough for me to have a ten minute break with you," Clare smiled and pulled out a chair.

Jo sipped her tea and said, "If anyone had told me before you came for that tarot reading, that I'd leave my job in the funeral profession to help run a bookshop, I'd have said they were mad. In fact, I'd have bet them every penny I had it wouldn't happen."

Clare grinned. "I still don't know why I asked you to join me, you were a complete stranger. At that point I didn't even know myself if it was a venture worth pursuing, which was why I came for the reading in the first place."

"I knew though. As soon as you walked in the room, I had a premonition that I'd go into business with you."

"You're weird," Clare said, wrinkling her nose.

"Hey," Jo pulled a hurt expression, "no I'm not, I'm just different."

"You're that alright," Clare said and moved out of the way as Jo went to slap her. "We're like chalk and cheese, I'm quiet and boring..."

"Clare, you are not boring!"

"Okay maybe not boring, but I was always a loner. I didn't want to do anything other than read books. My parents got so frustrated with me at times, because I never wanted to join in family days out. I preferred to stay in my room and read." Clare thought back to some of the arguments she'd got into with her mother. "Mum almost had a fit when I got a job as a librarian. But Dad stuck up for me and Mum eventually agreed that as long as I was happy, that was all that mattered."

"Aww, I love your mum," Jo said with a fond smile.

"She likes you too. It's amazing how well we all get on, even though we're nothing alike."

Whilst Clare was studious and quiet, Jo was gregarious and outgoing, but they balanced well and it made a good working relationship, as well as a great friendship.

"I do know I'm different," Jo admitted, "but at least I understand now that only a few people have psychic ability. I used to think it was something everybody did. When I realised they didn't, I thought there was something wrong with me."

"Aww, poor you, that must have been quite scary," Clare sympathised.

"I wasn't scared, but I thought I might have been a bit crazy. I'd always had premonitions – as far back as I can remember, a thought would pop into my head and later come true. How was I to know other people didn't do the same thing? It was only when I got a bit older that I realised it wasn't 'normal'." Jo made quote marks with her fingers.

"Was there nobody you could ask about it?"

"Only my grandma, and she did try to explain it all to me."

Jo had been really close to her granny and could talk to her about anything.

"What's wrong with me?" she'd asked one day, after explaining about the thoughts that came true.

Her grandmother had laughed. "Nothing's wrong with you, darling. My dear mother had the same ability. You're psychic, just like she was. You may not understand it now, but in time, you'll think yourself blessed to have such a gift."

At that time, Jo hadn't thought so.

She didn't like getting 'messages from beyond', especially when they were about bad things, like the time her mother's friend had called round for a chat. Jo had told Mrs Tomlin she was sorry her dog Benjy had died.

"But he hasn't," Mrs Tomlin said with a worried look, "Benjy's at home in his basket."

"I'm sorry, Jo must have had a dream or something and got a bit confused," her mother had tried to explain, shooting Jo an angry look.

Three days later when Mrs Tomlin opened her front door, Benjy had run out into the road, straight under the wheels of a car, and been killed instantly.

The shaken woman had told Jo's mother she thought it best if they didn't have anything to do with each other again.

Jo's mother had been furious. "In future, for God's sake keep your premonitions to yourself instead of going around upsetting people! We're going to end up being victimised," she'd said, afraid of repercussions from people who might think her daughter a freak.

In time, Jo learned to deal with her ability. She sometimes told her family and close friends the things that she saw, but she often kept her omens, as she called her premonitions, to herself.

When she was twenty, she bought a pack of tarot cards and

spent hours studying each one until she'd learnt their meaning. Then she put adverts in local shop windows offering her services as a tarot reader in the evenings and weekends. Through word of mouth, and because she didn't charge extortionate amounts – Jo believed if you had a gift you shouldn't abuse it by ripping people off – she soon built up a regular client list.

Now, nine years later, she still read the cards and still had premonitions, although not as often as when she was young. In a way, she was glad they were lessening.

"Did you always want your own bookshop?" she asked Clare now.

"Yep. Don't laugh, but when I was a little girl, I'd line up all my books and pretend it was a bookstore. I'd then walk my dolls up and down, as if they were customers."

Jo tried not to laugh, but couldn't. "I'm sorry, Clare," she said, wiping her eyes, "it's the image I have of you as a little girl. Blimey, you were serious even then."

"I think I was born serious," Clare sighed. "That's why Mum likes you so much, she thinks some of your fun-loving nature will rub off on me."

"Well, I like you just the way you are, we work well together, like..."

"Yin and yang?" Clare laughed. "Yes, you've said that before, only a few times." She got up and gave Jo a hug. "I'm so glad I came for that tarot reading and I'm delighted you agreed to go into business with me."

"Well, I know enough about my omens to take notice when I get one." Jo smiled.

"Hmm. I still can't believe how smoothly everything went, from the idea germinating in my mind, to actually opening Merrilies. It all happened so easily."

"Things happen for a reason, Clare. I truly believe our lives are mapped out and we're supposed to meet certain people and take certain paths."

"So I'm stuck with you then? Oh great!" Clare laughed.

This time Jo did playfully slap her.

"And I love how you came up with the bookshop name. When you suggested Merrilies, I knew it was just perfect. I'm rubbish at names. When I was little, I called my hamsters Hammy because I couldn't think of anything else. I had three in succession, and they were called Hammy One, Hammy Two and Hammy Three."

Clare looked at her watch and headed for the door. "Right, back to the grindstone. Some new books have come in which need sorting out."

"I'll be there in two ticks," Jo said as she finished her tea. It *was* strange how everything had fallen into place, but Jo was long past questioning the oddities of life. She just accepted that things happened, and believed there was a reason for everything, even if she couldn't explain it.

Chapter Two

When Clare had walked into the room for her tarot reading, the premonition had surprised Jo. She'd been working in the funeral profession ever since leaving school, and didn't want to do anything else, but her other omens had all come true, so she didn't want to ignore it. Maybe her life needed a change and she was being guided in that direction. Clare's reading had been extremely positive, pointing to financial matters and business development, the achievement of goals and a lifelong dream coming to fruition. As she finished, Jo had said, "Whatever it is you want to do, go for it. You're thinking of starting up your own business, aren't you?"

"Yes! How on earth do you know that?" Clare asked, astounded.

"It's all there in the cards."

"But I didn't even hint at anything. Wow, that's amazing!"

Jo never asked her clients why they'd come for a reading, she just asked them to think about the issue they needed guidance over whilst shuffling the cards.

Jo had smiled at Clare's reaction and said, "I don't have any other clients tonight, would you like to stay for a cuppa and tell me all about it?"

"You bet. I've been dying to tell someone." Clare liked Jo, she'd felt comfortable with her straight away.

Later they went from tea to a bottle of wine, as Clare outlined her plans for a bookshop.

Jo became enthusiastic too and found herself offering some suggestions. "You could have a children's area with a little table and chairs, and do you know what would be really nice?"

"What?" Clare asked, pushing her glasses along her nose.

"A café. Only a small one, but whenever I go into a bookshop, I'd love to sit with a coffee after browsing through the books."

"Hey, that's a nice idea. I reckon between the two of us, we'd run a pretty good business." Clare looked a bit taken aback, as if she wasn't sure why she'd just said that, but then she added, "What do you think?"

"Yeah, maybe we would."

"I'm serious, Jo. Are you interested?"

"I dunno, Clare, there's a lot involved."

"I know that. I've got a house an aunt left me, which I rent out. The tenants are keen to buy it, as the mortgage will be less than they pay me in rent, so I'll have enough money to get started. I can get a small loan if I need more, I've already checked."

"So you've thought things through?"

"Oh God, yes! I've dreamed of owning my bookshop for years. I've already planned how to fund it. We'd just need to find suitable premises and everything."

"*We'd?* We hardly know each other, Clare, and I have a good job already. This is madness!" Jo said.

Clare frowned. "I know, but, oh this is going to sound stupid, I feel like I've known you forever." She took a deep breath and went on, "Yes, it's mad and I can't explain it, Jo, but something's telling me this is what should happen."

"Hey, who's meant to be the psychic one here?" Jo had laughed.

Jo decided to go along with her omen – they'd never been wrong before, and Clare was obviously picking up on the vibes – so she agreed.

***

Over months of planning, the women had become good friends. Jo liked Clare's seriousness and her quiet confidence, and Clare liked Jo's enthusiasm for everything.

As she'd be the owner, Clare had to do the majority of the work, but Jo helped as much as possible by scouring the papers and estate agents for property, and looking in *The Bookseller* magazine for second-hand fixtures and fittings.

Once they'd sorted out most of the details, they felt it was safe to tell their families and friends, who were pleased for them, if a little worried that things might not work out.

"I might have known this was something you'd do. You and your books!" Clare's mum said. "But I am *so* proud of you; I hope it works out well."

"We've got some money put away for a rainy day, you can have it to put into the business," her dad told her.

"Thank you, but keep your money. Take Mum on holiday or something. I want to do this myself. It's my project, and I'll be responsible for it. That way, if it all goes wrong, I haven't let anyone down. You understand, don't you?"

"Of course I do, pet, we're very proud of you. But I can help look for premises. I've got that mate whose son is an estate agent; I'll get him to look for any suitable property that's coming on the market."

"Thanks, Dad," Clare said, giving him a hug.

***

Jo's parents were concerned that she'd be giving up the good job she'd had for years, just to work in a bookshop.

"Mum, you know I got an omen saying I'd go into business with Clare, and you know they always come true. The cards predicted success in business and financial matters, and they are never wrong, so don't worry."

Jo's boss was sad to lose her and had already told her if things didn't work out, she could have her job back.

"I might be with you for a while yet," she said, trying to cheer him up. "We've still got to look for a suitable property."

But as luck would have it, they didn't have to wait long.

Chapter Three

Through Jo's contacts, the women discovered a building had become vacant in the high street of Bewford, a pretty Cotswold market town just a few miles from where Clare lived in Chipping Norton. Jo lived with her parents in Oxford, but had been thinking about moving out for a while. She decided that once they'd got the bookshop, she'd look for a small flat or apartment.

After visiting the potential building several times, they agreed it would be ideal. It was a large two-storey structure, so they could easily fit in everything they needed. The previous owner had died, and none of his family wanted to take over his antique business, so they'd put the property up for sale. There was still a lot to sort out, but it looked like Clare's dream was becoming a reality.

***

Numerous phone calls, meetings, headaches and months later, they stood on the pavement and watched the sign-writer put the name of their new business above the door.

Jo put her arm around Clare and hugged her. "We did it, a couple more weeks and we open to the public."

"And I love the name," Clare said, looking up at it with a smile.

"I think it's brilliant," Jo agreed.

They'd been talking about poetry one evening over a shared pizza and bottle of wine at Clare's flat, and had been amazed to discover that they both chose John Keats as their favourite poet.

"I just love '*Old Meg*', it was one of the first poems I read in literature at school," Clare said.

"Meg Merrilies, yeah, I like that too. Hey Clare, that's it, I've just found the name of the bookshop!" Jo shouted, slapping her leg in a theatrical manner.

"What, 'Old Meg'?" Clare wrinkled her nose.

"No, Merrilies. What do you think?"

"Merrilies. Merrilies," Clare tried the sound of it out loud. "Merrilies Bookshop. I love it, it's perfect."

"Just right for an upmarket place like Bewford, don't you think? God, we were so lucky to be the first ones to view the property," Jo said.

Clare laughed. "I can't believe we were looking for a property, and the company you worked for handled the funeral of the antique shop owner in Bewford! If that wasn't fate, I don't know what is."

"See, it pays to know who's recently died. Merrilies should do really well. Bewford gets loads of tourists, even during the winter, and a steady flow of local trade too. With the amount of advertising we've done, everyone should know about us. I think we're going to be a great success."

"I hope so. Let's have some more wine, I think we deserve it," Clare suggested.

She'd topped up their glasses from the second bottle and clinked hers against Jo's with a loud "cheers". Then the pair of them had got shamefully drunk and woke in the morning with horrendous headaches, vowing *never* to drink that much again.

***

On the day of the official opening, Jo and Clare arrived at the shop extra early to put any last minute touches in place.

Among the many people attending were their family and friends, a rep from the wholesaler they'd be using, a couple of local authors whose books were on display, and people from the local newspaper and radio station. The girls had advertised well and made sure as many people as possible knew about the opening.

Then came the moment Clare had dreamed of for years.

She took the scissors Jo held out to her, and, watched by all her friends, family and local media, she cut the big blue ribbon and proudly announced, "I now declare Merrilies well and truly open."

The newspaper's photographer took photos, then Jo popped the cork on a magnum of champagne and everyone toasted their future success.

With Jo's help, Clare had spent a lot of time and effort getting the shop exactly how she wanted it. Jo had a lot of creative ideas and a good eye for colour, whereas Clare was practical, logical, and thought of all the necessary things and space issues. Not that space *was* an issue. The shop was on two floors and, even with every book you could think of lining the shelves, it was still roomy and light.

Whilst Clare was busy talking to people, Jo mingled with the crowd, listening to their comments.

"Oh wow!" gasped a woman who had wandered into the annexe at the back of the shop, which was the "Mind Body & Spirit' section. "They're going to give tarot card readings. I'd love to have that done."

Jo smiled. That had been her idea, one which Clare loved.

They'd put a round table and two chairs in there, and Jo would give her readings by appointment. She'd charge twenty pounds per reading and half the proceeds would go to Merrilies. Clare *was* running a business after all.

"Look, Jo," Clare had said when they'd discussed it, "you're giving up your time and talent, so you should charge for it. Would you expect an artist to do a painting for nothing? No, and it's the same thing, so start charging properly."

"Okay, but if it interferes too much with my job here, I'll go back to doing readings at home in the evenings or on my days off. Deal?"

"Deal."

To the side of the Mind Body & Spirit annexe was a small lockable room, which the girls were going to use as their office. The staff room was upstairs, out of the way.

Jo listened to another customer praising the children's area. "This is good," the woman said to her husband. "It's about time the children's section was on the ground floor. Most shops don't seem to care about women having to struggle upstairs or into a lift with a pushchair."

That was exactly what Clare had said, so the children's area had been tucked under the stairs on the left of the shop. They'd placed a child-sized plastic table and matching chairs there for the kids to sit at and read the books.

At the front of the shop, one of the local authors was admiring his book, which was prominently displayed on the New Releases table. "I like this, people can see our books as they walk in the door," he said to the other author, who had just signed a copy of his own book for the newspaper photographer.

People seemed to be enjoying themselves, but Jo wondered if she ought to tell them where everything was. She clapped her hands and said, "Sorry, can I have your attention a moment? In case you're looking for something specific, it is all clearly marked, but just to help you, down here is fiction and non-fiction, biographies and autobiographies, gardening, crime, cookery, crafts, address books and diaries. You'll see over by the till, there are a couple of turntable racks with bookmarks on, and a stand with gift vouchers. We have two local authors here this evening, giving away free bookmarks. Do please have a chat with them and maybe buy a signed copy of their books. Upstairs, you'll find the reference section, history and military history, art and photography, language, travel and maps, business, finance and law, and education. We also have a small café in the corner, which will be serving hot and cold drinks and biscuits, but we hope to branch out into sandwiches and things later on. I know that's a lot to remember, so if you need anything, just ask." She took a deep breath and said, "Phew, that's the most I've said all evening." Everyone laughed.

*****

Initially, as with any new business, they had a good stream of customers. People were curious to see what the new bookshop was like.

"Oh Jo, do you think they'll come back after the interest has died down?" Clare asked, biting her bottom lip. "We've employed four people, but we might not be busy enough to keep them all, and I poached Stella from the library. I'll feel awful if I have to tell her we can't keep her on."

"Stop worrying, of course customers will come back. We're what this town's needed for ages. There's only that one small bookshop around the corner; other than that, people had to go out of town for their books. They'll come back," Jo placated her.

"I hope so. What worries me, is that so many people buy books in the supermarkets or have e-readers nowadays."

"But there's still nothing like browsing in a bookshop. We stock much more than the supermarkets, and our advantage over an online store is that people can pick up the books and flick through them."

"That's true," Clare said dreamily. "There's nothing like holding a book in your hands; looking at the cover, the smell, feel and the weight of it, the noise as you turn the pages."

"You're a nerd, has anyone ever told you that?" Jo said. Then she continued, "And, customers can read the first couple of sentences or flick through and read a page to see if they think they'll like it, you can't do that online."

"Well, you can download a sample for Kindle books."

"Clare, stop worrying. People still like paper books and they make great gifts."

"You're right, as usual," Clare said, before adding, "about the books, not about me being a nerd."

"You reckon!" Jo laughed.

***

They'd been open for several months when Jo had another idea.

"Clare, why don't we have a reading group? We could put an advert in the local paper and one in the window."

"That's a good suggestion, but where would they hold it?"

"Well, we have that space over there," Jo pointed to the right of the shop. "We could probably fit in a table and about five chairs, six at a push. Think about the publicity it could bring us, and it would get people into the shop buying books."

"Brilliant! I'm so glad I asked you to be my manager," Clare grinned. "But," she continued, "we'd have to make them *want* to join; maybe offer a discount or something. What about a fifteen percent discount each on the books they read?"

"That's generous, can we afford that much?" Jo asked.

"If they are going through books on a regular basis, yes, it would be worth it. Right, you contact the paper, I'll get Stella to make up an ad for the window."

Clare was delighted. Merrilies was already a popular shop; the addition of a reading group would hopefully make it even better.

Chapter Four

Felicity Hughes flicked through a celebrity magazine while her mother got ready for their shopping trip to The Designer Village at Bicester.

Felicity wanted a new pair of shoes because Rupert was taking her out on Saturday, and she didn't have any shoes to go with her recently bought pink dress.

"Darling, you have hundreds of pairs of shoes in your room upstairs, several of which are pink, won't a pair of those do?" Eleanor had said before going upstairs to change.

"Mummy, it needs to be the right shade of pink, you know that. And besides, I can't wear pink shoes and a pink dress; I'll look like a flamingo. No, I need a new pair of black shoes to co-ordinate with the black lacy shrug I'm going to wear."

"Okay, I need a new handbag anyway. We can stop for lunch in that Italian restaurant we like. You'd better make the most of it though; this is your last shopping trip, you're meant to be looking for a job," her mother admonished.

"Yes, but I don't know what I want to do yet."

"Felicity," Eleanor said with a sigh, "you've just spent three years at university getting your law degree. What was the point, if you're not going to do anything with it? You should have carried on and taken the Bar Professional Training Course."

"And put up with another year of study? I'm sick of studying! I only went to bloody university because Daddy kept on at me."

"Don't swear, Felicity!"

"But it's not fair, Mummy. If Dom hadn't gone off and become a doctor..."

"Your brother's a consultant, as you well know," Eleanor said.

"Whatever! If he hadn't disappeared to that hospital in Devon, and had studied to be a barrister instead, Daddy wouldn't have pinned all his hopes on me. I only went to Uni to please him."

"Dominic didn't want to study law; he's more suited in the medical profession. I thought you enjoyed law school."

"I enjoyed it at first and law's very interesting, but I really hated all the study. Uni's nothing like people think – all partying and having a good time – it's bloody hard work, well, law school was anyway. I've decided I'm going to do what *I* want from now on. I can't live my life for someone else, even if it is Daddy."

"And have you told your father this?" Eleanor asked.

"I tried the other day, and he started lecturing me about the amount of money he'd spent to get me a good education, and how all he ever wanted was someone to follow in his footsteps, *blah blah blah*. I lost my temper and told him to shut up."

"Felicity!"

"Well, he gets on my nerves. And to moan about the money he's *wasted*," Felicity made quote marks as she said this, "is just tight. I'll bloody well pay him back, if that's all he's concerned with. It's not as if we're poor, Daddy's rolling in it. You don't work; why doesn't he go on at you to find a job?"

"That's different and you know it."

"Why is it different? You swan around shopping and spending his money – you haven't worked since you met him," Felicity stated.

"I'm his wife. Besides, I take care of the house and the garden."

"Mummy, we have a maid and a gardener."

19

"Okay – well – don't I throw the most splendid dinner parties?"

"How can you say that? You get the caterers in!"

Eleanor laughed. "Felicity, it's just different with me, that's all. You're a young girl; you ought to be doing something with your life and fending for yourself. I agree with your father totally. Now are we going shopping or not?" And that was the end of the subject.

Felicity was in a grumpy mood after their conversation, and Eleanor felt guilty, so they made the most of their day out and spent a lot of money. But Edward Hughes was one of the best barristers around. He dealt with many high profile cases, including the occasional celebrity, and he earned a fortune. So his wife and daughter regularly hitting the shops didn't dent his bank balance much.

A few days later as Felicity sprawled on the sofa idly watching TV, she leafed through the local paper, and spotted an advert for 'Merrilies Reading Group'.

That's the bookshop that opened up last year in the high street, she thought. Hmm, I need something to do, and I've always enjoyed reading. She could impress her friends by dropping it into the conversation, "Oh, I belong to this reading group, you know."

She grinned delightedly. What a great idea. I'll pop along and see about joining. It might even get Daddy off my back for a while.

Feeling much happier, she went into the kitchen to make herself a skinny latte.

***

Michael King was reading the local paper during his lunch break. He made sandwiches in a factory, which distributed them to various outlets in the area.

He also saw the reading group advert and thought about

joining. As an avid reader, he'd been a frequent weekend visitor to Merrilies since it opened. They had a much better selection than the small bookshop he used to visit, and he liked the bright airy building. He often went upstairs for a coffee to while away a bit of time until he went home to enjoy one of his mum's delicious dinners.

Michael's parents had tried for years to have a baby. They'd almost given up, when, at the age of forty-five, his mother discovered to her delight that she was finally pregnant. From the moment he was born, his parents doted on him, and he'd grown into a real mummy's boy. At the age of twenty–seven, he hadn't yet had a relationship, and was still living with his parents.

A quiet, private man, he didn't socialise a lot, preferring to stay at home. But on the odd occasions he did go out, he never drank alcohol. He couldn't see anything enjoyable about spending your hard-earned cash getting so drunk you were ill and couldn't remember anything the next day. He had no time for that sort of thing, and he thought the people who did were stupid.

What Michael did enjoy, however, was playing tabletop battle strategy games, like Warhammer. He'd taken over his parents' dining room, and had a long table laid out with miniatures of trees, buildings and little soldier figures. He had a couple of friends who regularly came to play and they'd spend hours setting up their fantasy figures and planning battle strategies.

If he didn't visit Merrilies at the weekend, he'd trawl the model shops for new figures, which he then took home and painstakingly painted, ready to play with once they were dry.

His work colleagues thought him a bit of an oddball. Michael knew this, but wasn't too bothered. Sometimes he thought it would be nice if they included him in their conversations, but all they ever talked about were their nights out drinking anyway. They didn't seem to have any other life or hobbies.

Michael considered himself rather interesting. He was well-read – he had a variety of books, from political stories to criminal psychology – and he had what he thought was a fascinating hobby. But if you'd asked the people he worked with what they thought of him, they'd have said he was rather strange.

***

Graham Anderson paused outside Merrilies to see why the traffic had come to a standstill. He smiled at the little family of ducks crossing the road, mum proudly leading her five little ducklings. When they were safely across, the cars moved off again.

He took a few moments to look around at the quaint shops, the Olde Worlde Tea Room, the little stream where the ducks lived, and the square of green with benches where the elderly stopped to rest their legs and catch up on any gossip. It was a pretty place. He'd retired early two years ago, so now had time to appreciate things like this.

Suddenly having plenty of time on his hands, he'd started taking a daily walk or going for a drive and stopping somewhere pleasant for lunch. But he struggled with the loneliness of retirement. He'd gone from being the managing director of a successful company, enjoying business dinners, trips abroad and meeting all sorts of interesting people, to nothing. He didn't expect the solitude to affect him quite so much, which was why he went for a walk every day.

To get out, meet people, see what was going on in the Cotswold town, and maybe have a chat with anyone willing to pass the time of day, all staved off the ultimate boredom.

Graham turned his attention back to the bookshop window, and, spotting a notice, went inside.

He approached the till area where a dark-haired girl in her late twenties was sorting the bookmarks in a rack. She looked up when he drew near, and smiled.

"Yes, sir, can I help you?" she asked.

"You certainly can. About this reading group notice in your window, how do I join?" Graham asked. He straightened his tie – he still couldn't get out of the habit of wearing a shirt and tie every day – and thought what an attractive young woman she was, with lovely green eyes.

"Oh, that's easy. We've had some other enquiries so what I suggested initially was, if you all meet here on Saturday afternoon about two, you can sort out amongst yourselves when it would be best to meet up again. You'll be sitting at that long table over there. I'm the manager, Jo, by the way."

"Graham Anderson. Nice to meet you, Jo. So I just turn up on Saturday then, do I need to bring anything?"

"Only a notebook and pen if you think you'll need it. Other than that, no, just yourself. Oh, see that lady walking down the stairs? She's joined too."

Graham turned to see who Jo meant, and smiled at the woman as she approached. She was about the same age as himself, quite plump but in a nice motherly way, with thick white hair and deep-set blue eyes.

"How do you do? Graham Anderson. I'm thinking of joining the reading group."

"Oh jolly good, at least I won't be on my own. I'm Mollie."

Mollie turned to Jo. "I see you only serve drinks and biscuits in the little café upstairs. That's a shame, I fancied a sandwich and maybe a piece of cake."

"Well, there's the tea room across the road if you want cake and stuff. We are going to serve more food, but we need to source a supplier first. So sorry, just drinks for the time being," Jo apologised, then turned her attention to a customer waiting to be served.

Mollie waited for the customer to leave then said, "I have

an idea, if you're up for it. I thought about it on my way downstairs. I love cooking, and used to bake regularly when my husband was alive. I could do some cakes for the café, and biscuits too, so you'd only have to get sandwiches elsewhere. If you think it's a good idea, that is."

"I think it's an excellent idea, Mollie. Let me talk it over with Clare and get back to you. Give me your number and I'll phone you later."

Graham had been listening to this exchange and said, "Well, if there's going to be cakes and biscuits made by your fair hands, I'll definitely join up. See you on Saturday, ladies." He saluted them both and left the shop.

"I think he was flirting with you, Mollie," Jo teased her.

"Nonsense, he was just being polite. Now, you will phone me about my suggestion, won't you?"

"Yes, once I've spoken to Clare. But if I don't, because it slips my mind or something, we'll see you Saturday anyway. Are you sure you don't mind? It'll be a lot of baking and we'll need it brought in on a regular basis."

"Heavens no, I wouldn't have offered otherwise. I'd do the sandwiches as well, but you'll need them daily, and I can't promise to get in every day. But I'm happy to do cakes and biscuits. It's been a while since I did any home baking, there's no point just for myself, so it'll be lovely to have someone to cook for again. Dear Victor used to love a nice fruit cake," Mollie said wistfully.

Jo had to serve another customer, so, with a quick wave, Mollie left the shop.

***

Graham took a slow walk home in the spring sunshine. It was quite a long way to his big house on the other side of Bewford, and he usually drove in, but in this weather he enjoyed the stroll. He took it easy and stopped whenever he needed to.

His spirits had really lifted. For the first time in ages, he had something to look forward to. Okay, it was only a small reading group, but it would get him out, and there would be people to talk with. That Mollie looked like a nice lady, and he expected the other members to be interesting too; this was an upmarket area, so they'd hardly be riff-raff. Yes, he was definitely looking forward to Saturday.

Chapter Five

It was quarter past four on Friday afternoon, and Clare was just tidying the children's area when, regular as clockwork, seven-year-old Annie Matthews entered the shop with her mother.

"Hi Alice. Hi there, Annie." Clare ruffled the little girl's hair.

"Hi Clare. Mum said I can have a new book today," Annie said with a big smile.

Each time Clare saw the child, she felt her heart contract, and she wasn't even maternal. Being born eight weeks premature had left Annie with a weak immune system and severe asthma. She had beautiful, long blonde hair and huge blue eyes, but looked ethereal with her thin body and pale complexion.

Yet she was always cheerful, and loved chatting to people in the shop before heading to the children's area, where she'd choose a book and settle herself in one of the chairs.

Clare only found out about Annie's illness when she noticed Alice looking frazzled one afternoon, and offered to get her a coffee. "You look worn out," Clare had said, and that was it. Alice had started talking and couldn't stop.

"It's a twenty-four hour job looking after Annie, and of course I don't mind, she's my daughter, but I'm just so exhausted at times."

Clare had patted her arm consolingly, as Alice explained about Annie's problems.

"She has a poorly functioning immune system so can't risk

catching anything from the other children at school; even a cold can have severe implications. If the teachers know a child in her class is coming down with something, I keep Annie at home for a few days to prevent her getting it. On top of that, her asthma means she has to be careful not to exert herself too much."

"Is she on any medication? Can the doctors do anything?" Clare had asked.

"She takes antibiotics regularly to prevent her getting any serious infections, carries an inhaler to ease symptoms if she gets wheezy or breathless, and uses another one every morning to stop an attack developing. Sometimes though, just playing with the other children makes her short of breath. It's hard to do everything at a snail's pace, children naturally like to run and dash about."

"Poor Annie, and poor you," Clare had sympathised. "It must be hard work."

"It is. I have to keep the house spotlessly clean and free from dust, so we've got leather sofas, and wooden flooring instead of carpets. We use anti–allergy bedding, and Annie's one and only teddy has to go in the freezer every night."

"Oh my word, I don't know how you cope with it all."

"Neither do I at times. Apparently, her immune system will improve as she gets older and she could grow out of the asthma. So life may get easier, but I'm not holding my breath," Alice had said with a sigh.

Clare now walked across to Annie, who was engrossed in a book, and said, "Guess what, Annie? Tomorrow we have some new people coming in. Remember I told you we were starting a reading group? Well, the first meeting is tomorrow afternoon. So when you come in on Monday, I'll be able to tell you all about them."

"How many people are coming?"

"About five, I think. Oh, I've got to go, honey, someone

wants an exchange." Clare ran over to her sales assistant who was beckoning her from the till. She took over and sent the girl for a break.

In between serving customers, Clare watched Annie. Alice had brought her in after school one day when Merrilies first opened, and it had become a daily routine ever since.

Alice occasionally bought a book if Annie took a particular liking to it, but the shop wouldn't get rich on their purchases. Clare knew it wasn't just about money though; it was also about happy customers who'd keep coming back, and, hopefully, tell other people about them too.

She dragged herself out of her thoughts as a customer approached the till.

"I'd like to book a tarot card reading, please."

"Certainly. Jo's upstairs if you'd like to go and see her; she's stocking the shelves at the back of the shop. She'll book you in."

Clare smiled as the woman walked off. It had been a great idea to do tarot readings in Merrilies. Jo's good reputation earned her regular appointments; at least three a week, often more. It was all extra money in the till.

The shop teemed with customers for the rest of the day. Fridays always seemed to be hectic for some reason. At five-forty, when the last of the customers had left the shop, Jo and Clare sat down together with a cup of coffee before locking up for the night.

"Well, it's the start of another phase in our business tomorrow – the reading group," Jo said. "I hope they'll all get on okay."

"Hmm, there does seem to be quite a mix of characters, that's for sure; it should be fun anyway. You should have seen little Annie's face when I told her about them. I've promised to let her know all about it on Monday."

Jo laughed. "She's going to be a real curtain twitcher when she grows up; she loves to hear all the gossip, doesn't she? She's such a sweet, affectionate kid. The other day when she was leaving, she gave me a hug, bless her."

"Yes, she hugs me too," Clare said. "I feel so sorry for Alice though, it can't be easy worrying about Annie all the time."

"No, I wouldn't want the responsibility. Right, I'll just make sure the table's ready for the reading group tomorrow. Wonder what book they'll start off with."

"They probably won't get round to reading anything, they'll be too busy introducing themselves and finding out about each other. Oh, Jo, I hope they don't argue over what to read!"

"Yeah, that's what I was thinking. Maybe we should choose books for them?"

"No, let them decide themselves; they can take a vote, or make a list and work through it. If they get stuck, then we can suggest some," Clare said.

"Hey, we could get them to review new books, maybe for the local paper or something; have a regular book review slot," Jo suggested.

"That's a good idea, remind me to phone the paper on Monday and run it by them. I'll speak to the same guy who covered the opening of the shop, get him to ask the editor. What would I do without you?" Clare smiled. "We make a good team, don't we?"

"Yeah. If only I'd known what I was letting myself in for that day you came for a reading." Jo laughed at the look on Clare's face. "I'm only joking. Come on, let's get out of here."

They took a last look around to make sure everything was ready for the next day, switched off the lights, set the alarm and locked up.

"I don't like leaving this place every night, I wish we lived closer," Clare said as they walked to the car park.

"Well, I'm looking for a flat, as it's about time I left home. I'm trying to find one around here. I know it's a pain not living nearby, especially if the alarm goes off and we have to drive all the way over," Jo said.

"Yes, we've been lucky so far, touch wood. What are you up to tonight, anything particular?"

"Nope, just having a night in. I told Mum not to cook as I fancy an Indian take–away. You?"

"Nothing special either."

"Do you want to come round?" Jo asked. "If you can stand more of my company after working with me all day, that is."

"Well, I was thinking about phoning Brad Pitt to see if he's free tonight, but I'll spend it with you instead." Clare grinned. "Okay, let me pop home, have a shower, grab a bottle of wine, and I'll be over about seven thirty to eight?"

"That's fine. Mum and Dad'll be pleased to see you." Jo giggled. "Mum always says how nice and sensible you are."

"I'm not sure how to take that," Clare said, feigning hurt. "I'll have to have a chat with your mum, accidentally let slip some shocking facts about my rampant youth. Trouble is, the worst thing I've ever done was take a library book back a week late!" she grinned. "See you later."

"Oh my God, I forgot, we've been so busy," Jo slapped her forehead dramatically. "Mollie made a suggestion. I was meant to talk it over with you and get back to her. I just haven't had the chance; to be honest, it slipped my mind. Remind me tonight and I'll run it by you, see what you think."

"Sounds interesting. Okay, see you in an hour or so."

Chapter Six

The following day, Mollie arrived first for the reading group, with a large fruitcake in tow. She took it over to Jo, who was behind the downstairs till.

"Mollie, I'm sorry, we've been so busy it slipped my mind until last night. Clare and I had a talk and she thinks it's a great idea. We need to sort out paying you and how much to charge customers for the cakes, etc. Any ideas?"

"Well, I took the liberty of checking out prices in the garden centre, the supermarket, and the tea room across the road. That nice lass who worked there must have left, because they're advertising a flat for rent. She used to live in the flat above the tea room so it must be hers that's now vacant. I wonder where she's gone. Anyway, I checked prices and..."

As Mollie spoke, an image suddenly flashed into Jo's mind of herself sitting in an L-shaped room listening to music. She hadn't had a premonition for ages, so butted in on what Mollie was saying.

"Hang on a minute, there's a flat for rent above the tea room?" Jo asked excitedly.

"Yes, there's an advert in their window. Now, about these prices, and take this cake, please, it's jolly heavy. You hadn't got back to me, so I thought you could sample my wares before making a decision."

"Thanks, Mollie. Can you hang on for a quarter of an hour? There's something I need to do." Jo beckoned a girl who was putting books on the sale table. "Stella, can you put this cake in the staff room and then cover for me until I get back?

Thanks."

Mollie gave the cake to the girl, who disappeared upstairs, then returned a few minutes later to go behind the till.

"I'll be back in two ticks," Jo said and ran out the front door.

Mollie shrugged and went to sit at the reading group table.

Twenty minutes later Jo came back with a satisfied smile on her face. "Stella, can you hang on there a bit longer while I go upstairs to see Clare?" She took the stairs two at a time.

"Oh there you are," Clare said as Jo approached. "The reading group will be here soon. Do you want to swap, you stay here and I'll go downstairs?"

"Yeah okay. Guess what?"

"Erm, you've won the lottery and Johnny Depp wants to marry you?"

"Ha ha, no such luck. But we won't have to worry about leaving Merrilies every night now."

"Why, you're not going to sleep here, are you?" Clare asked with a frown.

"No, don't be daft, but I've found a flat and it's really close."

"Oh brilliant! Where?"

"Across the road, above the tea room!" Jo clapped delightedly.

"Oh wow, Jo, that is close! How did you get it?"

"Mollie saw the advert and told me about it. As she was talking, I got a sudden premonition of me sitting in a room listening to music. When I went across to see Fran, she took me up to have a look and it was the room from my omen. How fab is that?"

"God, you and your psychic thoughts. So, Fran's let it to you then?"

"Yes. The ad had literally only just gone in the window. She's so pleased I'm going to take it because she was worried about renting to someone she didn't know. It's perfect. There's a big room, which is the kitchen and lounge, and there's a separate bedroom, shower room and loo. I can move in tomorrow if I want. And I'll save heaps of money because I won't have to drive to work!"

"Blimey, that's quick, but I know you trust your omens. What do you think your parents will say?"

"Well, they know I want to move out, so I don't think they'll mind. Mum might get a bit emotional, because it's so sudden, but Dad'll be cool."

"If you do move tomorrow and need any help, let me know."

"Thanks, Clare. Dad'll help I expect. I'll probably move in dribs and drabs, you know, take the essentials right away and get the rest over the following few evenings. Okay, you go downstairs if you want and I'll stay here. I know you're dying to see who turns up for this reading group. Mollie brought a cake for us to try, and I left her while I went to see the flat. Tell her I'm sorry but we'll sort out the details later."

"Okay, no problem. Well, this should be interesting," Clare smiled then and made her way downstairs.

"Erm, Clare," Jo called.

Clare ran back up the few stairs she'd descended. "What?"

"Don't eat all of Mollie's cake, save me a slice."

"Jo, I was halfway downstairs!"

"Ha ha, it'll do you good to burn off some calories, it'll leave space for the cake then." Jo grinned.

"You cheeky devil," Clare laughed. "See you in a bit." And she ran down to see who else, besides Mollie, had turned up for the reading group.

***

Tessa Parsons looked at her watch, and saw it was a quarter-to-two. "I better get going," she muttered. She picked up her bag and said to her daughter, "Amber, I don't know how long I'll be at this meeting, but I'll see you when I get back. I'll get a DVD for tonight, if you like. Will you be okay?"

"Yes, Mum, I'll be fine. Gran and Grandad are coming over at two, so I'll be on my own for a whole fifteen minutes – big wow!"

"There's no need for sarcasm, young lady. Make sure you behave yourself. I'll bring back pizza for dinner if you've been good."

"I'm not a baby, now off you go to your reading group and I'll see you later," Amber turned back to her magazine. Then she remembered what Tessa had said about the DVD. "Oh, Mum?"

"Yes?"

"Can you get the new chick flick that was advertised on TV the other day? You know, the one with that boy from *Holyoke*?"

"Yes, if they've got it. See you later, sweetie. Enjoy yourself with Gran and Grandad."

Tessa heard Amber mutter, "Oh wow, major laughs ahead' as she grabbed her keys and headed out the door.

She wondered if she'd have any trouble parking in the town's only car park. Usually, if she needed to go into the centre of Bewford, she went early to ensure a space.

It was only a short drive and Tessa got there in ten minutes, which she was relieved about, as she didn't want to be late for the first meeting. She wondered who else would be there. Oh heck, what if she was the only one? But Merrilies was a popular shop, something Bewford had needed for a long time, so she was sure there'd be other members too.

She spotted a parking space in the far corner and made for it. So did someone else in a rather smart car. Then she saw that there were actually two spaces. As she got out, the man who'd parked next to her spoke. "I thought for a moment I was late," he said.

Tessa just looked at him.

"Hmm late for what, you must be thinking," he laughed. "I'm attending a meeting in the book shop, for a reading group."

As he said this, the confused look vanished from Tessa's face and she smiled back at him.

"Oh, I'm going there too, I'm Tessa. I'm glad you're here, I was a bit worried I'd be the only one."

"Graham Anderson; pleased to meet you. And I know of another lady who's joined, so that'll be three of us at least."

"Oh good. Come on then, it's just gone two."

They crossed the road, walked around the corner to the main high street where Merrilies stood, and went in.

They approached the counter where Clare was putting some change in the till.

"We're here for the reading group," Graham said.

"Oh hi, there's one person already here and some more due, so just go down there." Clare pointed to a table where an older woman sat reading a newspaper.

The woman looked up as they approached. "Oh hello, we met the other day didn't we?" Mollie smiled at Graham.

He straightened his tie. "We certainly did. But in case you didn't get my name, I'm Graham. Pleased to make your acquaintance once more."

Tessa spoke. "And I'm Tessa, hi."

"I'm Mollie. Nice to meet you, Tessa. Oh, here's someone else."

They turned to see a young man walking towards them. He went red when he saw them watching him.

"Have you come for the reading group?" Mollie asked and introduced herself.

The others did the same.

"I'm Michael," the young man said shyly and sat down.

"Good grief, we can't do all these introductions every time someone turns up, I hope too many more don't arrive," Mollie said.

"We could make name cards, just till we've got to know each other," Tessa suggested.

"Jolly good idea. I'll ask Clare for some card and a pen." Mollie disappeared and returned a few moments later with some yellow card and a black marker.

"Here we go. Now write your name and put the card in front of you on the table."

The others did as Mollie suggested then sat back and looked at each other. There was a bit of an awkward silence, as they didn't know quite what to do next.

Graham looked at his watch. "Well, it's quarter past two, shall we get started?"

Just at that moment, a young girl arrived and plonked herself into the chair beside Michael. "Hello everyone, sorry I'm late! Well, isn't this fun? I see you've done place cards, can I have one too? I'm Felicity, by the way, but most people call me Flick." She paused for breath and grinned at them all.

As they all said their hellos, Mollie looked at the latecomer with her arm full of bangles and hippie-styled, but obviously very expensive clothes. Things will certainly be fun with her around, she thought.

"Right,' she said, drawing their attention back to the meeting, "if anyone else turns up, they'll just have to join in. Now, can I make a suggestion to get things going?"

Everyone nodded and Mollie continued, "Why don't we all take it in turns to tell a little about ourselves and why we're here?"

Michael didn't look too happy about this, but the others agreed.

"Okay, I'll start. My name's Mollie and I love reading. I didn't have a lot of time to read when my husband was alive, but now I have plenty. I joined this group to broaden my reading matter, and I thought it would be jolly nice to meet other like-minded people. I'll also be making cakes and biscuits for the café upstairs. I brought a cake for us all to sample later." She sat back in her chair and took her reading glasses out of her bag.

Graham went next. "I'm Graham, I retired two years ago and I also enjoy reading. Mainly military history, but..." He stopped because Felicity tittered.

"Is there a problem, Felicity?" he asked.

"No, I just wondered how anyone could read that stuff," she said with a shrug. "What?" she asked, as Mollie looked at her pointedly.

"I don't think we're here to question someone's reading tastes, and Graham was talking," Mollie replied.

"Sorry, I didn't mean to be rude, but I would find it an absolute bore to read something like that."

Graham continued, "Good job we're not all alike then. I was going to say, I'm not adverse to other reading matter; I'll try most things, even the odd romance novel." He looked pointedly at Felicity. "I have nothing more to add really, except thank you, Felicity, for your opinion."

"Tessa, you go next," Mollie said.

"Well, I love reading too, isn't that why we're all here?" Tessa went on, "But I'm also a writer. I write mainly short stories for women's magazines. I thought joining this group would do me good as I don't read enough – well, not as much as I should."

"How interesting," Mollie exclaimed. "Have you had any success?"

"A fair bit, yes. I'm published regularly in two women's magazines. I'm writing a novel at the moment, but I don't have a lot of spare time as I also work mornings in a doctor's surgery and look after my twelve-year-old daughter and the house."

"Can't Mr Tessa help out?" Felicity asked.

Tessa held Felicity's gaze with her own direct stare. "I'm a single mum."

Mollie intervened. "Well done, Tessa. I admire anyone who brings up a child single–handedly nowadays, especially when they hold down a job and look after a house as well. On top of that, you also write; you're obviously not afraid of hard work."

Felicity muttered something under her breath.

"Would you like to share that with us, Felicity?" Graham asked.

"No, just talking to myself," she said and gave him a big smile.

"So, can we get on with things?"

Michael went next, blushing as he spoke. "I'm Michael. I read a lot, but I'd also like to improve my reading material." He couldn't think what else to say, then added in a rush, "I'm twenty-seven, live at home with my mum and dad, and my hobby is war games."

"Do you dress up in funny costumes and have pretend fights?" Felicity asked.

Michael blushed even more. "No, it's called Warhammer. You paint these little figures and have battles with them. There's a lot of strategy to it..." he tailed off and looked down at the table.

Felicity tried desperately not to laugh and it came out as a snort. She pulled herself together. "Oh, is it my turn? Right, you know my name. I love shopping, sushi and shoes, and I can't abide cruelty to animals."

"Yes, but what about reading?" Michael asked.

"Well, yes, I do some of that as well, of course I do. Only last week I read the new celebrity magazine."

"I think you're meant to read proper books, Felicity," Michael told her.

Everyone except Michael knew that Felicity was teasing him.

An amused Mollie watched this exchange between the two youngest members of the group. Although Felicity was pretending to be ditzy, Mollie could tell from her accent that she was well educated and clearly came from a good background. She was rather outspoken and direct though. Mollie bet it made her a few enemies, but she doubted if Felicity gave a damn about that.

Everyone had finished speaking, so Mollie said, "Okay, that's the introductions over and done with, we can get on with the reason we're all here – books. We obviously read different genres, so how do we decide which book to read?"

Graham said, "Well, we could make a list and vote on one from the list, or we could ask the girls who run the bookshop to choose for us."

Tessa came up with a suggestion. "Why don't we ask them to draw up a list with some new releases, old favourites and classics, so there's a good mix? Then we can vote for the book we want to read and work our way through the list."

"Excellent idea, Tessa! Do we all agree?" Graham asked, looking at the others.

They nodded.

"Now, how fast or slow does everyone read?" Mollie asked. "We need to have a timescale; how about, say, one book per month, could everyone manage that?"

"Ooh, I'm not sure I'd manage that in between shopping, getting my nails done and lunching with my girlfriends," Felicity said.

Michael was about to pipe up when he saw the amused look on her face, so he closed his mouth again.

"Right, there's no point starting with a book today, so how about we have some of the cake I made and a cup of coffee? I'll ask Jo if she can make up a list of books for us when she's got time."

"Just the teeniest bit of cake for me, Mollie, I have to watch what I'm eating. I'd absolutely die if I couldn't get into my new white trousers," Felicity said.

"I'll bring it down and everyone can help themselves," Mollie said as she got up.

"Shall I come with you?" Felicity offered.

"That'd be lovely, dear, thanks."

As they were walking upstairs to find Jo, Mollie said, "You were a bit outspoken during the introductions, Felicity. Some people – I, for one – like directness, but others find it upsetting. Perhaps you could be a bit more careful what you say until you've got to know us all?"

Felicity tutted. "Okay, I'll be on my best behaviour from now on. Hey, that Michael's a bit weird, don't you think?"

"I like to reserve judgement until I've got to know someone properly and I suggest you do the same."

"Yes, Mother," Felicity retorted. "But it *was* funny when I said about the celeb magazines, and he was the only one who didn't know I was joking."

Mollie agreed it was funny, and they laughed.

Mollie liked the girl; she was energetic and fun. It would make things very interesting with her in the group.

They found Jo, and Mollie told her about Tessa's reading list suggestion.

"That's a great idea. I'll compile one with Clare, and you can collect it later in the week if that's okay?"

"Yes, that's fine. We can vote for which book to start with when we next meet up. Right, where's this cake I brought in?" Mollie asked.

"Hey, guys," Felicity said as she sat back down at the table. "We need to know what days we're going to meet. We can't go home without sorting that out. Which day would be best?"

They talked amongst themselves for a bit and came to a decision. Michael couldn't do weekdays because he worked; Tessa worked part-time, so it would be awkward for her. Felicity, Mollie and Graham were home during the day but there was no point them meeting up without the others.

Merrilies stayed open Thursdays until eight in the evening, and if Michael came straight from work, everyone could make that. So, they decided to meet twice a week, Thursday evenings from six until eight, and Saturday afternoons from two until four. They all seemed to like the two o'clock Saturday slot.

They ate Mollie's cake, which they agreed was delicious, chatted for a bit longer, arranged to meet up again the following Thursday, then said their goodbyes and left.

Mollie had parked in the same place as Tessa and Graham, so they walked there together. Felicity rushed off to do some shopping, and Michael went to the model shop for some new miniature figures.

Chapter Seven

"That seemed to go well," Jo said as she and Clare sat at the reading group table with a cup of tea and Mollie's cake, once the shop had closed.

"Hmm, it did. Five is just the right number too, I think; nice and intimate. They were a strange mix of people though," Clare said, pushing her glasses back along her nose.

"Yeah, it should make for an interesting time. We have to compile this book list for them, how many shall we put on it?"

"Well, if they're reading a book a month, let me think... If we put about twenty-five titles on it, that'll give them plenty of choice, don't you think?"

"Yep, that's probably enough. Let's have a look at the computer and pull off some titles from there." Jo got up and went over to the PC behind the till.

"Can you do it? I'm going to sit and have a rest, if that's okay. My feet are killing me today for some reason." Clare sipped her tea and ate her cake, while Jo scrolled through the list and highlighted titles on the screen.

Clare finished her drink and sighed. "Thank heavens I'm not out tonight. All I feel like doing is grabbing a pizza, curling up with the cat and watching TV."

"Lucky you! I'm meant to be going to that new club in Oxford with some friends tonight," Jo said with a grimace. "I don't feel like it at the moment, but I'll be fine once I get a couple of drinks inside me," she grinned.

"Honestly, I don't know how you do it, Jo. I'm whacked. But you're younger than me, that's why you can boil the candle at both ends."

Jo burst out laughing. "*Burn* the candle. You *must* be tired! Why don't you head home? I don't mind locking up. There we go," she said, printing off a sheet of paper.

"Okay, let's have a quick look at this list, then I'll get going. A nice bath, a pizza and an early night for me, I think."

Clare went through the list and added some favourite books of her own. They agreed they'd chosen a good mix. There were some classics, including Thomas Hardy's *Far From the Madding Crowd*, a few new releases, some general fiction novels and a couple of good crime reads. There was also a celebrity autobiography; *Lady Chatterley's Lover*, which Jo was adamant she wanted to put in for a bit of fun; a horror novel, a chick lit book – Clare wondered what the two men would make of that; *The Time Traveler's Wife,* and the latest release from a popular Japanese author.

"There's certainly plenty to keep them entertained. Right, I'm off. See you Monday morning, Jo, thanks for locking up." Clare walked towards the door, stopped and came back again. "Are you going to move into the flat tomorrow?"

Jo shrugged. "I was, but if I'm out clubbing tonight, I may not be up to moving my stuff out tomorrow. I'll do it next weekend; it'll give Mum and Dad a bit more notice. See ya Monday."

"Okay, I'll help next weekend if you like. Bye, have a good night."

Clare left, and Jo took the cups and plates up to the staff room, washed them up, checked that everything was ready for Monday, put the alarm on, locked up and went home.

Jo's mum was cooking her favourite meal, which made it even harder to tell her she was moving out at last.

As Jo expected, her mum cried.

"Oh, Mum," Jo said, getting up and putting her arms around her, "you've known for a while I wanted to move out and it's not as if you won't see me again. I'm moving to

Bewford, not Australia. I tell you what, why don't I get a bottle of wine, some chocolates and a DVD, and we'll spend the evening in together?"

Her mother wiped her eyes, blew her nose, and said, "That sounds nice," then busied herself getting the dinner ready.

Her father squeezed her arm and whispered, "Thanks, Jo." He knew she'd blown her plans for the night just to cheer her mother up.

Jo drove to the local supermarket, phoning her friend on the way to explain that she wouldn't be going out after all. She bought a bottle of wine for herself and her mum, some beer for her dad, a big box of chocolates, and on the way back she collected an action DVD from the video shop. The least she could do was spend this last weekend at home with her parents. She'd not really thought about things from their perspective, but yes, it would be strange not having her around any more. She'd lived with them for the last twenty-nine years, so it would be hard for them *all* to adjust. She stopped in the garage for petrol, and on impulse bought some flowers as well.

Over dinner, they chatted about Jo's impending move.

"So, I thought I'd move out next weekend if that's okay."

"Of course it is, love, I'll give you a hand with your things."

"Thanks, Dad, there isn't that much, just my clothes, music and stuff."

Her mum managed a laugh. "You'll need a truck for all your clothes. Oh, I'm going to miss you so much," she said, her bottom lip wobbling.

This time it brought tears to Jo's eyes too. "Aw, Mum, you've got me at it as well."

"No more wine for you two if it's going to make you maudlin," her dad said, removing the wine bottle.

"You'll put that right back, Richard Davis, if you know what's good for you," her mum joked.

"I'll still visit loads. You can visit me and I'll cook for a change. That'll be nice, won't it? It's going to be so handy, Mum, being right across the road from work. Besides, it's about time you and Dad had some time to yourselves, you don't want me around forever," Jo said.

"I love you being here, you're no trouble, Jo; never have been. So what's this flat like then?" her mum asked, trying to show an interest.

"Well, I've got the key, would you like to go round tomorrow and have a look? Then I'll treat you both to a pub lunch afterwards, how's that?"

"What do you think, love?" Jo's dad said to her mother. "We haven't had Sunday lunch out for ages, have we?"

Her mother smiled. "That would be lovely."

Her parents had obviously talked during the night, because when Jo went downstairs the next morning, her mum placed a cup of tea in front of her and said, "If we're going round to see this flat, it would make sense to take some of your things whilst we're at it."

Jo watched her mum's face as she replied, "Are you sure, because I can wait until next weekend?"

"Jo love, what difference does a week make? You might as well do it today. I've got to get used to you going, so there's no point putting it off."

"Well, if you're sure, and we'll have a nice lunch after. You choose where you'd like to go."

"No, I'm not sure, but you've got to go sometime. Ooh, can we go to Browns? We don't go very often and I like it there."

"Yeah, of course we can. I'll be around every weekend for your fantastic roast, so you won't be getting rid of me that easily." Jo wrapped her arms around her mother and kissed her.

After they'd had breakfast and done the crossword in the Sunday paper – something they all joined in with, it was part of their Sunday routine – Jo's dad went to make sure the car was empty, whilst Jo went up to her room to sort out what she wanted to take.

Her parents liked the flat, and her mum got quite enthusiastic about filling it. By the time she'd worked out what she could give Jo from the house, they needed to make another trip, and by one-thirty, they decided they'd done enough. Jo had all the essentials: bedding, kettle, crockery, her TV from her bedroom, clothes and music. She locked up and they drove into Oxford to have a late lunch at Browns.

**

Monday morning, Jo was already in when Clare arrived at work.

"Gosh, you're an early bird this morning," Clare said, when she saw Jo sitting down with a cup of tea.

"Well, I didn't have very far to come to work," Jo grinned.

"Huh? Oh, you've moved out already! How did your parents take it, especially your mum?"

"As I thought, she cried, but I took them to see the flat yesterday and she got quite excited and gave me a load of stuff. I took them both to lunch after they'd helped me move in."

"I'm surprised you were in a fit state to do anything after your night out."

"I didn't go. I thought I'd spend it with Mum and Dad seeing as it was going to be my last Saturday at home. Grr, will you *stop* doing that!" Jo said as Clare pushed her glasses along her nose.

"*What*? I haven't done anything."

"Yeah, you have; you keep pushing your glasses up your nose. If they're loose, take them to the opticians' and get them adjusted. They're only a few shops along the road."

Clare grinned at her. "I don't even realise I'm doing it. I'll go in my lunch break seeing as it annoys you so much. Good job you're my friend, that's all I can say! By the way, about phoning the Herald regarding the reading group doing reviews, maybe we should wait until they're a bit more established, then ask them. I'll phone the newspaper if they agree to it."

"Hmm okay, you're the boss. Stella's at the door; I'll let her in. We might be busy today, it's forecast for rain."

They didn't know why, but if the weather was bad, they always had a good day's trading. It was probably because people couldn't do much else in the rain except go to the shops.

The day passed uneventfully. They had a steady flow of customers, and it rained on and off all day; typical April weather.

At four-fifteen, Annie arrived with her mum. She went straight to see Jo who was on the downstairs till.

"Hi Jo, did the reading group come in on Saturday?"

Jo laughed. "Blimey, you've got a memory like an elephant. Clare's upstairs, if you go and find her, she'll tell you all about it if she's not too busy. Tell her I said you could have a piece of cake too – if that's alright with your mum?" Jo asked, looking at Alice. Alice nodded and made to follow Annie.

"It's okay, Mum, you stay here, I can go by myself," Annie said.

"Erm, I'd rather you didn't, sweetie," Alice said nervously.

Jo was already on the phone. "It's okay, Annie, Clare's waiting for you at the top of the stairs, so go now."

Alice smiled her thanks to Jo and went to browse round the books unhindered.

"Hello, Poppet, have a good weekend?" Clare asked as she met Annie.

Annie had stopped to catch her breath, and was wheezing a bit so she got out her inhaler and took a couple of puffs. "Yes, Mummy and Daddy took me to see a film, it was about these rabbits and it was really sad cuz one of them died and it played sad music. I cried, so did Mummy but she said she must have had a cold coming."

Clare smiled. "I was just going to sit in the café and have a quick break. Come with me and have a piece of cake and I'll tell you who came to the reading group."

And for the next fifteen minutes, Clare told Annie all about the people who'd turned up.

"I wish I'd seen them, especially that Fecility girl," Annie said, as one by one she ate the raisins she'd picked out of her cake.

Clare laughed. "It's Felicity."

"Fe-ci-li-ty," Annie tried again.

"Never mind, I like your version. You might just get to see them, because guess what?"

"What? What?" Annie cried, bouncing up and down in her seat.

"They're going to have one meeting on Thursdays, because we stay open until eight o'clock, and one on Saturdays at two. So, if Mummy brought you here later on Thursday, you could see them all."

"I'm going to ask her," Annie said, getting up from her seat and heading towards the stairs.

"Annie, wait for me," Clare called and she caught hold of Annie's hand. "You mustn't go wandering off on your own."

"Hmph, okay then."

Clare suddenly realised that she might have made things awkward for Alice. Maybe she couldn't come in later than four-thirty.

"Please, Mummy, can we come in later?" Annie wheedled.

"But, Annie, we stop in on the way home from school. It means we'll have to go home and then come out again."

"Oh please, Mummy, it's only Thursdays. Please, please, please?" Annie tugged on her mother's jacket. Alice looked at Clare, who made an apologetic face.

Alice sighed. "I suppose we could go home and you could have your tea, then we could come back later on for a bit. Daddy doesn't get home until seven anyway. If we came at six, then left at half past, we'd be home just before Daddy got in. Oh, all right then."

Annie reached up to kiss Alice. "Thanks, you're the bestest Mummy in the whole world."

"Right come on, you, we better get home. Can I pay you for this Clare?" Alice showed Clare the latest novel in a village series she enjoyed reading.

"Oh, do you like her books? She's also written a series set in a veterinary practice; have you read any of them?"

"Yes. I'm waiting for the next one to come out."

"Do you want me to reserve it for you?"

"Oh, yes please, not the hardback version though, that's too expensive. I'm waiting for the paperback."

"Okeydoke, I'll make a note. See you tomorrow."

The rest of the week passed in a blur of busy days. The weather was miserable with persistent rain, which seemed to bring people out in their droves to the shops.

Mollie popped in twice. Once to replenish the cakes for the café, and the second time to collect the book list which she'd forgotten to pick up the first time.

Jo was going to give it to the group at the Thursday meeting, but Mollie wanted to study it beforehand.

"I say, Jo, there's a jolly good choice of books on here, several I haven't read, and quite a few some of the others haven't read I should think, especially *Lady Chatterley's Lover*. Jo!"

Jo grinned. "I thought I'd have a bit of fun and throw that one in; I'll take it out again if you want."

"No, we'll leave it in, After all, it is meant to be a wide range of reading matter. I just hope they're broad-minded. Rightio, I'm off, see you Thursday at six."

Chapter Eight

Felicity had been shopping with her friend and they'd decided to stop in the mall café for a much-needed sit down and refreshments.

"Phew! I'm bloody exhausted. I really need a drink of water, I feel like I'm dehydrated," she said, pinching the skin on her hand to test it.

They found a table, plonked their bags on one of the chairs and sat down.

"I might have something to eat as well," her friend said.

"Yes, well you can, you're stick thin and never put on any weight. I only have to look at a cake and my trousers get tight," Felicity complained.

"Oh hardly! You're as thin as I am, Flick. You have to eat something. Shall I get a sandwich and we can have half each? That won't be too bad. I'll make sure it doesn't have mayo and is low fat. And a bottle of water each?"

"Yes, that'll do... Oh my God!" Felicity shrieked, turning around to hide her face behind her hand.

"What's up?" her friend hissed.

"Shh! See that guy coming towards us with the white overalls and hat on? Well, he goes to my reading group. He's a real bloody nerd. What on earth is he carrying?" She took a sharp intake of breath and tried to hide as Michael looked in her direction. Unfortunately, as she swung round, she knocked her bag off the edge of the chair it was balanced on, and it clattered to the floor, spilling its contents. This made Michael, who heard the noise, look straight at her. Recognising Felicity, he walked over.

"Hi Flick, fancy seeing you here."

"Oh, hi Michael. What have you got there and why are you wearing that funny hat?" Felicity thought she might as well turn the embarrassment of the situation back on to him.

Michael went red and started mumbling.

"What? I can't hear you. Speak up, Michael, don't be shy."

"It's to keep my hair covered. And this is a platter of sandwiches for the café."

"Ooh, so you're the delivery boy for a sandwich company then. My, what a high-level job you have. Do you get your own company vehicle?"

Felicity's friend was trying frantically not to laugh; Felicity could see her shoulders shaking slightly.

"Erm, I'm not the delivery boy. I work in the factory, making the sandwiches. I just have to drop them off. Be back in a minute," Michael said and took his tray around to the back of the café.

Felicity's friend couldn't contain her laughter any longer.

"You are awful, Flick," she spluttered. "That's hilarious! He doesn't even know you're taking the piss out of him."

"I know, wait until he comes back and when I've got rid of him, we'll get a drink. I don't want a sandwich now I know where they come from. Ugh, they've had his hands all over them."

"I expect he wears gloves, Flick."

"I don't care!"

Michael came back out and stood by their table.

"So, Michael, you make the sandwiches?" Felicity asked.

"Well, not just me obviously. There's a whole team of us and we all do different things."

"So what do *you* do?"

"I spread the margarine on them and put the tomatoes and cucumber on."

"Hmm, that sounds fascinating," Felicity said, while her

51

friend kicked her foot under the table. "But it's not exactly a challenge, is it?"

"Actually, it's quite a responsible job. You don't just spread the margarine any old how, you have to spread it right to the very edges; make sure all the bread is covered."

By now, Felicity wished she had a hanky to stuff in her mouth, she was so desperate not to burst out laughing. This man couldn't be for real, could he? Her friend had pretended to delve in her bag to look for something so that he couldn't see her face.

Felicity touched Michael's arm, making him blush to the roots of his head. "And?" she asked, playing up for her friend."

"Well, you have to put on two round slices of tomato or cucumber, one on either end. Not one or three, it has to be two. There are strict guidelines we all have to follow."

Now Felicity didn't care, she let out the laughter that had been bubbling up, and her friend did the same.

Michael stood there, hot with embarrassment. He looked at the girls, then said in a tight voice, "Well, you might think it's funny, but I take my job seriously. I'll see you at the reading group meeting tomorrow, if you can be bothered to turn up on time."

"Okay, Michael, see you then. Bye," Felicity managed to squeak, and she collapsed in a fit of giggles again.

***

The next evening, by quarter-to-six, all the members of the reading group were sitting at the table in the same places they'd sat when they first met up. Mollie had the book list with her, which she'd thoughtfully photocopied, so each person had one, and they were going through the list to decide which book to start with.

"Jo and Clare have kindly said they'll give us a fifteen percent discount on all the books we buy," Mollie told them.

At this, Michael looked up. "Oh, I thought they were lending us the books, I didn't realise we had to buy them."

"Bloody hell, Michael, of course we buy them. Otherwise what's in it for Merrilies? They're being good giving us a discount," Felicity said with impatience.

Michael went red. "Yes, of course they are, I just didn't realise we were buying them that's all. It's not a problem."

"Sure you can afford it on your wages?" Felicity smirked.

Michael looked down at the floor. He was still upset with her for laughing at him in the shopping mall the day before.

"Okay, everyone, which book shall we start with?" Mollie asked.

They talked it over and narrowed it down to three. A crime novel, the Japanese author, and Thomas Hardy's *Far From the Madding Crowd*.

"Let's take a vote, shall we?" Graham suggested.

Two voted for the Japanese author, two for Hardy, and one for the crime novel.

"Right then," Graham said, "the crime novel's out, so it's down to this Japanese gentleman or Thomas Hardy."

Hardy won.

"I'll see if they've got five copies," Tessa volunteered, and she went to find Jo or Clare. She saw Clare talking to a little girl at the front of the shop.

"Here's one of them now," Clare said as Tessa approached. "Tessa, this is Annie and her mum, Alice. Annie wanted to meet everyone from the reading group and came in especially. She's one of our regular customers aren't you, Poppet?"

Annie nodded and smiled. Tessa saw she had a tooth missing at the front.

"So, you come in a lot, Annie, do you?" Tessa asked.

"Yes, every day after school. Jo and Clare told me all about your group and said maybe if I came in today I could meet you all." She started wheezing as she finished talking.

"Use your inhaler, Annie, and try to stop getting excited,"

Alice told her. "She's got asthma," she explained to Tessa.

Tessa asked Clare for the books then, turning to Annie, said, "Come with me and I'll introduce you."

Annie followed Tessa back to the table and Alice hovered self-consciously behind.

"Everyone, this is Annie," Tessa said, beckoning the little girl to come forward and meet them. "Clare is just getting our books."

The group all said hi to Annie.

"I know who you are," Annie said to Felicity.

"Oh, do you now? Who am I then?"

"You're Fecility."

Felicity laughed, "That's almost right. It's Felicity, but I like the way you say it. Have you lost your tooth?" she asked, pointing at the gap in Annie's mouth.

"Yes, it was all wibbly wobbly and then it fell out."

Mollie spoke to the little girl. "You know what you have to do with it, don't you?"

"Yes, put it under my pillow."

"That's right," Mollie told her, "then the tooth fairy will come and take it away, and if you've been a good girl she might leave some money." Mollie looked at Alice and Alice said Annie *had* been good, so she might be lucky.

"Are you Mollie?" Annie asked.

"Yes I am. How did you know that?"

"Clare and Jo told me all your names and I remembered. I thought you must be Mollie cuz you're the only lady that's old with white hair."

"Annie!" Alice scolded. "I'm so sorry," she said to Mollie.

"Not at all, the child's right, and she has a good memory." Mollie smiled.

"Mollie, what does the tooth fairy do with my tooth and all the other children's tooths? I asked Mummy but she didn't know. You might know cuz you're old."

Everyone around the table laughed.

"Teeth, not tooths," Alice corrected her and apologised to Mollie again.

"Well, Annie, she files them down, shapes them, then polishes them until they're gleaming and turns them into jewellery for all the fairies and pixies."

"Wow, she must need lots and lots of too–teeth then," Annie said, her eyes wide with amazement.

"She does, which is why she goes round to all the children and collects them," Mollie told her.

At that moment, Clare came back with the books. "Here you are, one each. Jo ordered five copies of each book on the list in preparation for you."

"Okay, Annie, time to go and leave these people to study their books," Alice said, catching hold of Annie's hand.

"Aw, can we come again next week?" Annie looked up at her mother.

"We'll see. Say goodbye."

"Bye, Mollie, bye, Fecility, see you next week," Annie called, and she skipped ahead of her mother, then stopped and coughed. Mollie watched her take out her inhaler.

"Bless her, what a gregarious child, and so pretty with those big blue eyes."

"Hmm, as long as she doesn't pester us every week. We're meant to be talking about books," Michael grumbled.

"She only wanted to meet us, she didn't do any harm," Felicity said. "I thought she was sweet."

"Me too," Tessa agreed.

"Shall we get on with the proper reason we're here then?" Michael asked.

Mollie took charge. "Has anyone read this before?" she asked, picking up the Thomas Hardy book.

Tessa put her hand up, so did Graham. Tessa giggled, thinking it was a bit like school.

"I've read it too, although it was a long time ago," Mollie said. "When did you two read it?"

"It was a long time ago for me too," Graham replied.

"I studied it at school in English Literature," Tessa explained.

Mollie continued, "Jolly good. So Michael and Felicity, as you aren't familiar with the book, shall we give you a rough outline? Then we have a month to read it and we'll discuss it each week until we've finished it or the month's up."

They decided the best thing would be to make notes as they read and bring their notes to the meetings each week.

A member of staff asked them all what they drank, and a bit later, Jo came downstairs with a tray of drinks for them.

"This is jolly good of you, Jo," Mollie said.

"You're welcome. I just wanted to remind you that it's Easter next weekend. We'll be open Good Friday until four, Saturday as usual and Monday 'till four too."

"Are you girls working both days?" Graham asked.

"No, Clare's doing Friday and I'm doing Monday, that way we get one day off each. We're giving everyone who buys a children's book a free crème egg over Easter too."

"That's a great idea. You seem to work well together, this shop has such a lovely atmosphere," Tessa told her.

"Thanks, I think so too, I love working here. Strange, isn't it? I thought the funeral service was a brilliant job, but I like this more. Right I'd better go, we've got a new girl on the till upstairs, and she's not quite got the hang of things yet." Jo walked off.

One of their staff members had recently left to move with her parents to France. So Clare had advertised for a new assistant. They'd chosen Zoe because she had a bubbly personality and they thought customers would like her.

Unfortunately, so far she wasn't very good. She was a slow learner and kept making mistakes; even Clare's usually never-ending patience was wearing thin.

At ten to eight, the reading group finished their meeting, and lined up to pay for their books.

"How did it go?" Clare asked.

They all agreed they'd enjoyed the meeting, and Tessa said now they'd chosen a book, they were looking forward to getting the group underway properly.

"Next time you meet, remind me to ask you something," Clare told them.

"Sounds intriguing," Graham said, raising his eyebrows.

"It's to do with reviews, but I'll tell you properly later."

They couldn't pursue the matter because the shop was due to close and Clare still had customers to deal with. They said their goodbyes and left, clutching their books and speculating as to what she'd meant.

"They must want us to review the books we're reading or something," Mollie said as she stood outside the shop with Graham.

"Maybe they want us to review the new releases? We'll find out soon enough. Are you walking to the car park?"

"I am."

They walked along together, chatting about Merrilies.

"Will you be at this Saturday's meeting?" Mollie asked.

"Yes, but not next Saturday. Easter weekend, I'll be away," Graham said.

"Rightio, I expect we'll not bother until the following Thursday then. No point if we're not all together. Bye, Graham, see you Saturday."

"Yes, bye, Mollie, see you then."

Chapter Nine

Michael stayed at home on Easter Sunday, painting his figures and looking forward to lunch – roast turkey and all the trimmings.

He thought back over what'd happened on Friday. Although the factory closed over Easter, his boss had wanted volunteers to go in and give the whole place a clean through. They'd be paid double time. Most of the men and women declined the invitation, but a few of the single ones who didn't have much else to do – Michael included – agreed.

Everything was going well, until they had a tea break. A big mean-looking guy nicknamed Spike, because of his gelled-up hair, had sat reading one of the sensationalist tabloids. There were pictures of a female celebrity posing topless in it, and Spike was showing the other men.

"Oi, Michael, get a load of this." He shoved the paper towards Michael.

Michael, who was reading a catering magazine, didn't even glance at it.

"Oi, I'm talking to you. Have a butchers at that."

Michael looked up and said, "No thanks."

"Did you hear that? He refused," Spike said loudly, looking at the others with a cocky grin.

"Go on, have a look; she's got a lovely pair."

Michael blushed, but still refused to look, and said, "I don't look at stuff like that, it's demeaning to women."

"Ooh, hark at little Miss Proper, *it's demeaning to women*. The girl posing obviously doesn't think it's demeaning; she wouldn't have done it otherwise. Most red-blooded men love to get an eyeful, unless of course they're batting for the other side."

He leaned close to Michael and hissed, "That's it, ain't it? You swing the other way. Now I come to think of it, you never mention a girlfriend, not that you talk much about anything. You're a right weirdo; you don't go out anywhere, and rush off home to your mumsy every night. You're bent, aren't you?"

Michael continued to read his magazine, but could feel embarrassment flush through his whole body.

"I asked you a question." Spike's tone became more threatening, his voice louder, and he grabbed Michael's arm in a vice-like grip.

"Leave him alone, Spike," said one of the girls, who'd seen what he did.

Spike squeezed Michael's arm and whispered in his ear so that nobody else could overhear. "You perv. I don't want you on our table, go and sit somewhere else. None of the lads will want you working with them if they find out; they hate queers."

Their boss came in and told them to get back to work, but Spike picked on Michael for the rest of the day. He was relieved when, at four o'clock, their boss said they'd done a good job and could go.

He'd hurriedly got his things together and tried to leave without Spike noticing. He was halfway out the door when he heard a familiar voice yell, "Oi, Kingster!' – a name Spike used because of Michael's surname, King. He pretended not to hear and carried on walking, but Spike caught up with him and placed his hand heavily on Michael's shoulder.

"Don't worry, your secret's safe, for now," he said with a sneer.

"I am not homosexual, but my personal life is none of your business anyway," Michael muttered. He tried not to show it, but he was quaking with fear.

"Ooh, the little fairy is daring to answer me back. Too late," Spike snarled nastily, "You had your chance to deny it in there." He jerked his head toward the factory. "But you didn't, so in my book that makes you guilty. Now off you get, and remember, your skeleton's still in the closet, but for how long?"

He pushed Michael roughly away and walked off in the opposite direction.

Michael wondered now, what would happen when he went back to work on Tuesday? He sighed; he'd just have to deal with it when the time came.

***

Mollie spent most of the Easter weekend baking, but she enjoyed it. She found beating the mixture and stirring the ingredients very therapeutic. Sometimes though, her fingers would get a bit stiff and painful – arthritis, she assumed – so she'd thought about getting one of those food processor things to make it easier. But she enjoyed making cakes and biscuits by hand; it wouldn't be quite as satisfactory by machine.

Jo said her lemon drizzle cake, shortbread and Victoria sponge were always very popular.

"Jolly good," Mollie had told her. "Never mind all those fancy cupcakes, you can't beat a good old Victoria sponge."

She'd always loved baking, and had dreamt years ago of running her own tea room, but she'd never achieved her dream.

While she baked, Mollie thought about Thursday's meeting. They'd discussed a bit of Hardy's *Far From the Madding Crowd*, but then the conversation had turned to what they were going to do over Easter, and little Annie had come in again with her mother. The child had looked pale and unwell.

Clare had told them about Annie's illness before she'd

arrived.

"Poor little mite," Mollie had said. "I bet it's hard not being able to run around with the other children as much as she wants. And I feel for her mother. It's difficult enough to look after a child nowadays, but to be constantly worried about their health as well, must be quite draining."

Mollie rubbed some flour and butter together, and smiled as her thoughts turned to Graham, and how he'd steered them back to their book discussion.

It would take a while before the group found its feet and had a proper routine at these meetings, but things were shaping up nicely.

Without meaning to, she seemed to have taken charge of the group and Graham had backed her up. The others didn't mind though, and almost expected it now. It was probably because she and Graham were the eldest.

Was it just her imagination that Graham seemed to watch her a lot? She'd caught him looking at her when he'd thought she wasn't watching, but he didn't glance away again. Instead he gave her a slow smile. He had a nice smile; it made his eyes crinkle up at the corners. He had nice eyes too, soft and brown.

"You silly old fool," she chastised herself and got on with her baking.

***

Graham had an enjoyable Easter. On Good Friday afternoon, he drove up to Lincolnshire to spend the weekend with his sister and brother-in-law. They were delighted to see him, as he didn't visit often. On Saturday evening he took them out to dinner, and on Easter Sunday his sister cooked a roast. Graham missed proper home cooking. Although he was now sixty-two, he could still remember their mother's cooking, and made a mental note to visit his sister more often. He seldom cooked for himself; there didn't seem much point putting a roast in the oven for one. He usually opened a tin of salmon and had it with some new potatoes and salad, or made an omelette.

His sister had asked how he was spending his retirement and he told her about the reading group. He made her laugh with his descriptions of Felicity and Michael.

"Anyone your age there?"

"Well, it's only a small group, just the five of us. As well as Felicity and Michael, there's Tessa, and a lady who must be a bit younger than me, Mollie."

"Oh yes, and what's this Mollie like?"

"She's very nice, from what I know so far. She seems down-to-earth and quite motherly; she's taken charge of the group, with my help of course."

"Mm, anything else?" his sister asked.

"Well, I do know she's a good cook; nearly as good as you, my dear."

His sister pounced on this snippet of information. "Oh, how do you know that? Has she invited you for a meal?"

Graham tutted. "No, stop matchmaking. She makes the cakes and biscuits for the bookshop café. She brought a fruit cake in for us once. It was delicious."

"I thought you were looking a bit portly around the middle," his sister laughed.

"Talking about cakes, I don't suppose there's anything for pudding, is there?" Graham asked hopefully.

"I see you haven't lost your sweet tooth then. I thought you might want something, so I made a trifle."

His brother-in-law snorted. "Hmph, talk about favouritism. I'm never allowed dessert, but when you visit we get one," he said in a disgruntled manner.

"If he came every week, he wouldn't get it, but he doesn't visit that often, so it's a treat," his sister told her husband.

It made Graham feel a bit guilty. He'd never been very

good at this visiting business; he really should come more often. He phoned every few weeks, and his sister phoned him too, but it wasn't the same as seeing someone.

He knew it worked both ways, and they could visit him. But they only had an old banger of a car and not much money, whilst Graham's previous job as the managing director of a large international company had left him extremely well off. He had a big saloon car, plenty of money for fuel, and he enjoyed driving too, so it wasn't a chore.

Whenever he thought about the lifestyle he had, he felt very privileged. He'd travelled a lot on business, staying in the best hotels; had some lovely holidays, and eaten in all the top restaurants. His home was a beautiful converted barn, he had a riverboat moored near Henley, and he could afford to eat out every night if he wished. Mind you, he'd worked extremely hard for it over the years.

So he was the one who usually did the visiting.

He'd offered to buy his sister and brother-in-law a decent car, but they wouldn't hear of it. His brother-in-law had got quite worked up about it, so Graham had dropped the subject and taken them out for a meal instead. He guessed accepting dinner didn't seem so much like charity.

As he drove home on Easter Monday, he thought about the reading group.

He enjoyed the meetings. Felicity was a girl and a half. She teased poor Michael mercilessly at times, and she was so outspoken; but he could sense that she had a soft heart, and was actually a nice kid.

Michael was a bit strange. Graham couldn't decide if he liked him or not. Tessa was lovely, if a bit quiet, but she could hold her own and wasn't afraid to stand up for herself. She'd put Felicity in her place a few times. And then there was Mollie. Although he'd laughed off his sister's suggestions, he did have a soft spot for her.

I could get quite used to her home cooking every night and

snuggling up on the sofa, he thought. Then he chided himself for being so fanciful. She's a widow who must still miss her husband, and probably feels nothing at all for me; I'm just another member of the reading group. Nevertheless, he was looking forward to the next meeting when he'd see her again.

Chapter Ten

"Morning," Jo said as Clare let herself into the shop. Now that Jo lived across the road, she was usually first in, but Clare wasn't far behind her. "Good Easter?"

"Yes, lovely thanks. I went round to Mum and Dad's for lunch. I ate too much though." Clare laughed. "What about you?"

"Yeah, same really, had lunch with my parents on Sunday. God, aren't we boring? We did nothing interesting between us."

"I know. We need some excitement. The trouble is I'm so tired after working here that all I want to do is curl up with Angus and watch TV in the evenings."

"Yeah, I know what you mean, but we do need some fun. Why don't we have a night out together, let our hair down?" Jo said.

"Okay, that'd be good, we haven't been *out* out for ages, it's usually me coming to you for a meal or vice versa," Clare said as she leafed through some marketing brochures Jo had left on the counter.

"Meal! Pizza more like! When was the last time I cooked?"

"Ha ha, you know what I mean, but a proper night out would be good. We could start with a meal, then go to a few pubs afterwards," Clare suggested, and she pushed her glasses back.

"I thought you'd got your glasses tightened up."

"I did, why?"

"You're still pushing them along your nose," Jo laughed.

"It's such a habit, you don't even realise you're doing it."

Clare grinned. "Sorry, but at least it's harmless. I don't smoke or chew my nails, or anything equally as gross. Right, want a quick cuppa before we open up?"

"Please. I'll just finish putting the new releases on the table, and I'll be with you. I've got a tarot reading booked for eleven-thirty."

"Okay, I'll make sure I'm downstairs. Zoe had better buck her ideas up, she was worse than useless last week. I'm hoping it was just a blip, or she was unwell or something," Clare said.

"Let's give her the benefit of the doubt; she's still on trial. Give her one more week and if she's not on form, we'll let her go and find someone else. Agree?"

"Agree. '

The morning passed quite quickly, and Zoe seemed a lot better than the previous week. She'd mastered the till, and seemed good with the customers. She served them with efficiency and took the time to help with any queries. Clare breathed a sigh of relief; she didn't really want to go through the hassle of interviewing someone else again.

Jo did her tarot reading at the appointed time, then took over from Clare so she could go upstairs.

"That went well," she told Clare. "The woman was so impressed she's going to tell the members of her group. She's the president of some committee; the group who organise the town festival, I think she said. Hopefully it'll bring us some more business."

"Oh well done. I still don't know how you do it, or how the cards can be so accurate."

"Me neither and I've been doing it for years now. Blimey, I might have more clients than I can handle soon. I hope not, I'd hate it to affect Merrilies."

"Well, you're in charge of the bookings so don't take too many. If you do get a lot, you can do them at home. I won't mind. Don't feel that you're taking profit away from the shop.

Any you do at night are in your own time, so that's your money," Clare said.

"Okay, thanks. I might have to do that if it gets too mad."

They had a rush of lunchtime customers as they often did, usually local workers shopping in their breaks, then it settled down again in the afternoon. At four-fifteen, Annie and Alice came in, even though it was still the Easter school holidays.

"Hi Jo, guess how many Easter eggs I had?" Annie said.

"Two?"

"Nope, guess again."

"Erm, four?"

"Nope."

"Okay, I give up. How many?"

"Six."

"Six! That's a lot of chocolate for one little girl to eat. You'll get a podgy tummy." Jo gently prodded Annie's stomach.

Annie giggled, "Mummy helped me eat some of them, and I have three left."

"Yeah I bet Mummy helped too. I would if my little girl had been bought six Easter eggs."

"I didn't know you had a little girl," Annie said.

"I haven't, it was just a figure of speech."

"What's a vicar of speech?"

Jo and Alice burst out laughing.

"FIGURE of speech," Alice spluttered. "It means it's just something Jo said but didn't really mean."

"But why did she say it if she didn't mean it?" Annie asked with a frown on her little face.

"Oh never mind," Alice laughed. "Off you go and have a look at the books. We can't stop for too long tonight. I'll be there in a moment."

Annie made her way over to the children's area and Alice followed Jo, who took an armful of books to the fiction shelves, leaving Zoe on the till.

"Jo, can I ask a favour? You know Annie is dolphin mad,

well we've been reading up on dolphin therapy. It can help children with certain conditions, and even fit children get some benefits from it. We think it would do Annie the world of good and help boost her immune system. Tom and I are fed up seeing her so weak and ill. I know it's not her fault, but if we could try something that would help her…'

Alice stopped talking and looked near to tears. Jo's heart went out to her.

Alice continued, "Anyway, we'd like to send her to America for dolphin therapy. Apparently, the ultrasound they emit as part of their echolocation system can be beneficial, and interacting with them can help emotionally too. Annie would just love being in the water with dolphins. The trouble is it's expensive, so we need to raise the money somehow." She looked pleadingly at Jo.

"And you want us to help?" Jo asked. "I'll have to run it by Clare, but I'm sure she'll say yes. Why don't you get some collection boxes made up, and if Clare's okay about it, we'll put them on the counters. You could contact the Herald too. They always love a good local story. You could mention Merrilies, and that way we'll both get some publicity."

"Sounds like a great idea, but I don't want Annie made into some sort of charity case," Alice said.

"I'm sure it won't be viewed as anything except what it is; a family trying to help their sick child. Come on, Alice, people love to support local issues, and you may be able to take Annie to America sooner than you think."

"Okay I'll do it. Thanks so much, Jo. Talking of madam, I better go and find her."

As Alice made to leave, Annie came back and she was wheezing.

"Annie, for goodness sake, why have you been rushing? Okay, calm down and get your inhaler out. Annie, calm down."

The little girl took several puffs of her inhaler and her

breathing became more regulated.

"Why on earth were you running? You know not to exert yourself!" Alice shouted at her.

"I...was trying...to get back...to Jo," the little girl managed to say. She took a few more deep breaths then continued, "Jo, that girl on the till over there, put a ten pound in her pocket."

Jo looked at Alice then at Annie again. "Are you sure about that?"

"Yes honestly, Jo. I don't tell lies, I saw her. I did, I promise."

Jo didn't know whether to believe Annie or not, but she did seem certain.

Alice bent down in front of her daughter and held her hands. "Okay, sweetheart, don't get yourself worked up again, but tell us exactly what happened."

"Well, I'd gone to look at the books cuz you told me to. I choosed a book and went back to the till, but you weren't there. That girl was there but no-one else. She didn't see me. She looked around, opened the till, took out an orange money – that's ten, isn't it? – and put it in her pocket. Then I tried to find you. That's why I got out of breath cuz I was hurrying."

"Good girl, thank you for telling me. I must tell Clare. Alice, sorry to drag you into this further, but could you keep an eye on Zoe, make sure she doesn't go anywhere. If she's got money on her, I don't want her hiding it. We need to catch her with it still in her pocket."

"I'll go and talk to her," Annie offered.

"Good idea, darling, come on," said Alice. They walked up to the counter and started chatting to Zoe.

Jo ran upstairs to find Clare, and explained what Annie had told her. Clare asked Stella to mind the till and took Jo down to the office to watch the CCTV.

"Right, let's wind this back and have a look," Clare said.

She rewound the tape, and searched through the last fifteen

minutes of recording.

"Stop, back a bit. Okay, play it," Jo said. Sure enough, as damning evidence on the tape, there was Zoe furtively looking about her before opening the till, removing a note, and putting it in her pocket.

Clare exploded. "The thieving little cow! I am so angry, I could thump her. We trusted her, gave her a job, and this is how she repays us."

"Calm down, Clare. We'll deal with it."

"We'll sack her, more like; I'm not having a thief working for me."

"Okay, but we need to talk to her first, give her a chance to explain."

"Explain what! That she's stolen money from us? How many other times has she done it?"

"None, because the tills wouldn't have balanced, would they? Stop getting worked up until we've spoken to her. Come on."

They went out to find Annie and Alice still standing at the till.

"Thank you, Alice, we can deal with this now," Clare said.

"Can I stay and see..?" Annie blurted, but Alice managed to stop her just in time.

"Zoe, can you come with us, please?" Clare told her. "Can you cover the till for a bit?" she asked another assistant, who was putting away the books Jo had left.

"What's going on?" Zoe asked.

"We'll tell you in a moment, just come with us," Clare said.

Back in the office, she told Zoe to sit down. The girl still stood, so Clare grabbed her arm and shoved her into a chair.

"I think I better deal with this," Jo said.

Clare nodded and stood with her hands on her hips, her face like thunder.

"Zoe, is there anything you'd like to own up to?" Jo asked, sitting in the chair across from her.

"Erm no, like what?" the girl asked defiantly.

Clare hissed, "Like stealing from the till?"

Zoe looked uncomfortable. "No."

"Well, can you stand up and turn out your pockets then please," Jo asked.

"I don't want to."

"Right, I'm not asking, I'm telling. Turn out your pockets, NOW!" Clare shouted as she moved towards her.

Zoe hesitated, then slowly emptied her pockets onto the table. In her right pocket was a pen and a lip-gloss, in her left, a ten-pound note.

"Just as we thought, a ten-pound note," Clare said.

"But that's mine for bus fare home tonight."

"Zoe, please don't make this worse by lying. We know you stole it, you were seen," Jo said. She sat back and folded her arms.

"By who? They're lying!"

"But the camera doesn't lie; we've got it on CCTV. Do you want to see it?" Clare asked.

Zoe's face went white and she hung her head. "I'm sorry."

"Oh, so you did steal it then?" Jo asked.

Zoe mumbled something.

"Pardon?" Clare barked as she stood in front of the girl.

"Yes, I took it," Zoe admitted, tears now coursing down her cheeks.

Jo intervened again. "Why did you do it? We pay you a reasonable wage, you had no need to steal from us."

"I spent all my wages at the weekend on clothes, then remembered it's my gran's birthday. I needed some money to buy her a card and flowers. I've never done it before, honest."

"Then why the hell didn't you ask for a sub, instead of stealing it?" Clare shook her head in disbelief. "It may be the first time, Zoe, but it will be the last time you ever do anything for us."

"Wha– what do you mean?"

"I mean I'm sacking you."

"Oh please, Clare, don't fire me. Please, I need this job."

"You should have thought about that before you stole from us. You're not getting a second chance, what sort of message would that give the rest of the staff, huh? That they could steal from us once and get away with it? No, I'm sorry, Zoe, but I want you out straight away. Get your stuff please and leave."

Zoe put her hand over her mouth and, sobbing, went up to the staff room to get her coat and bag.

Jo stood up and got herself a glass of water from the tap, then poured one for Clare. "Don't you think you're being a bit hard on her?" she asked.

Clare took a gulp from the glass, swallowed the water and took a deep breath.

"No I don't. I'm not going to argue with you over this, Jo. You and I have never disagreed before, but I will NOT have my staff stealing from me. It's about trust, and once they've betrayed that, they're out, I'm afraid."

Jo shrugged. "Okay, but can we at least give her a reference so she can find another job?"

Clare slammed her glass down on the table, sloshing water everywhere.

"Absolutely not! Why should we give her a reference when she's a thief? No, it's up to her whether she tells anyone the reason she left, but I'm not hiding the truth. In fact, I might call the rest of the staff for a chat after work, just so they know we won't tolerate stealing. I hope I have your support on this, Jo."

"Of course you do. I just feel a bit sorry for her, that's all."

"Well, don't. Did she feel sorry for us when she took that money? You can bet your sweet arse she didn't."

"CLARE!" Jo gasped with shock, but laughed. "Blimey, remind me not to get on your bad side. And I thought you were such an easy-going person too."

"I am until something upsets me or makes me angry, and

this did. I don't like being taken for a fool."

Zoe came back with her belongings and stood in front of Clare, crying.

"Right, off you go, and I'd rather you didn't come into Merrilies again," Clare said.

Zoe sobbed even harder. "But what am I going to tell my parents and everyone?"

"That's not my problem, you should have thought about that before you stole from us. I suggest you tell the truth though. I don't want an irate father storming in here demanding to know why I sacked his daughter, because then I *will* tell him the reason. Now go."

And that was that; Clare dismissed her without another word.

At closing time, Jo asked the three remaining staff to stay for a quick chat, and Clare then explained what had happened. "So if you are ever tempted, I wouldn't advise it; we won't tolerate stealing. I like to think we have a happy band of staff and a good working relationship. Please don't let us down," she finished.

Jo said she and Clare appreciated all their hard work and it hadn't gone unnoticed. She told them they'd be rewarded accordingly at some point.

"What," Clare said, when she'd closed the door on the last member of staff to leave, "was all that about being rewarded accordingly?"

"I was just letting them know we appreciate them and that they might get a little bonus at some point. We haven't given them a pay rise since Merrilies opened, so they're due something," Jo said.

"Okay. Well, maybe after the summer we can see what our profit's like and give them a bonus in time for Christmas or something...maybe. Phew, I'm exhausted."

"Me too," Jo replied. "It must be the emotion of the last hour that's done it. At least everyone knows where they stand now. You tyrant, that's why I tried to sweeten it."

"Well, if they don't like it, they can find alternative employment, can't they? I think they'll stay though. Apart from Zoe, the rest have been with us since day one and are as good as gold. Right, I'm going home for a bath, a dinner for one and an early night in bed with a book."

"Sounds good. We must get a little something for Annie, bless her. If she hadn't spotted Zoe stealing, we wouldn't have known about it."

"Find out what she likes reading, and give her a couple of books."

"Hmm okay. Maybe there's something about dolphins, and I'll wrap them in pretty paper for her."

"You big softie."

"Aw, but she's such a sweet kid."

"Yes she is. Okay, I'm off. See you tomorrow."

"Yeah, see you, Clare."

They locked up and went their separate ways, Jo to her flat across the road and Clare to the car park to drive her little car home to Chipping Norton.

Chapter Eleven

The following Thursday the reading group met up again. They hadn't seen each other for a week, as they hadn't held a meeting over the Easter weekend.

For once, Felicity was early, and arrived at the same time as Mollie. They sat at the table and waited for the others.

"Did you have a nice Easter?" Mollie asked conversationally.

"It was okay; I didn't do much, and Mummy let the housekeeper off for a few days, so we had to suffer her cooking on Sunday – euck, it was dreadful." Felicity gave a shudder.

Mollie laughed. "I'm sure, Felicity, that your mother is a perfectly adequate cook and you're just making a fuss."

"No, really, it was bloody awful. She tried to do a roast lunch, but the meat was chewy and overcooked, the potatoes were hard and the vegetables mushy. As for the gravy...put it this way, Daddy said if Mummy ever attempts to cook again, he'll divorce her and marry Mrs Harris."

"Who's Mrs Harris?"

"Our housekeeper."

"Oh. Your mother can't be *that* bad. Surely she must have learned to cook when she lived at home with her parents."

"No she didn't. They had a cook, so Mummy never needed to learn."

"Oh dear. Well, I should jolly well hope you've learnt to cook. And if you haven't, it's about time you did."

"I can get by. I had to eat at Uni, so I did some cooking then. Nothing spectacular, but I can make a good chilli,"

Felicity said.

"Why didn't you help your mother cook the lunch then?"

"Because I didn't get up until late and besides, it was rather fun to watch her get in such a flap."

"Felicity, you are a terrible young lady, do you know that? If you were my daughter, I'd have woken you up at a reasonable time and made you help. You're spoiled rotten," Mollie told her, but she said it with a smile.

Felicity grinned then looked up as Tessa, Graham and Michael approached the table.

"Oh, I was hoping I'd have time to get a coffee," Felicity said. "Who else would like one? I tell you what, I'll get us all a drink, then we can start properly. Okay, who has what?" She wrote down how everyone took their coffees.

The others started digging in their pockets and bags for some change to give her.

"No, no, put it away, it's my treat," she told them.

Mollie looked at her affectionately. She might be an outspoken pain at times, but the girl was generous and had a good heart.

Felicity came down ten minutes later with five coffees on a tray and some biscuits. Once they'd sorted themselves out, and chatted a bit about their Easter, they got down to business.

"So what do we all think of the book so far?" Graham asked.

Felicity put her hand up.

"Yes, Felicity?"

"I think Sergeant Troy is a bit of a stud muffin. I wouldn't turn him down. I can just picture him in his uniform too. Mmm."

"What on earth is a stud muffin?" Graham asked with a look of puzzlement.

Felicity laughed. "It means I think he's a bit of a hunk."

"Flick, how could you? He's a womanising pig!" Tessa said in disgust.

"Mmm, but a charming one though."

"Ah, you are obviously taken in by charmers, Felicity, but you ought to be careful. They're usually the worst sort of men to get involved with," Graham admonished her.

"Sorry, Pops."

Graham raised his eyebrows at being called Pops, but didn't say anything.

Mollie joined in the discussion. "Well, it's perfectly obvious that Bathsheba would be much better off with Gabriel." She looked at Michael, who seemed quieter than usual, and asked, "Don't you agree, Michael?"

Michael looked up. "What? Oh yes, I agree...sorry, Mollie, what were you saying?"

"About Bathsheba and Sergeant Troy."

"Oh, the stupid woman. She'd be better off with shepherd Gabriel, he's much more her sort, and how she thinks she can run that farm all by herself too. A farm needs a man on it," Michael said with feeling.

"Nice to see you've been reading the book, Michael," Mollie smiled at him. There's something not quite right with the lad tonight she thought, maybe later if I get the chance, I'll ask him what's wrong.

They continued their discussion of the book until Jo came over to collect the coffee tray.

"Everyone happy?" she asked them.

"Yes fine, thank you," Tessa said.

They all answered except Michael. Jo bent down and looked at him. "You okay too, Michael?"

"Oh err, yeah thanks," he mumbled.

Mollie decided she was definitely going to have a word, but not in front of everyone else.

"While I'm here, there's something I want to tell you, and something I'd like to ask," Jo said and told them about raising money for Annie.

"And Clare was meant to ask you last week but forgot, we

also wondered if any of you would be interested in doing a review of the new releases for the local paper. We haven't run it by them yet, but I'm sure they'd be interested."

"What a jolly good idea. It's all publicity, isn't it? Do they know about the fundraising?" Mollie said.

"Not yet, Alice is going to contact them, and she'll let us know what happens."

"Anything we can do to help?" Tessa asked.

"You can tell your friends and family, and anyone else you know that Merrilies is raising money for Annie; every little helps."

"Okay and I'll see if I can get the surgery involved. I'm sure the doctors won't mind if we have a collection box on the reception counter."

"That's great, Tessa, thanks. Now, who's going to volunteer to do these reviews?"

Michael was listening this time. "Not me, I'm afraid, I have enough to do with my job, hobby and this group."

"Yes, you've got such a high flying career, eh, Michael?" Felicity teased.

Michael glared at her.

"Sorry, I can't spare the time," Tessa said. "With my job, daughter and writing, there aren't enough hours in the day. I only just manage these meetings, and then I have to get my parents to babysit," she sighed. "But it's so nice to escape for a bit!"

"No good looking at me, I'm afraid," Felicity said.

"But you have plenty of spare time, Flick, you don't work or anything." Michael, for once, had the chance to get his own back.

"So! I don't want to promise something and not stick with it. I don't know when I might be whisked off on holiday or asked out to lunch, and I don't want to be tied down to a regular task."

"But you come here regularly," Michael said.

"Yes, and that's as much as I'm prepared to do. Sorry, Jo."

"Don't worry, everyone, I'll do it," Graham told them. "I'm retired and have plenty of time on my hands."

Mollie felt sorry for him. "I'll help too, that way Graham won't have to do it all by himself."

"Can you spare the time? What about your baking?" Graham asked.

"I'm sure I can fit in the book reviews as well."

"You really don't have to, you know."

"I know, but I'd like to." Her eyes held Graham's for a moment.

He smiled his gratitude.

"Thanks, you two. I was going to ask whoever did it to review one title each month if they could, but I realise that may be a bit when you're reading a book a month for the group too. But with both of you, you could take it in turns; Graham do a book one month and Mollie the next. That way you get a free month in between. How does that sound?" Jo asked.

"I think I could manage that easily. I read during the day and in bed at night," Mollie said. She blushed when Graham looked across at her, hoping he wasn't thinking of her in bed; then she scolded herself. Why would he be doing that, she thought, you daft old woman!

Graham *was* imagining Mollie in bed though. He pictured her sitting up reading, with a pretty nightdress on and her face scrubbed clean.

He coughed and tried to concentrate. "Ahem, yes that's fine with me too, Jo."

"Oh that's great. Well, now we've sorted that out, I can phone the Herald and see if they're interested. I'll let you know what they say." She wandered off with the tray.

The meeting ended soon after. They'd almost finished reading *Far From the Madding Crowd*, so decided that at Saturday's meeting they'd vote for the next book.

They stood up to leave, collecting their books, coats and bags. Felicity said she had to meet a friend and rushed off. Tessa wanted to get home quickly because her parents were looking after Amber, so she rushed away too. Mollie hoped to catch Michael for a quick chat, but he mumbled goodbye and disappeared, which left just her and Graham.

They smiled at each other a little awkwardly.

"Are you walking to the car park?" Graham asked.

"Yes."

"Me too."

It was a lovely warm evening, unusually so for the end of April. Graham made small talk on the way to the car park. "So, what are you up to this evening?"

"Nothing really, I haven't even thought about what I'm going to have for supper. I don't always cook, being on my own."

"Nor do I, and I don't have anything ready for tonight either." He then blurted out, "I don't suppose you'd...no, don't worry."

"What?" Mollie asked.

"It doesn't matter, only a thought," he said and straightened his tie.

"Just jolly well say it, I'm intrigued now."

"Well, I was going to ask if you'd like to join me for a bite to eat. Heaven knows where though."

By now they were at their cars and Graham, feeling self-conscious, fiddled with his keys.

Mollie put her hand on his arm. "I'd like that, thank you."

She thought how attractive he was as his face lit up with delight.

"Oh that's good, right, where can we go? Shall we take my car and I'll bring you back here or do you want to drive your own?" Graham asked.

"It would make sense if I take my car, otherwise it's a lot of messing around. What sort of food do you like?"

"Italian, Indian, Chinese. I'm partial to a bit of fillet steak too; I'll eat most things really. You?"

"Pretty similar although I prefer sirloin to fillet. But I like Italian too," Mollie said.

"Well, I know a nice Italian restaurant not too far away, shall we try that?"

"Yes, why not? That would be lovely."

"Right," Graham said. "Follow me."

He couldn't quite believe she'd agreed to go for a meal with him, but was glad she had. He wondered how she felt about him. He was just being fanciful; after all, they weren't teenagers; they were past that sort of thing at their age.

He couldn't deny how he felt though, and knew he wanted to spend more time with Mollie. He hoped she felt the same, but even if she viewed him as just a friend, it was a start.

"Graham, old chap, there's life in the old dog yet," he said aloud and grinned.

Mollie carefully followed Graham's car, pleased at the turn of events. Even though it was a spur of the moment idea, she looked forward to spending time with him away from the group. She wondered if he also felt a spark between them, or if he was just being friendly and it was her imagination working overtime.

Chapter Twelve

Michael arrived home and went straight up to his room. He knew he'd been quiet at the meeting this evening and hadn't concentrated properly, but he had a lot on his mind.

Spike had cornered him in work yesterday and said he was going to tell everybody about him being "a poofter" unless Michael gave him fifty pounds. Michael told him to get lost, but Spike had grabbed him around the neck. Luckily, another worker unintentionally interrupted things when he shouted for Spike to sort out one of the conveyors. Michael had gone out on deliveries after that, so didn't see him for the rest of the day.

They hadn't worked together today as Spike was on deliveries, but they were both in tomorrow and Michael was dreading it.

Spike was a nasty thug; this bullying could go on for months.

Michael sighed and went down to answer the door to a friend who'd come round to play a battle game.

***

Meanwhile, Mollie and Graham sat at a corner table in the small but busy Italian restaurant. Graham wanted to order a bottle of wine, but they were both driving so they just had a small glass each. Mollie liked dry white wine, while he preferred red.

They talked about their past. Mollie told him a little about her life with Victor, and he told her a bit about his job.

He'd obviously worked hard and enjoyed the fruits of that hard work, but Mollie thought it sad that he'd never had anyone to share it with.

"It can't have been much fun being on your own, did you never long for company?"

"I wasn't alone that often. I attended business dinners, so was surrounded with colleagues day and night. Now I'm retired, it's different, but I don't mind my own company. I can do what I want, when I want," Graham said. He put down his fork and took a sip of wine.

"Colleagues aren't the same as friends though. It must be lonely at times," Mollie said.

"I'm okay. Living alone can make you selfish, and it's quite hard to change, especially when you're an old fogey like me."

"You're hardly an old fogey, and if you are, so am I. When Victor first died, I was devastated and felt so bereft. He was the love of my life and we'd been together a long time, but after a while, I learnt to live without him."

"Well then, you should understand what I mean about enjoying my own company."

"Yes I do, but I've experienced both sides of it. I've had a husband, and now I'm on my own. Have you never had anyone special in your life?" Mollie asked tentatively. She wanted to know all about him, but was aware of being too nosey.

"I've had a few relationships, but they didn't work. Because of my job, we hardly saw each other. I've got two cats for company though, and at least they don't argue with me," Graham said.

Mollie laughed. "That's true. I'm glad you like cats, so do I."

Graham changed the subject, not wanting to talk about his private life any longer. "Would you like pudding or are you watching your figure?"

Mollie tutted. "I'm well past that. Look at me, I'm hardly Twiggy. Yes, let's have something sweet."

"Just for the record, there's nothing wrong with your figure," Graham said. He looked at the menu the waitress had brought. "I think I'll have tiramisu."

Mollie looked through the menu then exclaimed, "Oh wonderful, they have lemoncello. That's my favourite."

The waitress took their order and they sat in silence for a few moments. Mollie looked around the restaurant, and whilst she did, Graham studied her. She looked back, caught him, and smiled.

"I like watching people and inventing scenarios for them. See that couple over there, do you think they're on a first date or celebrating an anniversary?"

Graham looked at a young couple who were holding hands across the table and gazing into each other eyes.

"First date, I would say. They wouldn't be so loving if it was their anniversary, would they?" he asked.

"Oh I don't know. They might if it was their first anniversary, or even their third. They look too young for any more than that. But some people are still as loving thirty years later as when they first met. The initial excitement of a new romance dies down, but your love deepens as you grow together." She stopped talking and blushed. "Listen to me, soppy old fool," she said laughing.

"You're not a fool, Mollie, and I like people-watching too. Oh great, here's pudding."

They ate in silence. Mollie finished hers first. "Mm, that was delicious. I haven't been to an Italian for ages. I'm glad I came."

"I'm glad you came too. Would you like coffee?"

"Only if they have decaf. I can't drink ordinary coffee, caffeine makes me ill."

The waitress stopped to collect their plates and Graham asked if they did decaffeinated coffee. They did, so he ordered two.

"Oh, do you drink decaf as well?" Mollie asked.

"Yes, I changed when I retired. I didn't need the caffeine to keep me going any more."

The waitress brought their coffees and the bill. Graham picked it up.

"How much is it?" Mollie asked.

"Why?"

"Because I'm paying half."

"No, it's on me," Graham said.

"It jolly well isn't. I'll pay my share!" Mollie said indignantly.

"Mollie, please, it was my idea to invite you, and I'd like to pay for it. I've had a nice evening in pleasant company. If it bothers you that much, you can pay next time." He then added quickly, "If you'd like to come out with me again, of course." He watched her face for any hints.

Mollie smiled then said, "I've had a lovely evening too, and yes, I'd like to see you again. But you're naughty for paying. I'm not happy about it."

"Well, you'll just have to put up with not being happy, I'm afraid, because I insist on paying. So there."

They finished their coffees and Graham paid the bill. He helped Mollie into her coat and they walked out into the dark street.

When they got to their cars, Graham said, "Thanks again for a pleasant evening, Mollie. I've really enjoyed myself."

"Thank you for inviting me. See you at the meeting Saturday?"

"Of course. Drive carefully, goodnight." He bent down and kissed her cheek.

She gave his arm a squeeze, said goodnight and got into her car.

Graham watched her leave the car park before he started the engine and drove off. He'd just had the nicest evening in a long time. He switched on the radio and sang along to the song that was playing.

***

At home, Mollie finished brushing her teeth, left the bathroom and sat on her bed. She'd had such a lovely evening, but she felt guilty, as if she was somehow betraying Victor's memory. Not in the mood to read, she sighed, got into bed, switched out the light and whispered into the darkness, "I've been so lonely. I hope you understand, Victor."

Chapter Thirteen

Jo and Clare were having an after-work drink in the local wine bar. It was a Saturday evening and neither of them had plans for the night ahead.

"Phew, I really needed this. It's been a busy week, hasn't it?" Clare took a huge gulp of white wine.

"You can say that again. I'm glad though. We'd soon complain if it wasn't busy and we weren't earning any money. We work really well together, don't we?" Jo said.

"Yes we do, we're a good team."

Clare asked the barman for a packet of crisps before saying, "I still have no idea why I asked you to join me that day. It just popped into my head at that particular moment and kind of seemed right. Does that make sense?"

"You're asking *me* does that make sense! The person who's acted all her life on the things that pop into her head." Jo raised her eyebrows.

"Ha ha, ooh yes, that's funny. But you know what I mean."

"Yeah, and I don't know, Clare. Maybe you had a premonition that day too."

"If so, it's the only one I've ever had, apart from things like humming a song then switching on the radio and the song's playing, or when the phone rings and you know who it is before answering it. Wish I could do what you do, it must be exciting."

Jo helped herself to some of the crisps and crunched a mouthful before speaking. "If you only knew! It might seem exciting, but it's been a real burden. People have treated me like a leper at times. I told you about mum's friend with the dog, didn't I?"

"The one that got run over?"

"Yeah, it was awful. She never spoke to us again, and actually crossed the street when she saw me. Kids at school called me Witchy, but I soon sorted them out; I said I'd put a curse on them."

Clare giggled, "Well, I'd only like to know good things, not horrible things."

"That's the whole problem," Jo sighed. "I can't choose what I know, it just happens; good and bad. It's lessened as I've got older, thankfully, and it only happens occasionally now. In fact, I haven't had an omen since the one about me sitting in the flat. Fancy another glass of wine?"

"I'd love one, but I've got to drive home," Clare said, looking at her watch.

"Why don't you stay with me tonight? You can have another drink then."

"That would be great. But what about Angus? He needs to be fed and locked in for the night. You know I don't like him out after dark. I could phone my neighbour, I suppose; she has a key to feed him if I go on holiday."

"Yeah, give her a ring. We can sit here and get drunk, then grab a takeaway and go back to my place. Go on, you've only got a boring night on your own else," Jo said.

"Oh thanks a lot, Jo! Mock the fact that I'm a boring individual who doesn't even go out on a Saturday night. Do you want to tell the whole pub whilst you're at it?"

"Okay." Jo went to kneel up on her stool.

Clare grabbed her arm to stop her. "Behave yourself and get the drinks in. I'll phone Sandy." Laughing, Clare got her mobile out to call her neighbour.

They worked through a few more glasses of wine each, and discussed whether to walk to the takeaway, or go back to Jo's and phone for a delivery. They decided the best option, considering their inebriated state, was to go back to Jo's.

They chose what they wanted from the takeaway menu and Jo phoned it through while Clare put a couple of plates in the oven to warm.

Eating their food sobered them up a bit, and they talked about the reading group.

"I think there might be something developing between Mollie and Graham," Jo said.

"No! Really? What makes you think that?"

"I don't know. The way they look at each other, and when they left today, Graham held Mollie's arm as he steered her out of the door."

"He might have just been being gentlemanly." Clare speared a prawn with her fork.

"Nah, it was the way they looked into each other's eyes as well. I reckon they're seeing each other."

"Well, good for them, I think they'd make a lovely couple."

"Yeah I do as well. I might ask when we see them next."

"Jo, you can't do that!" Clare exclaimed. "What if they want to keep it secret? Please don't ask; it might embarrass them. If they want people to know, they'll tell us in their own good time."

"Sorry, Mother. I forgot how proper you are." Jo made a face at her.

Clare frowned. "No, I just don't think we should interfere in their personal lives."

"I'm only kidding. I won't say anything. You're right; they'll tell us when they're ready."

"Yes they will, *if* anything is going on. Actually, I was going to tell you something. This nice looking guy came in today."

"Oh yeah, and?"

Clare looked down at her plate, suddenly shy for a moment. "Nothing really. I dropped some books and he picked them up for me. Our fingers brushed as he passed them back, and he looked right into my eyes." She tutted. "I'm being silly, but it was like a brush of electricity."

"Oh, you've just had too much to..." Jo broke off as an image suddenly came into her mind of Clare lying in a hospital bed. Jo looked at Clare in alarm, then shook her head, trying to clear the vision.

"Jo, what is it? What's wrong? You look like you've seen a ghost."

"N–nothing, I thought I heard a noise, that's all."

"What sort of noise?" Clare looked around worriedly.

"I dunno, it must have been my imagination. I was going to say you've had too much to drink, but I think I have too. My imagination's working overtime."

"Why have I had too much to drink?"

"Because you're getting all fanciful about that guy who picked up the books, talking about electricity and stuff."

"Well, I've never felt like that before. I wonder if he'll come in again."

"Clare, you're not usually romantic; you're one of the most matter of fact people I know, so get your head out of the clouds and get another glass of wine down you. Do you want to watch a DVD?" Jo asked, swallowing hard and trying to keep her face even.

"Yes okay."

"Scary, action, or chick-flick? Second thoughts, forget the chick-flick, let's have a scary film."

"I'm not sure I want to watch a scary movie if you're hearing noises, and I'm not sleeping on the sofa on my own if we do. I'll sleep in your room on the floor," Clare said with a shudder.

"I've got a double bed you can share," Jo offered.

"Erm, no thanks, I'll be fine on the floor."

Jo laughed. "Clare, for God's sake, I'm perfectly straight, and even if I was gay, I wouldn't fancy you. No offence."

Clare was outraged. "Jo!"

"Well, don't be so stuffy. It's only a bed, and we're friends.

Have you never shared a bed with a girlfriend before?"

"No I haven't, actually. And why wouldn't you fancy me if you were gay, what's wrong with me?"

Jo laughed out loud. "Nothing, you idiot, I only said it to pacify you. I should offer to sleep on the floor 'cos you're the guest, but I'm not into floors, especially when there's a perfectly comfy bed to sleep in. So, your choice is: the sofa on your own, the hard uncomfortable floor in my room, or the bed."

"Depends how scary the film is, but not the bed," Clare said.

Jo shook her head then went to search through her collection of DVDs while Clare refilled their glasses.

As she searched, Jo thought about the vision she'd had when Clare told her about the guy who picked up the books. She frowned, wondering what it meant. Like she'd said earlier, her omens had never been wrong before and she hadn't had one for a while. She hoped to God it was the alcohol fuelling her brain, and that her friend wasn't really going to end up in hospital. And was this guy connected? If so, how, and why?

Chapter Fourteen

Now that summer was almost here and the days were lighter for longer, Graham thought about using his boat again. He moored it at Wargrave, near Henley on Thames. He'd gone a couple of weeks before to give it a good clean and check it over. The boatyard had already run the engines, checked the electrics and given it a complete service ready for use.

He wanted to ask Mollie if she'd like a trip on it, but was scared she'd think him a 'flash sort' for owning a boat. There was also the fact that she might not like being on the water.

The boat was a beauty. A Fairline Phantom 37, she was a river boat but could also be used on the sea. She was a four berth, twin cabin boat, with a fly bridge and twin helms, so you could steer it from outside on the fly bridge in good weather or from the saloon below if it was raining. She was fully equipped with a kitchen – galley in nautical terms – a toilet, shower and lounge-saloon.

It only took Graham about an hour to get to Wargrave from Bewford, so if he got up early, by ten am he could be gently wending his way along the Thames, looking forward to a nice relaxing weekend.

And it *was* relaxing on the boat. He chatted to the people he met along the way and would moor up outside a pub, where he could either get off and have some lunch or sit up top with a cool drink and watch the world go by.

He was sure Mollie would enjoy it, but still didn't know how she felt about him. She'd been pleasant enough at yesterday's meeting, smiling at him a lot, but neither of them had mentioned another night out. He'd enjoyed Thursday evening and wanted to do it again, but didn't want to rush things. Damn it; he'd never been any good at this romance business.

He couldn't even call her for a chat because he didn't have her phone number. He decided that he'd ask her out next Thursday, if his courage didn't fail him.

***

Michael got home from work and limped into the kitchen where his mother stood preparing a salad.

"Had a good day, dear? Oh you're limping, what have you done?"

"It's nothing, Mum. I swung around quickly on my chair and bashed my shin against the edge of the conveyor."

"That sounds nasty, let me have a look," she said and tried to pull up his trouser leg.

He pushed her hand away. "Mum, I think I'm old enough to look after myself, leave it will you?" he snapped, then felt bad when he saw the hurt look on her wrinkled old face. "What's for dinner? Something smells good, as always," he said consolingly.

His mother smiled. "I've made your favourite – lasagne. So go up and change out of your work things and it'll be ready in about twenty minutes."

Michael limped up the stairs to his room and, as he took his trousers off, he looked at his shin. A huge angry bruise had formed. He hadn't bashed his leg at all; Spike had cornered him in the men's toilets and kicked him as hard as he could on the shin. The pain had been excruciating and Michael had almost fallen to the floor.

"Now, I want fifty quid, or there'll be more of that and I'll tell everyone you're a queer," Spike had spat at him.

To his shame, Michael had taken out his wallet, given him

the money and told him that was all he'd get.

Spike smirked. "For now anyway. I might feel like blabbing next week, and I might be skint too. Another fifty quid will come in handy."

Michael tried to flex his leg. "I can't afford to give you any more money, so just go ahead and say what you like."

Spike had grinned menacingly. "Remember what I told you about Barry and his mates? It won't just be me you'll have to worry about. So what's it to be?"

Michael was scared. Spike had told him that Barry and his mates went "queer bashing" on their nights out. He knew he shouldn't give in to blackmail, but he had little choice. If what Spike said was true, and Barry thought Michael was gay, a kick in the shin would be the least of his worries; his life wouldn't be worth living.

"I'll give you some more next week," he'd mumbled.

"Correct answer." Spike had slapped him on the back and laughed at his own joke as he'd said, "But you are the weakest link, goodbye." Then he'd pushed Michael out the door.

Michael didn't know what to do. He hated giving in to Spike. He didn't earn much as it was, and fifty pounds a week was more than he could spare. By the time he'd paid his mother housekeeping, bus fares to work and back, and bought his models, there was little left, which was the main reason he still lived at home. He often thought it would be nice to have his own flat; not that he hated living with his parents – they doted on him – but he was twenty-eight years old and had decided he'd like his own space.

Spike's blackmailing would leave him with even less money now.

Michael changed into his tracksuit and rubbed his forehead. He could feel a headache coming on. Probably stress, he thought. He wasn't usually a worrier, but this had really got to him. He'd eat his dinner then come up to his room and try to think of a way out of this mess.

He couldn't tell his parents. They were both in their seventies and didn't need the worry. No, it was down to him to sort out.

***

Mollie sat at home trying to read her book, but her thoughts kept wandering to Graham. He'd been perfectly pleasant at the reading group meeting yesterday, and had held her arm as he'd shepherded her out of the door when they left. He'd walked to the car park with her, but had just got in his car with a "Goodbye, Mollie, have a nice weekend", then driven off.

She'd hoped he might ask to see her again. They'd had a lovely evening last Thursday. The meal in the Italian had been superb, and it'd been very kind of him to pick up the bill. Perhaps he thought she'd now expect him to pay every time they went out. No, she'd made enough of a fuss about paying her share, and he'd said she could pay *next* time. So why hadn't he asked her out again?

"Oh how jolly disappointing," she said aloud, and threw her book on the sofa.

She went into the kitchen to make a cup of tea. It's probably too soon, she told herself, it's only Sunday today. I'll wait and see if he asks next week. But what if he doesn't? a little voice in her head said. Then I'll ask him. We do live in a society where a woman can ask a man out. But, whispered the nagging voice, what if he says no thank you? "Well, at least I'll know where I stand," she muttered aloud again.

She'd actually had a bit of a battle with her conscience about courting again. Victor had been her true love, and although she'd enjoyed herself immensely with Graham, she'd felt bad when she got home, as if she was betraying her husband's memory.

But she'd had a long hard think. Victor had been dead for

five years now, and she knew he wouldn't want her to spend the rest of her days alone. She could imagine him telling her to stop feeling guilty and start living again.

Yes, she thought to herself now, I'll wait and see if Graham asks me out and if he doesn't, I'll invite him round for lunch. He'll probably appreciate a home-cooked meal, and I can say it's payment for Thursday.

Satisfied with her decision, she took her tea into the lounge and settled down with her book.

Chapter Fifteen

On Monday morning, Jo phoned the Herald and asked to speak to the reporter who'd covered the opening of Merrilies.

"Nice to talk to you again, Jo. I hear Merrilies is doing well. What can I do for you?"

"Hi Rob, have you heard yet about a little girl called Annie Matthews?"

"Ah yes, her father contacted us to see if we'd do a piece in the paper. They're trying to save up to send her off for dolphin therapy."

"Yeah, that's right. Did he tell you Merrilies is helping with the fundraising?" Jo asked.

"No, he didn't say much on the phone but I'm seeing them tonight."

"Right. You don't fancy popping in for a coffee, do you? I might have something of interest if you want it."

"That'll be great. Until Mr Matthews called us, we were short on stories for this week's paper. In fact we've struggled for the last few weeks," Rob said.

"The town show is soon though, isn't it?"

"Yep, next month, so we'll have plenty of articles and photos then."

"That's good. When can you come in?" Jo asked.

"How about this afternoon? Wednesday is our deadline day, so if you want it in this week, today's the best day. How about one-ish?"

"Yeah that'll be lovely. See you then." Jo rang off then phoned upstairs to tell Clare about the visit.

"Well done, the more publicity the better. Do you have any tarot readings booked in for today?"

"Nope, none. Do you think you'll be able to sit in on this visit with Rob? I know we're still one short with Zoe gone."

"I'd like to, but if it gets busy, we'll just have to leave him whilst we help out," Clare said.

"We should think about taking on another member of staff, you know," Jo said.

"Yes, but managing without has saved us one wage. I know we need someone else, especially when it's manic in here. Maybe we can ask Rob to stick another advert in for us. Oh, gotta go, someone needs serving." Clare hung up and dealt with her customer.

They were quite busy for a Monday morning, but it calmed down just before noon, so they hoped they'd have a quiet lunchtime for once.

Clare came downstairs with a coffee for Jo and saw a familiar face – the man who'd picked up the books for her.

"Hello again, dropped any more books recently?" he asked.

"Hello." Clare laughed shyly, "No, I must have had butterfingers that day."

"You should do that more often."

"What?"

"Laugh. It's pretty."

Clare blushed; she'd never been called pretty before. "Thanks. Are you looking for anything in particular? Something I can help with?"

"No, I was just browsing. I'm on my lunch hour. Nice to see you again though," he said and gave her a big smile.

"Erm yes, you too. I better go; I've got a meeting soon."

"For another job, is it? Mustn't tell the boss?" he whispered in a conspiratorial tone.

Clare laughed again. "I *am* the boss."

"Oh, really? You own this bookshop?"

"Yes. Sorry, I've really got to go, things to do."

The man watched her walk away and smiled to himself. He bought a bookmark and left the shop.

***

The meeting with the reporter went well. Luckily, Merrilies was quiet for a change so both Clare and Jo were able to talk to him.

Rob was happy to do an article in that week's issue about Merrilies' fundraising for Annie, and a regular monthly one covering the book reviews. It would be good to have a monthly slot as the paper was sometimes short on stories, so he could make more of the review in a particularly newsless issue.

Jo watched him write hieroglyphic type symbols in his notebook. "I can't make head nor tail out of that shorthand, does it take a long time to learn?"

"It did take a while, but in my job, you couldn't do without it. If I had to write everything out in full, I'd be there all day and the stories would never get printed," Rob explained.

When they'd finished talking business, he asked how things were going and Clare told him about Zoe.

"I might just be able to help you out," he said.

"How? You're not changing jobs, are you?" Jo asked.

"Not likely. I love being a reporter. You never know what story you're going to get next. No, my sister's just left college, and doesn't want to go to university. She's looking for a job, but isn't sure what she wants to do. One thing I know about my little sis though, she's book mad. She's always reading. I reckon she'd be ideal."

"I'm not being funny, Rob, but is she reliable?" Clare asked. "I know some kids of that age aren't. We need someone who's going to turn up for work on time, and who we can trust."

"She's sensible and reliable, and will turn up on time every day."

"You're bound to say that, she's your sister," Clare pointed out.

"No, if she was unreliable I wouldn't put her up for it. Go on, give her a chance. You trust me, don't you? Look at this face," he said, and made puppy dog eyes.

Jo laughed at his soppy expression then said, "Clare, we can take her on a trial period and see how she does, can't we? We do need someone desperately, and it's better to have someone recommended, isn't it?"

Clare thought about it for a bit then said, "Oh okay. Tell her to come in tomorrow morning for a chat, assuming she does want a job here."

Jo was pleased, she had a feeling Rob's sister would fit in well.

"I can do better than that and phone her now if you want," Rob said, reaching inside his jacket for his mobile.

"No, tomorrow morning about ten will be fine. What's her name?"

"Hermione, but we all call her Hemmy. And it's not from Harry Potter; she was born before Potter mania was invented!"

"I love her name, it's so romantic," Jo said.

Rob laughed. "Romantic is *not* a term I would use to describe my sister. Tomboy, more like."

"Ask her to phone and let us know if she's not interested," Jo told him.

"She'll be interested. Right, I better go and write up this article. It'll be in Thursday's issue. See ya."

"Yeah bye, Rob," Jo said, watching him leave.

"He's nice, isn't he?" Clare said.

"Yeah, he's okay."

"Only okay?"

"Clare, I am not interested in Rob in that way. Besides, he's younger than me."

100

"So, it's only by a couple of years. I think he likes you."

"He's just being friendly, now back to work you!" Jo pushed her friend towards the stairs.

Clare went up to take her turn in the café and Jo refilled the bookmark rack.

A couple of hours later, on time as always, Annie and Alice came in. Clare was downstairs this time, and Jo was in the Mind Body & Spirit area giving a reading to someone who'd seen the "Tarot Readings" notice in the window and walked in. Usually Jo insisted on an appointment, but the lady was on holiday and going home the following day, so she'd agreed this once.

"Clare, Clare! Guess what?" Annie said, bouncing up and down.

"Easy, Annie," her mother warned.

"What, sweetie?" Clare said.

"A man from the newspaper is coming to see me to take photos, and Mummy and Daddy are trying to get people to give their spare pennies so I can swim wiv dolphins."

"Yes, I know about that. Now *you* guess what?"

"What?" Annie asked.

"Merrilies are fundraising for you too."

"I know, Mummy told me. Does that mean I'll be able to swim wiv dolphins very soon?"

"Well, not really soon like next week, it'll still take a while to get enough money, but hopefully it won't take too long," Clare said.

"I can't wait, dolphins are my bestest animal in the whole world." She swept her arms in a wide circle to demonstrate the world.

Clare smiled and ruffled the little girl's hair then turned to Alice. "Have you got any collection boxes for us yet?"

"They're nearly finished. Annie's drawn dolphins on them so that people know what the money's for."

"Oh that's lovely. Well, as soon as they're ready, bring them in and we'll put them on the counters. Tessa wants one for the surgery where she works; the doctors have agreed to have one there."

"That's great. We don't expect people to put a lot in, especially with the economic climate at the moment, but it all helps, doesn't it?" Alice said.

"It does, even if it's only their odd coppers," Clare added.

"I hope people put in lots of pennies, cuz it will be the bestest thing ever to see real dolphins and get in the water with them," Annie said. "I've only seen them in books and on telly. Can I go look at the books now?"

Alice said yes and Annie went across to the children's area.

"She looks a bit pale today, is she okay?" Clare asked.

"She's overexerted herself in the last couple of days. It's hard trying to stop her doing things; she's a little girl and wants to do what the other kids do. She knows her limits, but does get carried away sometimes."

"When's the reporter coming?"

"Tonight, which is why Annie's so excited. We can't stop for too long, he's coming at half six, but Annie wanted to come in and tell you. She just *has* to come here; it's her daily routine." Alice tutted and shook her head.

"Aw, we don't mind. Good luck later. You'll like Rob, he's nice."

"Thanks for your help, Clare. Say thanks to Jo as well."

"I will. I hope you get good results from this, Alice. It would be lovely to see Annie improve."

"Yes, it would be wonderful. The doctors say her immune system should get better as she gets older, but they don't know when. But I want to know, when she's ten? Fifteen? Twenty? I know that's unrealistic and they can't give an accurate date, but I just want her well."

Clare squeezed Alice's arm, "It must be such a worry."

Alice smiled thinly. "It's not as bad as it sounds. We've had seven years to get used to it, but sometimes you know, I just wish... Oh never mind, we're dealt the cards we're dealt. I'd better go; she has to have her tea before the reporter comes. I'll let you know tomorrow how we got on. Thanks again for your help, it's appreciated."

Alice collected Annie, who'd been reading a book about three skeletons. Alice bought the book then, holding Annie's hand, waved goodbye and left the shop.

Chapter Sixteen

Tessa was editing her latest short story when the phone rang. She tutted at the interruption and picked it up.

"Mrs Parsons?" enquired a voice on the other end.

"Miss, but yes that's me. Can I help you?"

"It's Sergeant White from the police station. We've got your daughter, Amber, here."

"Oh my God, is she okay? I mean, what's happened?" Tessa was already on her feet.

"She was caught shoplifting in the arcade, and the store manager called us. Are you able to come and collect her?"

"Erm..." There was a long pause whilst Tessa struggled to take in the news. "Sorry, yes of course, I'm on my way."

Tessa hung up the phone, sat back down and put her head in her hands. She hadn't expected this. Shoplifting! She couldn't believe it. Amber was a model daughter. Good at school, well behaved at home. No, surely the shopkeeper'd got it wrong, got the wrong girl. Oh poor Amber, she must be terrified. Tessa got up, searched for her car keys, grabbed her bag and flew out of the door.

She arrived at the police station about twenty minutes later and rushed up the steps into the reception area.

"Someone phoned me a while ago, regarding my daughter, Amber."

"And you are?"

"Tes... Miss Parsons."

"Ah yes, have a seat for a moment," the policeman behind the desk told her.

Tessa looked around then sat on a long bench facing the desk. She hugged her bag to her stomach and looked at the posters on the wall. She'd never been in a police station in her life, and wasn't too happy about being here now. The posters warned about the dangers of drugs, pickpockets, drink driving, and leaving valuables in your car. She shuddered.

The door to her left opened, and out came a policeman with Amber at his side. Tessa stood up as they approached. "Amber, what on earth's going on? Didn't you tell the shopkeeper it wasn't you, that they must have made a mistake?"

"Mum…"

"They ought to get their facts right before they start calling the police on innocent young girls, I mean…"

"MUM!"

Tessa stopped talking. The policeman spoke. "The manager didn't make a mistake, I'm afraid. It was Amber. We've got CCTV footage of her."

Tessa looked at her daughter in horror. "But why? What did you steal? You've never…" She turned to face the policeman. "She's never been in trouble before. I can't understand this, she's always been so good."

Then anger overtook disbelief and Tessa grabbed hold of Amber's arm and shook her.

"What in God's name did you go shoplifting for, you stupid girl? You ought to be ashamed of yourself. Oh hell, what on earth are your grandparents going to say?"

Amber began to cry. She looked at her mother. "I'm sorry, Mum," she mumbled.

"Yes, well, we'll talk about this at home, young lady. What happens next?" Tessa asked the policeman.

"Luckily nothing. The manager's got the item of clothing back, and banned Amber from her store, but won't press charges. She could see how scared Amber was and knows she hasn't been in trouble before. We checked up on her."

The policeman turned to face Amber. "But, if you commit a second offence, you *will* be prosecuted; which means going to court and facing a judge. So I don't want to see you in here again. Okay?"

Amber hung her head to stare at the ground and nodded.

"Go out to the car, it's just outside, I'll be there in a minute," Tessa told her, then said to the policeman, "I am so sorry, I'll get to the bottom of this if I can."

"Her mates probably dared her to do it. Anyone can see she's not a bad kid. Hopefully this will be a lesson to her."

"I'm sure it will, thank you. Do I have to do anything else or sign anything?"

"No, you can go. I hope we don't meet again, and I mean that in the nicest possible way," the policeman said and smiled at her.

Tessa smiled back, even though she didn't feel like smiling at all.

All the way home, Tessa kept quiet. She knew if she spoke, she'd lose her temper and start shouting, which she didn't want to do. She needed to concentrate on driving.

Amber sat huddled in the front seat staring at her lap and didn't utter a word either. She knew she was in deep trouble; she'd never seen her mum so angry before, and the worst thing was her silence. Amber wished she'd shout and scream at her, this hush was so unnerving.

It was only once they'd pulled onto the drive that Tessa spoke, just the one word, "IN!"

Amber clambered out of the car and ran into the house. She was about to go upstairs to her room, when Tessa shouted, "Oh no you don't, young lady. Get in the kitchen. I think you have some explaining to do."

Amber huffed, threw her bag onto the stairs and slouched into the kitchen, with Tessa following.

"Right, what did you steal, and why?"

Amber didn't respond. She sat at the table, staring down at

her hands as she picked the skin around her nails.

"I asked you a question. Please do me the courtesy of answering. What the hell did you think you were playing at?"

"I took a top from that clothes shop in the arcade. It didn't cost much."

"It doesn't matter how little it cost, you stole it. Why, Amber? I know we don't have a lot of money, but I go without to make sure you get what you want, and this is how you repay me." Tessa raked her hands through her hair. "I haven't had any new clothes for ages, and when did we last have a holiday? All my money goes on keeping a roof over our heads, food on the table and things for you." Tessa knew her voice had risen several octaves, but she couldn't help it, she was so damned angry.

Amber looked up defiantly. "Oh for heaven's sake, Mum, it was one little top, not such a big deal... OW!" she cried as Tessa slapped her across the face.

For a moment, neither of them moved or spoke, then Amber got up and tried to run out of the kitchen, but Tessa grabbed her arm.

"Let go of me. Let go. Let GO!" Amber screamed, hot tears coursing down her cheeks, then she slumped sobbing into her mother's arms.

"Darling, I'm sorry I hit you, but how can you say it's no big deal? I am so angry with you. Stealing? I've brought you up better than that. Why did you do it?"

Amber tried to speak, but the words came out in shuddering gulps. She took a deep breath as Tessa stroked her hair away from her forehead like she'd done when she was a little girl. "There's a new gang at school. I wanted to join them, but they said I had to prove myself first. My challenge was to steal something without being seen, except I got caught."

"But why do you want to be in the gang? I thought you were friends with Cathy and Georgia."

"I am, but they've joined the gang, so I wanted to be in it too," Amber sniffed.

"What happened to them when you got caught?" Tessa asked, already knowing the answer.

"They ran away."

"Yes, leaving you to take the rap by yourself. Nice friends, huh? Did Cathy and Georgia have to shoplift too?"

"No, they did the other girls' homework for them, but I wouldn't do that. I said it was cheating."

"And shoplifting isn't? Oh Amber, you silly girl, you should have refused to do the shoplifting too. You don't need friends like that."

"But then I wouldn't have anyone at school to sit with in lunch and break."

"You must have other friends besides Cathy and Georgia. I'm surprised at them both; I thought they were nice girls." Tessa sighed. "I expect they thought the group was fun and exciting. They'll soon realise it's not clever to steal and get into trouble, and I bet they'll leave and be friends with you again. If they don't, then they're not worth it. Are they?" She held Amber away from her and looked into her eyes. "Are they?"

Amber shook her head then said, "Mum?"

"What?"

She started sobbing again. "I'm really sorry. Are you going to tell Gran and Grandad?"

"Well, I should, but they'll be so disappointed in you, I couldn't bear to see the look on their faces. So it'll be between us. But don't you ever do anything like that again, promise me," Tessa said.

She waited.

Amber wiped the back of her hand across her eyes and nodded. "I promise. I'm really sorry. I was so scared when the security guard stopped me, and took me into the room with the CCTV. Then when the police came, I thought I was going to wet myself. I was terrified they'd arrest me and lock me up for the whole night. And I was scared of what you were going to say..." She took a shuddering breath.

Tessa remembered the thought of being in trouble with her own parents and managed a grin. "Well, let that be a lesson to you. Now if you've got any homework, do you want to get it done while I start dinner?"

"Yes I'll do it now. Can I use the study?"

"Yep, just clear my stuff to one side. Jacket potatoes or new?"

"Jacket please, with lots of butter." Amber gave Tessa a hug then said, "Mum?"

"Yes?"

"Love you."

"Love you too. Now off you go."

Amber went into the hallway, picked up her bag and walked upstairs.

Tessa took a deep breath and let it out slowly. She hoped with all her heart that that was an end to things. She couldn't bear it if Amber went off the rails. Until now, she'd been such a well-behaved child. Hopefully she'd had such a scare that she'd never do anything like that again.

***

At Merrilies, the interview with Rob's sister Hermione went well. She was a remarkably bright young girl who was keen to be in employment. Jo and Clare liked her immediately and offered her a job, saying she could start the following day.

Annie turned up on Wednesday afternoon, full of her visit from Rob and the photographer.

"Two people came just to see me. I thinked, I mean I *thought* Rob was going to do the story and take the photos, but they have a man who just takes photos, and he said I can have one when he's printed them. You're meant to buy them, but he's going to *give* me the best one. I'm going to be in the paper this week, ooh tomorrow achally." She finally stopped talking and took a big breath.

"Well, good for you. I hope lots of people see it and donate their pennies," Jo said.

"Did I tell you dolphins are my very bestest animals in the whole world?" Annie asked.

"Erm, yes only about a hundred times." Jo rolled her eyes. "There's no customers upstairs at the moment, so if you want, go up and tell the girl in the café I said you could have a glass of orange and a bit of cake...is that okay?" she asked Alice.

"Yes that's fine," Alice replied.

When Annie had gone, Jo asked why she hadn't been in the afternoon before. "She never usually misses a day."

"She didn't go to school yesterday. She had an asthma attack after the photographer left Monday night, probably from all the excitement. She was still a bit weak when I woke her yesterday morning, so I thought it best to keep her off. She wasn't too happy about not coming in here, but I told her if she didn't rest, she wouldn't come in for the whole week. She was a lot better today and I couldn't keep her off anyway, she wanted to tell everyone her news."

"Ah bless her. Is that the finished boxes? Lovely, I'll get them put on the counters and give one to Tessa."

"Oh, talking about the reading group, Annie wanted to come in tomorrow and tell them about the photographer's visit. Do you think they'll mind?" Alice asked.

"Well, I know they like to get through the meeting on Thursdays as we close at eight, so it might be better if she comes in on Saturday? They'll have more time then."

"Okay, I'll see if I can put her off until then." Alice made a face, obviously not relishing the thought.

"I'll tell her if you want. It'll sound better coming from me perhaps," Jo said.

"Yes, otherwise she'll think I'm just saying it because I don't want to bring her."

110

When Annie came back downstairs, Jo told her that the reading group would be busy the following evening, but she could she come in on Saturday when she'd have lots more time to tell them about her visit from Rob and the photographer.

Annie screwed her face up and for a moment, Jo thought she was going to get upset, but she smiled her toothy smile and agreed it was a better idea. "Cuz I might even have my photo and I can bring it and show them all."

"Yes, that's a good idea," Jo agreed. She was sure the reading group would be thankful. Much as they liked seeing Annie, they didn't get a lot done when she came in on Thursdays.

Clare felt bad because it had been her initial suggestion that Annie meet the reading group members, but she'd started turning up every Thursday. Then it dropped to every other Thursday and the occasional Saturday. If they could now get her to come in Saturdays only, it would be much better.

Alice was trying to explain that to Annie on their way home. "So you see, darling, they really have quite a lot to do in those couple of hours. They have to talk about the book they're reading, make notes, choose another book and all sorts of things, so Saturdays would be a better day to pop in and say hello."

"Okay. I know you don't really like going all the way home then coming out again on Thursdays. Sometimes I don't want to go home and come out again either, but I like seeing everyone, especially Fecility and Mollie." Annie made a face. "I don't like Michael cuz he doesn't talk to me, well, only sometimes. Graham talks to me now, and he says funny things."

"What do you mean funny things?"

"Well, he asks if I've been a good girl, and do I like school, things like that, just as if he's my granddad."

Alice laughed. "He probably doesn't know what else to say. I don't think he's used to children."

"Why not? He must have big children your age and they must have children." Annie wound her long blonde hair around her fingers.

"Darling, not everyone has children. Some people don't want or like children."

"Why not?"

"I don't know, Sweetie. Because they don't."

"But if people don't have children, then the world won't have any people in it, just animals and trees," Annie said with a frown.

"Well, that won't happen, darling, because there are more people who do have children than people who don't."

Annie thought for a while. "But..."

Just then, Alice's phone rang, which saved her from having to answer any more of Annie's questions.

Chapter Seventeen

Thursday evening found everyone except Felicity sitting at the table for the meeting. This was the first discussion about the new book, which they'd chosen the previous Saturday. Felicity turned up five minutes late.

"Hi, everyone. Sorry I'm late, Pops," she said to Graham with a grin.

"You cheeky thing. I am old enough to be your father, I suppose, but not your grandfather surely?"

"How old are you?"

"You should never ask an older person their age," Graham said.

"That only applies to women, sorry," Mollie chipped in.

"Ah, so whose side are you on then, the female side or the oldies' side?" Graham asked teasingly.

"Nobody's, just stating a fact," Mollie replied, giving him a warm smile.

"In answer to your question, Felicity, I'm sixty-three."

"So... hang on, let me work this out. I'm twenty-three, well, and a half, my father was twenty-five when I was born. So-o-o, oh damn, not quite old enough to be my grandfather. I'm still calling you Pops though, it suits you."

Everyone laughed except Michael, who sat at the table flicking through his book.

"Okay, let's get down to business. How much, if anything, has everyone read since Saturday?" Graham asked, and the meeting got underway.

Mollie noticed how quiet and on edge Michael seemed

again, and decided she was definitely going to tackle him about it this week, as well as asking Graham if he'd like to see her again. She thought the best way was to call a halt halfway through for refreshments. She spoke up. "If I might suggest it, I feel in need of some sustenance. I haven't had a drink for ages. Can we have a break for coffee about halfway?"

Everyone agreed.

"Jolly good, who's volunteering to get them?" she asked, knowing Michael wouldn't and that Tessa and Felicity probably would, leaving her with Michael and Graham. Who to tackle first? She decided to wait and see what happened when the time came.

As she expected, Felicity and Tessa said they'd get the drinks when they stopped for a break.

Satisfied, she tried to concentrate on what Tessa was saying about the chapters she had read so far.

About an hour later, Graham checked his watch. Declaring that it was ten past seven, he asked if everyone was ready for a break. They agreed. Tessa and Felicity went upstairs to get the drinks and Michael stuck his head in his book, obviously avoiding any communication, so Mollie made 'go away' motions with her head to Graham, who took the hint. He coughed and said, "I'm just nipping over to look at the new releases, see what we might be reviewing soon."

When he'd gone, Mollie touched Michael's arm, making him jump.

"Michael, please don't think I'm prying, but I can't help noticing you've been quiet and withdrawn the last couple of weeks. Is anything wrong?"

Whether it was the sympathy in her voice and the kind way she was looking at him, or the need to offload the burden he was bottling up, he didn't know. But to his shame, Michael felt his eyes well up and he blurted out, "I'm being blackmailed at work."

Mollie moved her chair closer. "Do you want to tell me

about it?" she asked gently.

Michael nodded then sniffed. "It would be such a relief to tell someone, but not here."

"Is it okay if we involve Graham in this? I feel sure he'd know what to do, he's such a sensible knowledgeable chap."

Michael nodded again, so Mollie quickly called Graham over to the table. She explained that Michael had some trouble and needed to talk to someone about it. Graham suggested going for a drink somewhere after the meeting.

"Not to any pubs around here," Michael said in alarm.

"No, it's alright, I know a quiet place a little drive away. Shall we go there? We can go in my car and I'll drop you back here after, is that okay?"

Michael said that would be fine, and even managed a small smile.

The girls came back with drinks for everyone, and Felicity had bought some of Mollie's chocolate-topped flapjacks.

She gave one to Michael. "Here you go, misery guts. You've been a frightful bore for the last couple of weeks, even more so than usual. Maybe some chocolate and carbohydrate will cheer you up."

Michael accepted the cake and muttered, "Thanks, Flick."

Mollie almost laughed aloud. Good old Felicity, she'd obviously spotted that Michael was down about something but, as usual, had approached it in her direct way. Michael seemed a bit more at ease now, so maybe the knowledge that he was going to get his problem off his chest, and Felicity's kindness, had done the trick for the moment.

After the meeting, Mollie, Michael and Graham walked to the car park.

"Nice vehicle," Michael said as he got in the front passenger seat of Graham's car.

Graham opened the back door. "Would you rather sit in the front, Mollie? I'm sure Michael won't mind getting in the back, will you?"

Mollie interrupted before Michael could answer. "It's okay, I told Michael to get in the front. I'll be quite comfortable in the back, thank you." And as if to prove the point, she got in and settled back into the seat.

Michael, feeling a bit awkward, tried to make conversation to ease the silence. "So this is an Audi S8, right?"

"It is," Graham said.

"What engine?"

"The V10, five point two litre."

"Whoa, it must drink tons of petrol. Isn't that the engine that's in the Lamborghini?"

"Yes. Right, we'll be there soon. You okay in the back, Mollie?"

"Perfectly, thank you. Michael's right, this is a jolly nice car; very spacious and comfortable."

Michael couldn't help asking, "How come a guy who's retired can afford a car like this?"

Mollie was appalled at such an impertinent question. "Michael!"

"It's okay, Mollie. Because, Michael, I had a good job when I did work, and was shrewd with my money."

"Lucky," Michael said with a mixture of admiration and envy.

"It may sound great to have a job that earns you lots of money, but it's hard work and there are sacrifices. The good side is I now have a comfortable lifestyle. But money isn't everything, Michael." Graham looked in the rear view mirror at Mollie, and she could see the wistfulness and – was that regret – in his eyes.

In the pub, Mollie spotted a vacant corner table. "Shall we sit there? It's nice and quiet and we can chat."

"Yes, sit down and I'll get some drinks. What would you both like?

Mollie asked for an orange juice, and so did Michael.

"Want any help?" Michael asked.

116

"No, I'm alright. You go and sit with Mollie, I'll be there in a moment."

Michael trudged after Mollie, wondering, now that he was here, if he was doing the right thing. What could these two old people do about his situation? But he might as well talk to someone, he couldn't tell his parents and his friends would be no help. Besides, he didn't want them knowing, they might not want to be his friends any more.

He sat in the chair opposite Mollie, feeling shy and awkward.

She smiled encouragingly at him. "Don't worry, Michael, we'll sort you out."

Graham approached with their drinks. "Here we are, three orange juices. Now, what's the problem, Michael? You've been in a world of your own for the last couple of weeks."

Michael hesitantly told them about the day over Easter when he'd volunteered to work and Spike had told him to look at the topless girl in the paper. With Mollie and Graham's encouragement, the whole story came tumbling out. "Now I don't know what to do. I can't afford to keep paying him fifty pounds a week and I don't want to be kicked and punched again. But if I don't pay him and the other lads find... think I'm gay, they'll beat me up even more than Spike does." Michael looked thoroughly miserable.

Mollie was appalled. "What a nasty piece of work! Blackmail is against the law, Michael, why on earth don't you go to the police?"

"Because I have no proof, and Spike will put me in hospital, that's why!"

"Okay, calm down. Now, when are you due to pay him again?" Graham asked. He'd been deep in thought during the tale, and had an idea.

"Next week. He'll come looking for me on Monday, I expect."

"Right, I have a plan," Graham said. "I've got a

dictaphone, you know, one of those dictation machines. I'll bring it in on Saturday. Before you go into work on Monday, switch it on and put it in your pocket. It's only small, and, unlike some, you can't hear it whirring so Spike won't know you've got it." He leaned closer to Michael and continued, "Try to get him to drop himself in it. The more threatening he is the better, so refuse to give him the money and see what he says. Then, when you're alone, go into the lavatory or something, play back the tape and make sure it's recorded."

Michael was sitting forward, his hands on his knees, concentrating intently on what Graham was saying.

"Then take it to your boss and remind him that blackmail, assault, bullying, and harassment in the workplace are all serious issues and that you're leaving it to him to sort out before you take the matter to the police. Do you think you'll be able to do that?" Graham finished.

Michael nodded. "Are you sure it will do the trick? What if Spike's angry with me for going to the boss, and waits for me outside work?"

"I don't think that will happen. If your boss has any sense, he'll warn Spike that if he or any of his friends touch you, the tape will go straight to the police. In fact, you need to make sure of that, so tell your boss you're afraid Spike will get you for dobbing him in or whatever you call it nowadays."

Mollie then spoke. "Michael, it's none of our business, but can I ask, are you gay?" She tutted and said, "I really don't like that word, it meant bright and happy when I was young. Are you homosexual?"

Michael went red and looked away. Then, biting his top lip, he nodded. He looked down at his hands, which he was twisting in his lap.

"Michael," Graham said quietly.

Michael kept his head down. Graham spoke again, louder and in a more authoritative voice. "Michael, look at me."

Michael slowly lifted his head up and Mollie's heart went

out to him. The boy – that's all he was compared to her and Graham – had tears sliding down his cheeks and looked very uncomfortable.

"Right, my lad, there is nothing to be ashamed of. Your sexual orientation has no bearing whatsoever on the type of person you are. Look at Spike, for example; he's a real thug, and heterosexual. Does anybody else know you're gay?" Graham asked.

Michael shook his head. "I've told no-one until now. I didn't want to tell you really, I thought you'd be shocked."

"Why on earth would you think that?" Mollie asked.

"Because you're old! I dread to think what my parents would say, they'd probably disown me. I couldn't bear to see the shame on their faces." He hung his head.

"Just because we're older, don't assume we haven't lived. We've probably seen and done things that would shock you. We grew up in the swinging sixties don't forget." Mollie grinned to try to lighten the mood.

"I think you're worrying unnecessarily," Graham told him. "Good grief, there was a time in my life when the house was full of gay men."

Michael's head shot up at this revelation and Graham laughed. "My mother was a cabaret singer and often worked the gay circuit. She had lots of homosexual friends, and often invited them back to the house after her shows. Even my father got on well with them. We held some wonderful parties."

Michael was astounded. "Really? And did you not think they were, well, disgusting or anything?"

"Not at all, they were people. I judge individuals on their personality, not their looks or sexual preferences. It's what sort of person you are that counts, Michael. If you are kind and respectful to others, that's what matters. Nothing else."

"Jolly well said! I completely agree. Now, young man, don't you think it's about time you told your parents or 'came out', as they say? I think you'll feel a lot better when you don't have to hide your real self any more," Mollie said.

"But what if they tell me to get out? Apart from my parents and a couple of friends, I have no-one else and nowhere to go." He looked as if he was going to cry again.

Mollie felt so sorry for him. It must have been awful trying to cope with his feelings and keeping it secret all these years. She laid her hand on his arm. "You do have someone else; us. If your parents kick you out, you can come and stay with me."

"Honestly?" Michael rubbed his right eye as if he had something in it.

"Honestly. But I'm sure they won't. You're their son, Michael, and they love you unconditionally. All that matters to them is that you're happy and healthy." She knew this was true because it was how she'd feel if he were her son. "Now let's have another drink, and stop those tears or you'll start me off." She reached in her bag for a tissue and blew her nose.

"Right," Graham said. "Same again, or would we like something stronger?"

"I'm going to have a small glass of wine, I think," Mollie answered. "Michael?"

"I don't usually drink alcohol, but I'll have a small glass of red wine please, it might give me a bit of courage. Here, I'll help you, if you don't mind sitting on your own, Mollie. It's my turn to get them."

"No, you're not paying and neither is Graham. I am, so you can help me."

Graham tried to protest but Mollie slapped away his hands. "It's my turn to pay, especially after you paid for our meal the other week."

Michael picked up on this news. "What's this? You two been seeing each other?"

"Tsk, no, we just went for dinner after the group meeting one evening, as neither of us had eaten," Mollie answered.

"Yes, and it was a very enjoyable evening, one I'd like to

repeat again," Graham smiled into Mollie's eyes.

"Really?" she asked.

"Yes really..."

"Shall we get the drinks, as I'll have to get back soon?" Michael said.

"Yes, sorry, Michael. Come on, give me a hand."

Mollie and Michael went to the bar, each with a whirl of emotions going on. Mollie was delighted at Graham's words, and Michael felt a mixture of relief but trepidation at what would happen when he got home.

Graham sat at the table feeling pleased that he'd managed to let Mollie know he'd like to see her again.

On the way back with the drinks, Mollie asked Michael to keep quiet about her and Graham seeing each other. "We're friends at present, and we don't know how far it's going to go, so I'd rather people didn't find out yet."

"What are you two whispering about?" Graham asked.

"Mollie asked me not to say anything about you two yet."

"Yes, if you don't mind, for the moment anyway."

"Well, I guess that's all of us with secrets. The same applies to you both, please?" Michael pleaded.

"Michael, I wouldn't dream of saying anything. You can rest assured that anything you tell me will be in the strictest of confidence," Mollie said.

"That goes for me too, of course. Michael, about the tape machine, I think the best thing is to give it to you after the meeting on Saturday. I'll leave it in the boot of the car and if you walk to the car park with me afterwards, I'll hand it over. Nobody will see it and ask questions then."

"Okay, can I just say thanks to you both. You're alright for a couple of old fogies."

"Oi, you jolly well watch the *old* bit," Mollie laughed.

"Seriously though, I didn't know what to do, and was thinking of giving my job up. I'm still afraid of facing Spike on Monday, and of telling my parents, but I know it's got to be done. I'll tell them tonight. I'm glad I talked to you both. Thanks."

"I meant what I said, Michael. If your parents do react badly, give me a call. I've got a spare room, so take my number in case."

Mollie told him her mobile number, which Michael put into his phone. He leaned over and kissed her cheek. "Thanks, Mollie."

They talked about the reading group and the book reviews while they finished their drinks, then Graham drove them back to the car park so Mollie could collect her car.

"How are you getting home, Michael?" she asked.

"Bus."

"I'll take you home," she offered.

"No, it's okay, I've got a return ticket."

"Yes but you don't want to sit around waiting for a bus. Come on, get in."

Michael looked at his watch. "There's a bus due soon, and I'd like to have some time to think, if it's alright."

"Are you sure? It's no trouble to drive you."

"I'm sure, thanks."

"Okay. Let me know how you get on with your parents. I'll be thinking of you."

Graham shook his hand and said he'd see him at the meeting on Saturday afternoon.

Michael thanked them again and walked to the bus stop, his heart beating rapidly.

Chapter Eighteen

Jo arrived at work late on Saturday morning, which was unusual for her, especially as she only lived across the road.

"Ooh had a late night, did you? What did you get up to?" Clare asked her.

"I didn't go out. I just overslept that's all," Jo snapped.

"Sorry, I was only joking. I'm going upstairs, but we can swap after lunch. That okay with you?"

"Yeah, fine, see you later."

Clare walked upstairs feeling puzzled. It wasn't like Jo to be snappy; something was wrong. Clare didn't have chance to dwell on it though, because she had a lot to do and didn't stop until it was nearly lunchtime. She ate her lunch in the café, then asked Hermione to cover the till while she went downstairs.

"I'm very sorry about that, but I won't be doing any for a few weeks," Jo was saying to a woman as Clare approached.

"Won't be doing any what?" Clare asked.

"Tarot readings."

"What do you mean, you won't be doing any? Why not, what's happened?"

"Nothing, I just want a break for a while, that's all."

"Jo, you've never refused to do a reading, there's more to it than that. Come on, what's up?" Clare tried to put her arm around her friend and colleague.

Jo shrugged her off. "Honestly, it's nothing. I just fancy a break. Shall I go upstairs now? There's a pile of new releases here that need to go out and some orders have come in, but I haven't phoned the customers yet." Jo smiled weakly at Clare and went upstairs.

Clare knew there was definitely something wrong. There had to be for Jo to stop reading the tarot, but she didn't want to push it. Jo obviously didn't want to discuss things yet, she'd tell Clare in her own time.

They had the usual lunchtime rush, and then it settled down again. Clare was just finishing a phone call to a customer, when she looked up and saw the man who'd helped pick up her books. He was browsing through the sale table. He looked across, saw she was finished on the phone and walked over.

"Hello, I just thought I'd nip in and see if anything caught my eye. Any cheap books, I mean." He gazed at Clare intensely, making her blush.

"Oh erm hi, nice to see you again."

"What's your name? I need to know your name if I'm going to keep talking to you?"

"It's Clare."

"Hello, Clare. So, what do you do when you're not running this place?"

"Oh, not a lot really. I usually stay in and watch TV, or sometimes at the weekend I go out with Jo, she's my manager and best friend."

"No husband or boyfriend to take care of a lovely damsel like you then?"

"No, I'm young free and single." Clare wanted to kick herself. Why had she said that? He'd probably think she was angling for a date.

"So, if someone, say someone standing very near you now, was to ask you out for a drink, would you say yes or no?" he teased.

Despite her shyness, Clare enjoyed their flirting and decided to be a bit bolder. "Well, I couldn't say yes to someone whose name I didn't know," she replied.

The man took in a sharp breath. "Oh, forgive me, fair lady, my name is William of Oxford." He bowed theatrically.

Clare giggled as he continued, "Actually it isn't. I'm Dan Sullivan, and I'm a sales rep for the new car showroom on the main road."

"Pleased to make your acquaintance, kind sir," Clare said and curtsied.

Dan laughed. "But you still haven't answered my question. Would you like to come out for a drink with me some time?"

"Yes, I would, thank you."

"Well, I'm a spontaneous kind of guy, so how about tonight? If you're free, that is."

"Let me see. I did have a date with Johnny Depp, but I'll cancel it. So yes, I'd love to."

"Okay then, shall I pick you up or shall we meet somewhere?" Dan asked.

Clare thought about it. "How about we meet in RJs wine bar? Do you know it?"

"I do. What time? Obviously you need to clear up here then go home and get ready, not that you need a lot of time to do that of course," Dan added quickly.

Clare laughed. "I know what you mean. Well, by the time we cash up and everything and I drive home, shall we say eight-ish?"

"Eight-ish is fine. We can have a bite to eat too if you like, while we get to know each other."

"That'd be really nice," Clare said.

"Okay, I'll see you then."

A customer was waiting, so Clare said, "Yes see you later, Dan," then smiled at him and got on with her job.

The afternoon passed in a blur, with a visit from Annie, the reading group and several customers, including one who wanted a refund. Clare wasn't sure the woman had bought the book in Merrilies, but she refunded it nonetheless. She worked on autopilot, her mind more on her date that evening than her job.

At four o'clock, Jo came downstairs with a coffee for her. "Sorry about earlier, Clare, I was just grumpy 'cos I'd overslept. Hey, why are you grinning like that?"

"Because I've got a date tonight."

"You haven't! Who with? How did that happen?"

"He's called Dan. Remember the guy I told you about a while back? Well, he came in earlier and we were chatting and being silly, and he asked me out."

"Oh, Clare, be careful. You don't know anything about him."

"Jo, what are you – my mum? I think at thirty-nine, I'm old enough to make my own decisions. And if I don't go out with him, I can't get to know him, can I? I'll be fine. We're meeting in RJs."

Jo remembered the vision she'd had the night Clare had first told her about Dan, but she'd had none since, so it probably wasn't linked to him at all. "How about we meet for lunch tomorrow and you can tell me all about it?" she said.

"Yes, that would be great. Ooh, I've got a full diary this weekend, that makes a change! I'm so looking forward to it, but I'm a bit nervous. I haven't been on a date for ages. Oh God, what am I going to wear?" Clare wailed.

"Don't panic about it now. Wait 'til you get home and look through your clothes. Don't go over the top though, no low-cut tops or short skirts," Jo teased. She knew Clare didn't have a single item like that in her wardrobe.

"But you know my dress sense; I haven't got anything remotely sexy, let alone short or low-cut. I can't go out looking like Plain Jane."

"You are not a Plain Jane. If you are, why did Dan ask you out?"

"Good question, I'm still trying to work it out." Clare frowned.

"Stop it. He obviously likes the look of you. It takes all

sorts, and when two people click, that's it."

"Takes all sorts? Thank you very much!"

Jo giggled. "I didn't mean it like that. Oh, you know what I mean."

"If the shops stayed open late I could maybe buy a new top to go with those black trousers of mine. Maybe I just shouldn't go," Clare said nervously.

"Stop getting yourself in a state. Why don't you leave at four-thirty? I can see to the cashing up and stuff. I'll get Hermione to stay and help, I can say it's a bit of training. Then you can look in the shops."

"Really? Oh thank you, you're an absolute angel."

"On one condition."

"What's that?"

"That you buy something really nice; treat yourself. Go for something you wouldn't normally buy, not the typical blouse done up to the neck, I mean."

"But then he isn't seeing the true me, I don't want to pretend to be something I'm not."

"Clare, it's only a top, it's not going to change your personality! You just said you don't want to wear your usual boring stuff."

"Okay you're on, I'll see what I can get. If I buy it before you close, I'll come in and show you. Ooh, it's twenty past four, only ten minutes." Clare grinned excitedly.

Jo rolled her eyes. "Oh for goodness sake, just go now."

"Thanks, Jo, you're the best friend anyone could have."

"Yeah, yeah, yeah. Off you go and have a good time. I want to hear all about it tomorrow. And I mean ALL."

Clare rushed off to get her bag, and Jo thought it was the happiest she'd seen her friend look in a long time. She hoped Clare would enjoy herself, she deserved some happiness.

At a quarter past five, Clare flew back into the shop.

"Jo, I've bought it!"

"Let's have a look then."

Clare opened her bag and took out her new top.

Jo gasped. It was beautiful. Jade green silk, with a 'V' neck and three-quarter length sleeves, it had an exquisite bead detail around the rim of the 'V' and the sleeves, and fell away in a loose caftan style.

"That's gorgeous. Where did you get it? It must have cost an absolute fortune."

Clare held up the bag showing the name of the very exclusive boutique down the road.

"Oh my God! Hold it against you."

Clare did and Jo saw that the colour totally transformed her complexion.

"I've still got some trial contact lenses, I'll use them. I'm going to wear my hair loose, and I bought this eye shadow." Clare showed her a pot of deep green metallic powder. "Do you think it will go?"

"You are going to knock him dead, that colour really suits you. How much was the top? Go on, tell me." Jo nudged her.

Clare looked a bit sheepish. "Seventy-five pounds. But I haven't bought myself anything in ages, and I'll wear it with lots of stuff, and you did say to treat myself."

"That's right," Jo laughed. "Blame me! It's a lot of money, but it does suit you. It brings your complexion to life and really brightens up your hair and face. Hey, why don't you dye your hair too? Go blonde."

"Erm, I think I've done enough for the moment. It'll be drastic enough with this top and eye shadow, seeing as I don't usually wear make-up. Right, I'm off, wish me luck," Clare said with a huge grin.

"Yeah, have a great time, and good luck. But you won't need it, you'll look stunning. See you tomorrow." Jo hugged Clare and watched her bounce out of the shop.

Chapter Nineteen

Sunday afternoon, after a delicious roast lunch, Michael walked to the petrol station down the road. He came back and presented his mother with a huge bunch of flowers.

"Oh thank you, love, but what are they for?"

"To say thanks for being so understanding about my problem."

"Michael, it isn't a problem, it's the way you are. What did you think your dad and I were going to do, really?" she asked.

"Disown me, kick me out of the house. I thought you'd be disgusted."

His mother's eyes filled with tears. "You're our only son. Nothing you could ever do would make us disown you or not love you."

"That's what Mollie said."

"Mollie?"

"She's the woman at the reading group who persuaded me to tell you. She said you wouldn't disown me, and to prove it, she said if you did I could move in with her."

"She's obviously a mother herself."

"No, she doesn't have children. She's on her own. Her husband died a few years back, but she's seeing Graham, another member of the group. No-one's supposed to know though," Michael said.

"Well, I'd like to meet this Mollie and thank her for her help. But, as we told you on Thursday, we already knew deep down. We were just waiting for you to tell us."

"But what about grandchildren? You won't have any. I'm

sorry, Mum."

"It doesn't matter. If you'd been heterosexual, by the time you'd got round to having children, your father and I probably wouldn't be around anyway."

Michael gasped. "Please don't say that."

"Well, face it, son," his mother said gently, "we're neither of us getting any younger. I'm seventy-two and your dad's seventy-five, we won't be around forever." She patted his arm. . "I'm glad you told us the truth about everything. I still wish you'd go to the police about that horrible man at work though."

"Mum, let me deal with it. I told you Graham has given me some advice. I'll do that first and see if it works. If it doesn't, then I promise I'll go to the police. But hopefully, I won't have to. Now are you going to put these in water?" Michael indicated the flowers.

"Yes. Thanks again. You didn't have to buy them, but they're lovely." His mother kissed his cheek.

She went into the other room to get a vase, and Michael ascended the stairs.

His mother called out to him. "Michael."

He stopped. "Yes?"

"Your father and I do love you, you know."

Michael swallowed the lump that appeared in his throat. "Yeah I know, Mum. Love you too."

***

Mollie hummed as she put the final touches to the lunch table. After Michael had gone last Thursday, she and Graham had stayed for a while and she'd invited him over for Sunday lunch. To her delight, he'd accepted.

So it had been a productive evening all round. She'd helped sort out Michael's problems, and arranged to see Graham again. She set down a wineglass as she heard the doorbell chime. She looked at her watch; he was exactly on time, as she'd known he would be. She guessed they had many things in common, punctuality being one of them. She looked in the mirror and smoothed down her hair then took off her apron to answer the door.

Graham greeted her with a kiss on the cheek and a bottle of wine. "I've brought a nice white wine, seeing as you're not keen on red."

"Oh lovely, thank you. Do come in."

Graham entered the hallway and immediately took his shoes off.

"House-trained too. You can come again," Mollie teased.

"Wait until we know each other better, I'll bring my slippers."

"You could have brought them anyway, it's better than walking round in socked feet."

"I have a pair in the car actually."

"Well, go and get them." She laughed at the look on his face. "Go on, there's no standing on ceremony with me, it's better to be comfortable. Go and get them, and I'll put mine on too," she said, shoving him out of the door again.

"Mollie, hang on. I can't walk to the car in my socks, I need my shoes," he wailed.

Mollie burst out laughing. "Oh, Graham. I'm sorry, but you do look funny standing there with that indignant look on your face. Here are your shoes."

He put them on and walked to the car.

Back in the house, he followed Mollie to the kitchen and sniffed appreciatively. "What's that wonderful smell?" he asked, as the aroma wafted around the room.

"Roast lamb. I hope you eat lamb. I tried to remember what you said you liked."

"You must have read my mind. I was thinking I hadn't had roast lamb for ages. I love it; it's probably my favourite. I don't suppose there are Yorkshire puddings to go with it too?"

"I should say. I do them with all my roasts. There's also roast potatoes and parsnips, cauliflower cheese, green beans and peas. Is that okay?" Mollie asked.

"Good grief that's plenty, and you've done another of my favourites, parsnips. Mm lovely. My mouth's watering. Right, is there anything I can do?"

"No, you sit down, you're a..."

"Don't say I'm a guest, I think we can dispense with the civilities, don't you? You told me to make myself comfortable and I've got my slippers on, so please let me do something," Graham said.

"Okay, you can open the wine and pour us both a glass. Oh, does it need to go in the fridge for a while?"

"No, I took it straight out of mine, and it's still cold. Where are the glasses?"

"In the dining room. There's a bottle of red wine in there for you. I know you prefer red."

Graham walked though to the small but tasteful dining room and picked up the red wine. "Rioja, good choice. May I pour a glass?" he called out.

"Help yourself. I must confess I had a hard decision about which red to get. I know my white wines, but don't know a lot about red. It was a choice between that or Merlot," Mollie answered.

Graham walked back into the kitchen with their glasses of wine. "Either are good, but you didn't have to worry about getting me any wine; I'm quite happy to drink white with you, and you're providing lunch."

"That's okay, if you don't drink the whole bottle, you'll have to come again and finish it off," Mollie said with a twinkle in her eyes.

Graham handed her the wine. "Ooh, you devious woman, I might have known there was a reason behind buying it."

Mollie took a sip of wine and laughed up at him.

Time stood still as they looked at each other, then very

gently, Graham took the wine glass out of Mollie's hand, put it down with his, leaned towards her and kissed her; a soft gentle touch on her lips. Initially, Mollie put a hand on his chest but then she relaxed against him, enjoying the feel of his lips against hers, and the manly smell of him as he kissed her again.

Then the oven buzzer went off, and they pulled apart.

Graham smiled. "Do you know, I've wanted to do that for ages, probably since the time I first saw you."

"It's a jolly good job you didn't, you'd have got a slap," Mollie told him with mock indignation. Then she smiled and went on, "I hoped to see you again after our meal in the Italian. Then when you didn't ask me out again, I thought you'd changed your mind. I was so disappointed."

"Tsk, what are the pair of us like? I'd have liked to see you again the next day, but I didn't want you to think me pushy, so I waited," Graham admitted.

"Well, I'd already decided I'd ask you out if you didn't mention us getting together again," Mollie told him boldly, as she prepared the cauliflower cheese.

"Oh you had, had you? I'm not sure I like independent women who take charge."

Mollie flapped the tea towel at him, laughed and took another sip of her wine. "Dinner will be ready in about half an hour. Can you carve the meat when it's ready?"

"Of course, I'm always happy to make myself useful. Have you heard from Michael? Did he tell you how it went with his parents?" Graham asked.

"I didn't get a chance to speak to him in depth, but he said they took it well, and in fact they'd already suspected."

"That's what he told me when I gave him the tape machine yesterday. I said we'd go for a drink after the meeting next week, and catch up with what's happened. You'll come, won't you?"

"Yes. I'm so pleased for the boy, and will be even happier if this thug leaves him alone. I knew his parents wouldn't disown him, how could a mother disown her child? It just wouldn't happen."

"Hmm, I don't know; I'm not used to children. Did you never have children, Mollie? You'd have made a lovely mother."

As soon as he'd spoken, he could see it was the wrong thing to say. A cloud came over her face, and for a moment he thought she was going to cry, but she pulled herself together, grabbed the oven glove and said, "I just need to check the potatoes."

Graham knew when someone didn't want to talk about a subject, so he said, "Here, let me get them for you." He took the glove from her and opened the oven door.

The potatoes were perfect, crispy and golden, and the parsnips were doing nicely too. He put them back in the oven and sat on a chair while Mollie busied herself with the vegetables. They chatted about various things, and he asked what she liked to do with her leisure time. She said that as well as baking and reading, she liked going to the theatre.

"There's a Noel Coward play on soon, would you like to go? I think Honor Blackman's in it," Graham said.

"Oh yes, that would be lovely. Could you carve this meat now please?"

Graham carved the meat and poured himself and Mollie another glass of wine.

"Shall I dish up straight onto the plates, or do you want it done properly and put into serving dishes so we can help ourselves?"

"Don't do that, it's too much hassle. Just dish it up, if you like."

Mollie served up the meal and they carried their plates into the dining room.

"Cheers. Thank you for a lovely meal," Graham toasted her.

"You haven't eaten it yet."

"No, but I can tell from the smell that it's delicious." Graham stuck his fork into a potato.

Three-quarters of the way through the meal, Mollie excused herself and went into the kitchen. Graham heard her doing something, but didn't know what. She came back five minutes later.

Graham finished his last forkful and sat back with a deep sigh of pleasure. "That has got to be the best roast lamb I've ever had. Absolutely delicious. You're an excellent cook."

"Thank you. I hope you have room for pudding."

"Pudding as well? My, you're wonderful, but I need to let this settle a bit."

"Of course, why don't you have a seat in the lounge while I sort out the dishes?"

"I'll help."

"No you jolly well won't, you're a guest," Mollie said.

"But we agreed I wasn't a guest. Do you have a dishwasher?"

"No. There isn't any point when I'm on my own."

"Right, that settles it then, I'm helping. Show me the kitchen!" Graham marched ahead of Mollie.

Once the dishes were done, Mollie took a jam roly-poly out of the oven.

Graham sniffed it in delight. "Ooh, I haven't had that since I was a boy. You are really spoiling me. What a treat."

After washing up their pudding bowls in the leftover water, they relaxed on the sofa until early evening, chatting, getting to know each other, and finishing the wines.

Graham looked at his watch and sat up straight. "Well, I suppose I'd better get going. I can't drive after all that alcohol, so I'll get a taxi." He took out his mobile phone.

"You don't have to get a taxi. Why waste money? I have a spare room; you can stay here and drive home in the morning. It'll also save a taxi back again to pick up your car."

"Money's no problem, Mollie, and I don't want to put you

to any trouble. You've been kindness itself inviting me for lunch."

"It's no trouble. The bed's made up for guests anyway, and I wouldn't ask if I didn't want you to stay. I'm enjoying your company and don't want it to stop."

Graham relaxed back against the sofa again. "I don't want it to stop either," he said, his voice hoarse. He gazed into Mollie's blue eyes as she snuggled closer, then he brought his lips down to meet hers, and watched as she lifted her face and closed her eyes to receive his kiss.

Chapter Twenty

Felicity woke up with a pounding head. Ouch, that's the last time I drink so much, she thought, then smirked because she said that every time she got a hangover. She snuggled back under the duvet and thought about last night.

She'd been sitting on a barstool in RJs laughing at something one of the boys had said, when the door opened. She'd looked up to see if it was anyone she knew, and watched as a woman who seemed vaguely familiar walked in.

"Wow, look at her top, isn't it gorgeous? I love the colour, and it looks frightfully expensive," Felicity whispered to the girl next to her.

She frowned, trying to place her as she watched a man greet the woman and lead her to a table. "I'm sure I know her from somewhere, but I can't think where." Felicity said to the friends she was with. "Oh, it'll come to me in a moment. Edward, be a sweetie and get me another drink, would you? I'm nipping to the lavatory."

Felicity'd slipped elegantly off her stool and made her way to the Ladies. On the way, she passed the table where the woman was sitting with her man friend. The woman called out when she saw her.

"Hello, Flick, fancy seeing you here."

Felicity looked down, and her eyes widened in astonishment, "Clare? Oh my gosh, I didn't recognise you! You look amazing. I love your top; fantastic colour, it really suits you," Felicity looked at the man beside Clare, waiting for an introduction.

"Oh sorry, Flick, this is Dan; Dan, this is Flick, one of the reading group members."

"Nice to meet you," Dan said.

"You too," Felicity smiled at him. "Sorry, Clare, must dash. I need the loo. Have a lovely evening, see you next week," she said, and dashed off to the Ladies.

She'd made her way back to her friends, and found a glass of Chardonnay waiting for her. "Thanks, Ed, I'll get you one later. You'll never guess what?" she said. "That girl in the green top is the owner of Merrilies. I couldn't believe it, she looks so different. Usually she's quite plain-looking with her hair in a ponytail and dreary clothes, but she looks fantastic tonight; talk about ugly duckling into a swan. Bloody hell, she must have taken lessons from a personal stylist or something."

"Hey, maybe she saw that Gok Wan bloke from the TV," Edward said.

Felicity laughed, took a sip of her wine and looked across at Clare. "Yes, I can just imagine him saying, 'Dahling, you need to let your hair down, get rid of those glasses and get some decent clothes, Sweetie'." She waved her hands around theatrically as she said this.

Her friends laughed.

"And the guy she's with is a bit of a stud too. Well, good for her. Come on, you lot, drink up, let's go to another bar."

"Flick, I can't get drunk again tonight, I have to drive to my mother's for lunch tomorrow don't forget," one of the girls said.

"Yes I know, but *I* don't have to drive anywhere."

"I don't know how you do it, Flick, your organs must be pickled."

"I'm preserving myself, darling," Felicity replied, and her friends roared with laughter.

"Come on, last one to Barneys buys the drinks," she yelled and, knocking back the rest of her wine, she grabbed her bag and left, with her friends rushing to keep up.

Well, well, she smiled now. Who'd believe that the priggish owner of Merrilies turned into a diva at night? And that top she'd worn wasn't cheap; Merrilies must be doing all right if Clare could afford clothes like that!

Felicity rubbed her thumping head. It had been a blinder of a night. They'd stayed in Barneys for a bit, then moved onto another bar, and eventually got a taxi to a smart nightclub in Oxford. At first, the taxi driver had refused to take them when he saw the state some of them were in, but Felicity pressed some notes into his hand and he'd agreed.

That was the good thing about Daddy being wealthy; money came in useful for getting your own way.

She couldn't remember getting home, and assumed they'd caught a taxi again.

She groaned and stuck her head under the duvet, knowing her father would call her soon. She was in no mood for one of his "You must get a job and do something with your life" lectures this morning, and was very likely to tell him to naff off.

Her mobile phone rang and, huffing, she got up to find it. "Yes yes, I'm bloody coming!" she yelled at its continuous ring.

Then, finding it under her bed, she grabbed it and pressed the answer button. "What?" she snapped.

"And good morning to you too, sis. What's up? Heavy night again?"

"Hi, Dom, you know me so well. What are you doing?"

"Calling you, you dope."

"Yes I bloody know that! Ooh my head. Why are you calling me?"

"I just thought I'd say hi, that's all. Can't a brother call his favourite sister occasionally?"

"Ha ha. Just think yourself lucky you've only got one," Felicity said.

"Too right. It was bad enough growing up with you, another would have been ghastly," her brother laughed.

"Oh thanks!"

"You asked for it. So, how's things? Got a job yet?"

"Has Daddy told you to phone me?" Felicity asked suspiciously.

"No, why?"

"Because that's all he asks me and I wouldn't put it past him to get you onside too."

"Oh come on, Flick, you know I wouldn't do that."

"Sorry, but the only time Daddy talks to me now is to moan that I don't have a job."

"Well, I'm not sticking up for him, but he does have a point. You've got to do something if you're not going back to Uni," Dominic said.

"Oh for heaven's sake, YES I KNOW! But if you'd trained to be a barrister instead of swanning off to yokel land, Daddy would leave me alone," Felicity yelled.

"Hey, don't shout at me! That's not a fair comment, Flick, and you know it. And don't talk about Devon like that. You should come down here, it's lovely. I'm sitting on top of some rocks at a place called Burrator. It looks out over the reservoir, forest and moorland. It's beautiful."

"Mm, I'll take your word for it."

"Philistine! Where are *you* then?"

"Erm...well..." Felicity ran her fingers through her dishevelled hair.

"Oh, Flick, you're not still in bed on a beautiful day like this? You shouldn't drink so much. Go out and get some fresh air."

"Bloody hell, Dom, all that country air's turned your head to mush. You're far too sensible. You used to drink more than me, what's happened?"

"I've grown up, that's what. I'm a consultant now; I can't risk getting out of my head all the time. Well, I'd better go, I've got to go home and change. I'm taking someone out to lunch later."

"Ooh, by someone I take it you mean a girl?"

"Yes."

"Is it serious?"

"It's early days but I like her, so we'll see how things go. I'm losing the signal. Bye, sis, take care. And get a job!"

"You take care too, Dom, and...oh." The call cut off.

She sighed, threw the phone on the bed and walked into her en-suite to have a shower.

Bloody hell, she thought, both Daddy and Dom are pestering me to get a job now. I am rather bored actually, so maybe I'll have a look around and see if anything interesting comes up.

***

Thursday's meeting came round again.

Tessa didn't know how the days went so quickly. What with working in the surgery, her writing, and looking after Amber, there was hardly enough time for anything else. But she'd decided she would *not* give up the reading group. It was her little bit of me time to mix with like-minded people and talk about one of her great loves – books.

When she arrived at Merrilies, Mollie was, as usual, the first one there.

"Hi Mollie, had a good week so far?" Tessa asked.

"Not bad, what about you?" Mollie answered.

"Yes quite good thanks, apart from Amber."

"Oh dear, what's she been up to?"

"Well, I had to collect her from the police station. She'd been caught shoplifting." Tessa said with a sigh.

"No! I thought she was a good girl. You've always spoken highly of her," Mollie said in surprise.

"I know. But hopefully it was a one-off. She was dared to do it by a gang she wanted to join and, just her luck, she got caught. Mind you, when the police came and took her to the station it frightened the life out of her, so I don't think she'll do it again. And...well, I lost my temper and slapped her across the face. I'm so ashamed of myself now, but I think it shocked her rigid." Tessa looked a bit sheepish.

"Hmm, don't feel too bad about it. If more parents gave their children a slap, they wouldn't be such little horrors in my opinion. But with all this political correctness or whatever it is, parents no longer have any control and the kids get away with all sorts."

"I know. Even teachers can't discipline them any more."

Mollie tutted and went on, "It was so different in my day; children knew how to behave. Oh sorry, Tessa, I do get carried away sometimes. How are things now?"

"Well, she's been good so far and even offers to help around the house." Tessa grinned. "But I don't expect it will last much longer. Anyway I have some other news. You know that story I was working on, the crime one?"

"Yes."

"Well, I'd contacted a new women's magazine with the idea, and someone phoned me back during the week. They want to publish it as a serial. Their rates of pay are excellent too."

"Oh that's jolly good news, Tessa. You never know, you might make a name for yourself, be able to leave the doctors' surgery and write full time. Would you like that?"

"You bet, that's my dream; all I've ever wanted." Tessa's eyes were shining.

"I'll keep my fingers crossed for you, my dear. Oh hello, Felicity, how are you?".

Felicity flopped down in the chair next to Tessa and sighed. "Hi, I'm fine. Fed up, but fine."

Tessa laughed, Felicity could always make something out of nothing. "Why are you fed up?" she asked.

"Well, not only does Daddy go on at me to get a job, but my brother, Dom, phoned at the weekend, and even he

142

moaned at me to do something. It's all very tedious."

Mollie couldn't help speaking up. "Well, they do have a point, Felicity. Look at Tessa here. She works in the doctors' surgery and writes too. You should be working, not freeloading off your parents."

"Yes," Tessa agreed with Mollie. "Especially with your high standard of living." She grinned to show she was only half-serious.

"But I'm not sure what I want to do. I know what I *don't* want to do; any more studying. Can you see me as something like a checkout girl? I mean, puhlease!" Felicity tossed back her hair dramatically.

"Well, what would you really like to do, if you could?" Tessa asked.

"Work with animals. I've wanted to do that ever since I was a little girl."

"So why didn't you study to be a vet?" Tessa said.

"Because my bloody father wanted me to study law and become a barrister. Especially once my brother became a doctor and disappeared down to the depths of Devon." Felicity folded her arms grumpily.

"I wouldn't have thought anyone could make *you* do something you don't want to. Why didn't you just tell him you didn't want to study law?" Mollie asked.

"You haven't met Daddy. Nobody says no to him!"

"Hmm, maybe it's about time someone stood up to him then," Mollie said, her mouth set in a grim line. "Anyway," she went on, "why don't you train as a vet now?"

"It's too much work. I don't want to go back to Uni and study any more, I've had enough."

Mollie thought for a bit, then said, "What about Animal Saviours? Their headquarters are here in Bewford, they might have something."

Felicity clapped with delight. "Mollie, you're brilliant! Yes of course, why the bloody hell didn't I think of them? I'll phone them tomorrow."

At that moment, Graham arrived with Michael behind him.

"Hi Pops. Hi Mikey," Felicity said.

"Hiya, you lot," Michael said with a big smile.

"Er Michael, are you okay?" Felicity asked.

"Yep, why?"

"Because you're smiling. You hardly ever smile."

"Oh ha ha, Flick, very funny. Well, if you must know I'm happy because I've got rid of a problem that's been bugging me for ages." He looked at Mollie and Graham, then went on in a quieter voice, "And, erm, I admitted to my parents that I'm gay."

The table went quiet. Felicity's eyes widened in surprise as she stared at him, speechless for once.

Tessa spoke first. "Good for you, Michael. I bet it was a relief to come out, wasn't it?"

Felicity found her voice. "I knew you were weird, but I didn't have you down as a poofter."

Mollie was astounded. "Felicity!"

Felicity held her hands up and laughed. "Hey I was joking, guys. Well done, Mikey, perhaps now you'll stop being so bloody grumpy and smile more often; it suits you." She grinned at him.

Michael grinned back. "Thanks, Flick. Yes, it was a relief, Tessa. I feel as though a big weight has disappeared. I also had a problem with a guy at work, but that's been sorted out now too."

"What, fancied you, did he?" Felicity snorted with laughter.

"No, he was blackmailing me actually."

Felicity's face changed. "Oh hell, Michael, I'm sorry. I knew you weren't very happy a couple of weeks ago when I bought the flapjacks, but didn't want to pry."

"Well, it's a good job someone did." He nodded at Mollie

and Graham. "These two helped me sort things out, and I'm so glad they did. Thank you both."

Graham changed the subject, disliking praise. "Right, can we get onto the reason we're here?"

The reading group got underway.

Halfway through they had their usual break for coffee, and Felicity bought some cakes. After she'd bought the coffees and flapjacks that first time, it had become a routine, and she bought drinks and cake or biscuits for the group every Thursday. She came back with the tray containing their coffees, and Tessa carried the plate of cakes.

"I don't know what's up with Jo tonight, but she's very quiet," Tessa told the group.

"Yes, I noticed that. She's been a bit quiet for a while now," Mollie said.

"Perhaps she's gay and needs to come out too." Felicity laughed.

Michael groaned. "Oh great; are we going to have this referred to for the next six months now?" he asked, but his question was good-natured.

"For the next year, Mikey. It's the best bit of gossip I've heard for ages."

"You're the only one who thinks you're funny, Flick, and you know what they say about someone who laughs at their own jokes," Michael answered.

Mollie enjoyed the banter between the two youngsters; she couldn't believe the change in Michael. She'd never seen him this animated. It suited him, made him seem less, well, nerdy, she supposed.

Felicity spoke again. "I haven't seen Annie for a while, has anyone else seen her?"

"Not since she came in to tell us about the photographer," Tessa answered.

"Hmm, I'll ask Clare or Jo about her when I get chance," Felicity said. "Talking about Clare, I saw her out at the

145

weekend, and she looked gorgeous. I didn't recognise her."

"Really?" Michael asked. "I wouldn't describe Clare as gorgeous, she's rather plain."

"Michael, don't be cruel. She looked lovely. She must have had contact lenses in, her hair was down, she had make-up on, and a gorgeous jade green top. The guy with her was pretty hot too."

"You sure it was her and not a more attractive lookalike?" Michael joked.

"No, it was Clare. I spoke to her."

"Well jolly good for her," Mollie said. "She deserves some fun; they work damn hard to keep this bookshop running. Now, talking of work, let's get back to ours."

"Okay, Attila," Felicity replied and they laughed.

***

When the shop closed, and Clare and Jo were getting things ready for the following day, Clare decided to risk asking her friend what was wrong again, even if she told her to mind her own business.

"I know something's up, Jo, you've been quiet or snappy for a couple of weeks now. Sometimes you manage to hide it, but I know you well enough to see you're unhappy."

To her horror, Jo started crying. Clare had never seen her cry in all the time she'd known her.

"Oh my goodness, what on earth's wrong?" Clare put her arm around her friend.

"I've been so worried," Jo sniffed. "I've got... I found a lump in my breast."

"Oh God, when and where?"

"About three weeks ago. Just on the side of my right breast, below my armpit."

"What has the doctor said?"

Clare saw the look on Jo's face. "You haven't been to the

146

doctors, have you?"

Jo shook her head. "I'm too scared of what he might tell me."

"For heaven's sake, Jo, you've got to go! If it *is* something nasty, don't you see that the quicker they can deal with it the better?"

"I know." Jo sobbed, twisting the tissue in her hands. "But I'm so scared it might be cancer."

Clare made her a cup of tea to calm her down a bit. When Jo was more composed, Clare asked, "Have you told your mum?"

"No, I haven't told anyone except you."

"Right, first thing tomorrow I want you to make an appointment with the doctor, do you hear me? You have to get this looked at as soon as possible." Clare shook her head in exasperation.

"But I'm scared and don't want to go alone," Jo said, her face anguished.

"I'd come with you, you know I would, but we can't leave Merrilies without one of us here. Why don't you tell your mum, she'll go with you."

Jo shook her head. "No. I don't want to upset her unnecessarily. She doesn't have to know unless it is something bad."

"But she's your mum, Jo, and she'll be terribly hurt if she finds out you kept it to yourself because you didn't want to worry her. You need someone with you. Promise me you'll talk to her tonight and make an appointment tomorrow. Don't worry about work – take as long as you need. In fact, why don't you take the whole day off?"

"Thanks, Clare, but I'll come back to work; I'll need to keep occupied."

"Okay, but I'm going to phone you later to see if you've told your mum, and if you haven't, I will. So you better do it. And don't fib either. Now let's finish up here and get off home."

They locked up and, before she could change her mind, Jo got into her car and drove to her parents' house.

Her mum answered the door. "Hello love, nice to see you. Why didn't you phone to let us know you were coming? Dad and I had shepherd's pie for tea, but there's some left, would you..? What's wrong, darling?" she asked as she got a proper look at Jo's tear-stained face."

"Oh Mum," Jo managed to blurt out before she started crying again.

"Come inside, sweetheart, and I'll put the kettle on." Her mother ushered her inside with a worried frown.

Chapter Twenty-One

The following morning, Felicity was up, showered and dressed by eight.

"Good grief, what's got you out of bed this early? You usually sleep until at least ten. Are you feeling all right, darling?" her mother asked.

"Oh *tres amusant*," Felicity said, rolling her eyes.

"And you're all dressed up. You normally look like a grungy hippy. You can't possibly be Felicity in that pencil skirt and sensible blouse, and what's happened to your hair?"

Felicity had put up her long hair, which she often wore loose and wild around her shoulders, using a pretty flower-shaped clip.

"Mummy, you are *so* not funny. I'm going to see someone this morning, is that okay, Mrs Nose Ointment?"

"Oh, who? Good heavens, don't tell me it's about a job!" Eleanor asked with genuine shock.

"Okay, I won't then. What's for breakfast?" Felicity looked around the kitchen.

"Anything you want as long as you get it yourself."

"I was going to, Mother. I don't expect you to chip your nails doing it for me."

"If I'd offered, you'd have happily sat there and let me get it."

"Well, that's what mothers do," Felicity said.

"When their children are young maybe, when they're older they can do things for themselves."

"What did you do for us when we were young? We've

always had cleaners, gardeners and nannies." Felicity got bread out of the bread bin.

"Don't exaggerate, Felicity. I did my fair share of bringing you and Dominic up," Eleanor replied.

"What, in between the lunches and beauty sessions, you mean?"

Her mother pulled a hurt expression.

"Oh, don't look at me like that, I'm only teasing. You're a wonderful mother and I love you," Felicity said and kissed her mother's cheek.

"Oh God, now I know you're not my daughter. You're an alien impostor."

Felicity grinned and put two slices of bread in the toaster.

"Want a coffee?" she asked.

"No thanks, what I do want though, is to know where you're going."

"Well, I don't want to tell you yet; you'll find out later maybe, depending on what happens." Felicity stuck her nose in the air.

"Okay, have it your way. Right I'm off. I'm meeting Penny at the health club then we're having lunch. See you later, sweetie, and good luck, whatever you're up to."

"Thanks, Mummy. Bye."

Felicity sat down to drink her coffee and eat her toast while flicking through the Telegraph. She'd decided that rather than phone the animal shelter, she'd appear there in person and plead with them to give her a job. She adored animals, and if she could do some sort of work with them she'd be happy. And maybe it would stop her father nagging her; although Felicity felt that where she was concerned, he'd always find something to moan about.

***

Alice took a tray with a bowl of Rice Krispies and glass of

150

milk up to Annie, who was lying in bed with a book. "How are you feeling this morning, sweetheart?"

"I'm okay. Can I get up and watch telly please?"

Alice felt Annie's forehead and looked at her face. She certainly seemed brighter and the colour had returned to her cheeks. "Yes, when you've eaten your breakfast. Have you used your inhaler yet?"

"No."

"Well, take a couple of puffs please. You know you should use it as soon as you can to help your breathing."

Annie reached for her preventer inhaler, which was on her bedside cabinet, and took a couple of deep lungfuls. Then she coughed a few times. Alice rubbed her back.

"I'm alright, Mum. Can I go back to school on Monday?"

"I'll see, Annie."

"Please, I miss my friends, and I miss going into Merrilies."

"Honey, they'll all still be there when you return. I want to make sure you're properly well before you go back to school. You know you can't risk getting another infection on top of an existing one."

"But I'm okay, I feel tons better."

"That's why you just had a coughing fit, is it?"

"No, that was cuz I breathed in too much inhaler. Pleeease, can I go back?" Annie stuck out her bottom lip.

"I'll see how you are over the weekend. If you're okay, then yes you can return on Monday."

"Thanks, Mum, can I go watch telly now?"

"Yes, but put your dressing gown on."

Alice wished she could keep Annie at home permanently. She'd caught a nasty cold, which had gone straight to her chest, and then she'd had an asthma attack as well.

She'd been quite poorly, and they had feared she would need to be hospitalised. But the doctor had come to see her and given her an extra course of antibiotics. Thankfully, her chest had eased, her breathing improved and she seemed to have bounced back well.

Alice knew it was unfair to try to keep Annie at home for longer than necessary, but she so wished she could protect her little girl from the outside world.

Later that day, Annie said, "Mum, I feel loads better, and seeing as I've been in bed all week and not had any fresh air, can we go to Merrilies?"

"No, sweetheart, just stay at home until after the weekend."

"Aw please, Mum, please please please. We can see how much money they've got for my fundraising. I want to see Jo and Clare. The must wonder where I am cuz I haven't been in for ages."

"You're still not well enough, honey," Alice said.

"I haven't coughed all day."

"What about earlier this morning?"

"I told you, that was just cuz I had too much of my inhaler."

"No it wasn't, Annie, and you know it." Alice hated being the bad guy, but as the adult, she had to be the sensible one.

"But I'm bored, and no-one could visit me in case they had a cold or something. I'm okay now...pleeeeease!"

Alice looked at her daughter's pleading face and her beautiful big blue eyes, and gave in. "Annie Matthews, you know how to wind me round your little finger. Go up and get dressed. Make sure it's something warm and we'll pop into Merrilies for half an hour."

"Thanks, Mum, you're the bestest." Annie made for the stairs.

"Annie, don't run!" Alice said in a panic, waiting for the wheezing to start, but Annie was already halfway up the stairs, singing to herself.

Luckily it was a quiet Friday afternoon in Merrilies, and Jo was sitting at the till reading a Bookseller magazine. She looked up as someone came in the door. "ANNIE! How lovely to see you. Where have you been?" She went round the counter and gave the little girl a hug.

"I've been poorly in bed all week, but I'm much better now," Annie told her.

Jo looked at Alice. "Is she okay?"

"Well, I'd rather she stayed in until after the weekend, but she seems a lot brighter than she was." Alice turned to her daughter, "Go and look at the children's books if you like."

Alice waited until Annie was out of earshot. "I was really worried this time, Jo. We've had some scares in the past, but even Tom panicked and called the doctor. She nearly ended up in hospital."

"Oh no, what happened?" Jo asked.

"There was a bug going round at school, but the teachers didn't know until it was too late and Annie had caught it as well. It's not their fault; it's so hard to tell if a child's ill and they often have the virus before any symptoms show."

"It must be really difficult," Jo agreed.

Alice rubbed a hand across her forehead. "Annie had an asthma attack when she got home from school one afternoon, and was poorly all that evening so Tom called the doctor out. He wanted to monitor her in hospital but she got all worked up because she didn't want to go, so he prescribed some different antibiotics and advised complete bed rest. After a few days, thankfully she improved."

"She knows her own mind, doesn't she?"

"Yes. She may be weak physically, but she's a strong-willed little madam. She pleaded with me to bring her here today, by saying she hadn't had any fresh air or seen anyone all week. I'd rather she'd stayed at home in bed, but...'

"But you can't wrap her up in cotton wool, much as you'd like to?" Jo asked.

"Something like that." Alice smiled weakly.

Annie came back and waited to interrupt, "Jo, is Clare upstairs?"

"Yes, she is. Shall I tell her you're on your way up?"

"Yes, please."

Jo picked up the phone. "Clare, you have a visitor...wait and see...yeah it is."

"Aw, does she know it's me?" Annie asked.

Jo laughed. "Yeah, she guessed."

Annie pulled a face.

"Well, how many other people come in to see us?"

"Lots and lots. The people who buy the books," Annie said in her simplistic way.

"But I'd have said I was sending a customer up, not a visitor."

"Oh I see. Okay can I go up now?"

"Yeah off you go while I chat with Mummy. Hermione's on her way to meet you."

Jo served a couple of customers, then turned her attention back to Alice. "I've got some great news about Annie's fundraising. Two local businesses are going to put some money in. The bank across the road and that exclusive boutique a bit further down."

"That's fantastic, how did they get involved?"

"Clare bought a top from the boutique the other day and the woman serving her recognised her from here. They got chatting and Clare told them about Annie. They offered to sponsor her, so to speak. And you know our new girl, Hermione? Her boyfriend works in the bank, so she asked him to tell his boss and see if they'd help, and his boss agreed."

Alice was delighted. "Oh, that's brilliant news!"

Jo continued, "They'd seen it in the Herald and were going to do something anyway. They want to contact you about it, and I thought maybe you could speak to the paper again as it's a story they'd like. I can imagine the headline, '*Local Businesses Help Annie's Dolphin Dream*' or something like that. You need to ask the bank and boutique first though, because they might not want the publicity."

"When are they going to get in touch?" Alice asked.

"Well, as soon as they have your details, I guess. We were concerned because we haven't seen Annie all week. I was going to leave it a few more days then phone and see if everything was okay. But now I know things *are* okay, can I give them your phone number?" Jo asked.

"Of course, but why don't I nip in and see them on Monday?"

"Yeah good idea, but phone beforehand and make an appointment, that way they might be able to spare you a bit more time."

"Jo, thank you so much. Hopefully with all this help it won't take long until we have enough money for the trip. Oh this is great, aren't people kind?" Alice's eyes filled with tears. "Tom and I could really do with a holiday as well, so this will be great for all of us. Okay, I'm going to get Annie back home in the warm." She headed upstairs to find her daughter.

Poor woman, Jo thought, as she watched her go. But she didn't dwell on it, as she had her own worries. Over a cup of tea the previous evening, she'd told her mother about finding the lump in her breast.

"Jo sweetheart, why didn't you say anything earlier?" her mother said.

"I wasn't going to tell you at all," Jo sniffed, "but Clare made me promise to tell you, and to go to the doctor tomorrow morning."

"Well, hooray for Clare, she's a very sensible girl. What time does the surgery close?"

"I'm not sure, half past six I think."

"It's too late to phone them now, but make sure you phone first thing in the morning and tell them you need an urgent appointment."

"Oh Mum, I don't want to go. I'm scared of finding out what it is," Jo said, her bottom lip trembling.

"It's okay, love, I'll come with you. I wouldn't let you go

through something like this on your own. Now go and say hello to your dad, then have something to eat."

Her father had made himself scarce when he'd heard her crying, giving her the chance to talk to her mum. She found him in the lounge, pretending to read the paper. She saw his dear concerned face and knew he must be worried, but also knew he wouldn't ask what was wrong, so she sat down and told him. He said pretty much the same as her mother and Clare, that she must get it sorted out.

Jo felt a little easier having told her parents, and realised how ravenous she was. She'd not eaten properly for a couple of weeks, so she sat in the lounge with a tray on her lap and ate a healthy portion of shepherd's pie.

It was gone half past ten when she arrived home and heard the bleep of the answer phone informing her she had a message. She knew it was Clare.

Clare usually went to bed around ten. Knowing she'd switch her phone on in the morning, Jo sent a text to say she'd told her mum, and would make an appointment with the doctor first thing in the morning.

After examining Jo, the doctor said she ought to have a biopsy, and the hospital would send her an appointment soon. She explained that most breast lumps were benign, and, as there was no history of breast cancer in the family, Jo's was probably benign too. "Try not to worry," she'd said with a reassuring smile.

It's okay for *you* to say that, Jo thought, you're not the one with this lump.

"Why don't you stay home with us?" Jo's mum said on their way back from the doctors.

"Thanks, Mum, but I'm going into work."

"But if Clare said it's okay, why don't you take the rest of the day off?"

"Because I need to keep occupied. It'll take my mind off things. Otherwise, I'll just sit around worrying, and that won't do me any good. Do you mind?"

"No, I understand," her mother said patting her arm.

She did understand, but she'd have liked Jo home so she could make a fuss of her. "Well, have a good day and if you need anything, you know where we are. We do love you, you know."

Jo pulled up outside her parents' house. "Mum, I love you too, now stop talking as if I'm dying already..." She broke off as she saw the look on her mother's face, and gave her a hug. "Go on, in you go, I'll be okay. I'll tell you as soon as the appointment comes through. You will come with me, won't you?"

"Of course I will. Bye, dear."

Jo watched her mother wave goodbye, then she drove around the corner and stopped to let the tears that had been threatening all morning, overflow.

Chapter Twenty-Two

Saturday morning Felicity breezed into the shop and rushed up to Clare who was on the till.

"Clare, you couldn't give me Mollie's home phone number, could you?"

"Well, I'm not sure about giving it out."

"Oh Clare, she won't mind *me* having it, we're friends. I've got her mobile number, but it's switched off. '

"Leave a message then."

"I want to speak to her now. Just give me the number, she won't mind," Felicity said.

"Maybe not, but let me phone her first and ask if I can give it to you."

Felicity rolled her eyes. "Okay can you hurry up though please?"

Clare got out a book and looked up Mollie's number then dialled it. "Ah, Mollie? Hi, it's Clare from Merrilies. Felicity wanted your phone number, but I wanted to check that it was okay to give it to her. Yes, hang on a mo." Clare passed the phone over to Felicity.

"Hi, yes I know I did tell her." Felicity looked pointedly at Clare, who busied herself with some gift cards. "I've got some news for you. Are you sure? Okay, give me the address. Yes, about half an hour? Fine, see you then." Felicity handed the phone back to Clare and said sarcastically, "Ooh, now I have her address too."

Clare refused to acknowledge that maybe she was being a bit too cautious. "I'm sure you'll understand, Felicity, that we have to adhere to the rules at all times. We do not give customers' personal details to anyone."

"What, not even the police if they asked?"

"Well, that would be different of course," Clare replied.

"Exactly. You can use your discretion when you want to. Anyway, I'm not standing here arguing with you, I have much more interesting things to talk about with Mollie. See you." And with a cheery wave, Felicity flounced out of the door.

About twenty-five minutes later, she rang Mollie's doorbell.

Mollie answered, an apron tied round her middle. "Come on in. Don't mind me, I'm in the middle of baking."

"Mm, something smells delicious."

"Cakes for the café. I've made an extra one, so we can have a piece with a cup of tea." Mollie looked Felicity up and down then said, "If you're not dieting this week."

Felicity laughed, "No, not this week. I've given up dieting for the time being."

"Jolly good. Have a seat. I hope you don't mind if I carry on cooking, I need to get these cakes finished to take to Merrilies later."

"No, that's fine. Shall I put the kettle on?"

"Good idea, you can come again if you carry on making yourself useful. Use water from the filter there please. Now what's this news?"

"I've got a job!" Felicity stated as she filled the kettle.

"Felicity, that's wonderful! Tell me all about it. How, where?"

"It's thanks to you really. I went to the animal shelter yesterday and spoke to a very nice man. He showed me around and asked what I'd been doing so far, then told me about the different jobs. As luck would have it, they had a couple of vacancies."

"Doing what?" Mollie asked as she stirred a bowl of cake mixture.

"Well, they had one in marketing, which is what he

thought I'd be interested in. He was a bit concerned about me wanting a job with animals when I've been studying law, but I persuaded him that working with animals is what I really want to do, and that I want to be much more hands on."

"*You*, get your hands dirty?" Mollie looked at her in surprise.

"Yes. I'm not as posh as everyone thinks you know. I can get my hands dirty, I'm just choosy about the type of dirt." Felicity stole a fingerful of cake mix.

Mollie slapped her hand away then roared with laughter. "You are an absolute delight, do you know that? The teabags are in that cupboard, put three in the pot."

"Three?"

"Yes, one per person and one for the pot. So, what will you be doing?"

Felicity found the teabags, put three in the teapot then answered, "I'm going to be an Animal Welfare Assistant. I will be responsible for the day-to-day care of the animals; doing things like walking the dogs, grooming the animals, their general care, and, with supervision initially, feeding them and giving them their medication. I'll also help to re-home them. I can study for an NVQ in animal care too if I want, which after studying law, should be a doddle." She filled the teapot with boiling water.

Mollie looked at Felicity's happy face and could see this really was something the girl wanted to do. She gave her a hug. "I'm very pleased and proud of you. When do you start?"

"Monday morning. I can have Saturday afternoons off. I told them about the reading group. I know it's not much, but I've come to enjoy our meetings and I like the people in it, well, most of you. I don't have to work every Saturday morning either, but if I do, I get half a day off in the week to compensate. I'm really looking forward to it, Moll."

"Well, jolly good for you. I didn't realise you were so fond of animals."

"I've always loved them. I got arrested once." Felicity made a face and looked a bit ashamed. "It was while I was at Uni. I and some other people protested about animal experimentation at this big lab. I did the typical thing, chained myself to the gates and threw the key away, then shouted out that they were torturers and murderers. Someone called the police, and after cutting the chains, they told me to go away; but I picked up a huge stone and threw it at one of the windows. It broke and the police arrested me."

"Felicity! While it's admirable of you to stand up for what you believe in, there are other ways of doing it. What happened?" Mollie said.

"I phoned Daddy, and they released me without charge. They were going to do me for criminal damage and disturbing the peace or something, but Daddy is very influential. I knew he'd get me off."

"Well, let that be a lesson to you, young lady, and you shouldn't always rely on your father to bail you out. Now how about a piece of chocolate cake?" Mollie cleaned her hands and took her apron off.

"Yes please! I am so grateful to you. If you hadn't thought of Animal Saviours, I wouldn't be starting work on Monday. I don't know why I hadn't thought about it really. Well, to be honest, I didn't think about work at all. I enjoyed just hanging around and shopping, but after a while that gets very dull. At least Daddy can stop moaning at me now."

"Oh yes, what did your parents say?"

"Well, Mummy says she doesn't want me coming home stinking of awful animal smells, and Daddy said that with my education I could do much better for myself. But I think they're secretly pleased I've got a job; they just like to make a fuss."

"Hmm, not unlike someone else I know. She's a jolly nice girl when you get to know her, but you wouldn't believe it sometimes, especially when she's an outspoken little madam."

Mollie raised her eyebrows.

Felicity laughed and took a bite of her cake. "I couldn't believe it when Clare wouldn't give me your phone number. I told her I had your mobile already, but she wouldn't budge. What a jobsworth."

"Yes, but she was just being careful, that's all. Sorry my mobile was off, I don't switch it on if I'm at home, but I should do, I suppose. Anyway, would you want us all having your phone numbers?" Mollie asked.

"I wouldn't mind you and Pops, or even Tessa. Ugh, but not nerdy Michael! I would *not* be happy if Clare gave him my phone number without asking me first, and if she did ask, I'd say no."

"He's not that bad, Felicity, have some tolerance. He's got my mobile number, I gave it to him when we helped him out that time, but he's never used it."

"He's been a lot happier since he 'came out'. I did actually feel sorry for him when I found out about the blackmailing, and he's okay in small doses I suppose." Felicity wrinkled her nose. "I better phone a taxi as I need to leave soon, I've got some shopping to do before our meeting. I'm going to buy some clothes for work."

"What, nice sensible ones you mean?" Mollie said eyeing Felicity's outfit.

Felicity looked down at her grungy clothes and laughed. "Yes. See you at the meeting later."

"I'll be there. You've got both my phone numbers now, so if you have some spare time, give me a call and pop in for a chat, I'd love to see you."

"Thanks Mollie, I'd like that."

They chatted until the taxi came then Felicity thanked Mollie and kissed her on the cheek. Mollie smiled, waved her off, and went back to her baking.

***

Michael *was* feeling much happier. His life seemed to have taken a turn for the better. He only wished he'd told his parents the truth sooner. Everyone had been brilliant about the whole thing, especially his boss.

The conversation he'd managed to record with Spike was cracking.

Spike had cornered Michael on Monday morning just as he came out of the men's toilet. Michael had already switched the tape machine on and tried to calm himself down and not let nerves get the better of him, this was his one chance to stop Spike and he didn't want to blow it. He just prayed that Spike wouldn't notice the machine or hear anything; although Graham was right, it didn't make a sound.

"Well, have you got the money?" Spike growled.

"Pardon?" Michael said, hoping Spike would speak up. He looked around to see if anyone had noticed them.

"No point looking for help, Kingster, we're the first ones in. Now give me the money."

"This is the last fifty quid you're getting from me, Spike."

"You'll keep paying, otherwise I'll tell everyone you're a queer." He snatched the money out of Michael's hand. "Now, I'll expect another fifty quid, same time next week."

"I told you, that's all you're getting. I can't afford to keep paying you. This is blackmail; you're making my life hell!" Michael shouted knowing the machine was recording it all.

Spike sniggered, "You think I'm making your life hell? You'll know what hell is if Barry and the boys find out. They'll do to you what they do to all homos. So, call me your protection if you like. Yeah that's good, you're paying me to keep your little secret and stop you being pulverised. Now scram, perv." Spike pushed Michael away and walked off whistling.

Michael went back into the toilets and locked himself into a cubicle. He took the tape machine out, rewound it and pressed play. YES! The whole conversation had recorded loud and clear. Now all he had to do was take it to his boss.

Mr Simmons was on the phone, but as soon as he'd finished, Michael went in and asked if he could have a word in private. He sat in the office and explained what had been happening, and then played the tape. He watched his boss's face go from shock to disbelief and then contort in anger while he listened to Spike's clear threats.

"How long has this been going on, Michael?"

"It started at Easter."

"Why on earth didn't you come to me sooner?"

"Because I didn't think you'd believe me, I didn't know what to do."

His boss rubbed his hand over his chin and sighed. "Michael, I just wish you'd told me what was going on. I would have believed you, and I will not tolerate bullying of any kind in my company. What Spike has done is discrimination and blackmail and it's against the law. Can I ask you, are you gay? Don't answer that if you don't want to, it's none of my business after all."

"No it's okay, Mr Simmons. Yes I am, and I'm not ashamed of it."

"Good for you, lad. One of my nephews is gay. Took him a while to tell us all, but we already knew really."

"That's what my parents said." Michael couldn't believe how kind people were being. He really hadn't expected this reaction.

"Right, leave it with me. Do you want to press charges? I'm more than happy to contact the police, it's what Spike deserves," Mr Simmons said, his face red with anger.

"No, I don't want the police involved, but I'd like my money back."

"Don't worry, Michael, you'll get your money back."

"What if because I've told you, Spike tells Barry and his mates? They go 'queer bashing' on their nights out. If they knew I was gay, my life wouldn't be worth living, that's what

Spike says; you heard it on the tape." Michael looked worried.

"Don't believe a word of it. I think it's all lies and he said it to frighten you. And don't worry about repercussions either. I'll warn him that if he says anything or touches you, this tape will find its way to the police station. Now go back to work and don't worry, you'll have no more trouble from him."

About half an hour later, Mr Simmons called Spike into his office.

Ten minutes after that Spike came out again his face etched with worry. He collected his belongings and left without a word.

Mr Simmons then came out and addressed the rest of the staff. "Just to let you know, Spike has been dismissed for bullying and blackmailing another member of staff. I hope you all take note now, that I will not, under any circumstances, stand for bullying or harassment in this company. Anyone suspected and found guilty of it will be sacked on the spot."

To Michael's astonishment everyone clapped, even Barry and his mates.

Since then, things had improved dramatically. It was altogether a nicer, more relaxed place to work.

His colleagues talked to him more and they'd even invited him out for a drink. Although he'd declined, he was delighted because they'd never invited him before. He discovered he wasn't the only one Spike had picked on. He'd tried it on with one of the girls, and Barry'd had a run in with him on more than one occasion. It also wasn't true about Barry and his mates 'queer bashing'. Spike had just said it to frighten Michael.

Michael had decided to tell his colleagues he was gay. They'd only be speculating anyway, so he'd plucked up the courage to speak out one break time while sitting round the coffee table with the rest of the crowd. "It was me who was being blackmailed by Spike," he told them.

"What on earth for?" Barry asked.

"Because I'm gay. He said he'd tell you, and that you went queer bashing, and you and your mates would beat me up."

"He said WHAT? The little git! If I ever see him, he's for it. Michael, I swear to you, I do *not* do things like that, and I don't hang out with the sort of people who do either. Okay?"

"Okay."

"Although I might make an exception if I ever see him." Barry was fuming.

One of the girls, who'd stopped Spike grabbing Michael before, put her hand on his arm. "It doesn't matter to any of us whether you're gay or straight. You're a million times better than Spike. We're glad he's gone."

With things settled down, Michael decided it might be a good time to get a flat. He could afford it now he didn't have to pay Spike any more, and he'd recently had a pay rise. He realised he couldn't stay tied to his mother's apron strings forever, so he bought the Herald each week to look in the 'Property for Rent' section.

He also thought he'd buy Mollie a bunch of flowers and get something for Graham. If it wasn't for them, he'd still be paying Spike and hiding who he really was. He owed them both such a lot.

***

Jo felt a bit more stable emotionally too. Her appointment for the hospital had come through; she'd done some research on the internet and wasn't as scared as she'd initially been. She still had the odd worry, but realised there was no point getting into a state until she'd seen the consultant and heard what he had to say.

She focused on her job again and decided she could concentrate on the tarot once more. She had some ideas for a late night opening on the twenty-first of June to celebrate the

Summer Solstice and, as part of it, she'd give tarot readings.

Clare loved the idea. They'd stayed late at work one night to plan the evening and had come up with some great ideas. They got in touch with a few people, and were quite excited about the forthcoming event.

Jo had friends who ran a mystical shop, and as they weren't making their usual trip to Stonehenge this year, she'd persuaded them to come along. They were going to offer Indian Head Massage, Reflexology, advice on Feng Shui and talks about Guardian Angels.

There'd be mystical music playing in the background, a table laid out with finger food, courtesy of Mollie, and a glass of wine or elderflower pressé for those who were driving.

"I hope the evening goes well, and plenty of people turn up," Clare said.

"They should do. Rob's advertised it in the paper for us, and there are always people walking up and down the street in the evenings, especially at this time of year. If they see the shop open and hear music playing, curiosity will make them come in," Jo said.

"Hmm, hope you're right."

"Yeah, course I am. What about when we stayed open on Halloween? We had a fantastic evening. All those parents who brought their kids in dressed up, and we sold loads of children's books, especially the new Spooky Stories series."

"Yes that was fun, wasn't it? Remember little Annie? Didn't she look great as a zombie?" Clare said.

"Yeah she did. It was so funny when that little boy pulled of her piece of fake dangly skin, so she pulled his false nose off and stamped on it." Jo laughed.

"Oh my God, I thought I was going to wet myself. I saw a new side to Annie then, the little madam. The look on his face when he picked the nose up and it was all squashed, and then he ran crying to his mum." Clare giggled at the memory.

"Well, it should be mostly adults this time, so let's hope

they're better behaved." Jo grinned.

"I've had a thought. You know the local writing group? Well, why don't we ask them to write some Summer Solstice poems?"

"Hey, nice idea. In fact, why don't we set them a little competition to see who can write the best one? We could give a prize to the winner."

"How about offering that new anthology of poems as the prize?" Clare suggested.

"Fab idea."

Clare's face became serious for a moment. "Jo, are you going to be able to cope with all this organising? You've got your biopsy next week; the Solstice is only two weeks after that. I don't think you'll be fit and back at work by then."

"Clare, it's only a tiny op. I'll be back to work after a couple of days, stop worrying."

"But what if... I mean, if the doctor finds..."

"What if it's cancer?" Jo said.

Clare winced at the words. "Yes."

"I'll still be back at work. Don't look at me like that. Yeah I know when I first found the lump I was a wreck, but I've got over that and come to terms with it now. Even if it is cancer, I'm not staying at home moping, Clare. I love my job, and will need to do something to stop me dwelling on it."

"Hmm. Well, let's wait until next week and see if you still feel the same. Your mum's going to go with you, isn't she?"

Jo smiled. "Yes she is, worry guts. I'll be okay."

"Jo, you're my best friend in the whole world, of course I worry about you." Clare bit her lip and looked down at the floor.

Jo put her arms around Clare and hugged her. "Hey, no getting maudlin on me. Blimey you're as bad as my mum; and I tell her I'm not dying for a long time yet. By the way, I meant to tell you, you look great without glasses. I assume you've got your contacts in?"

"Yes. I've been wearing them at the weekends for a few weeks now and I put them in when I go out with Dan, so I thought I might as well wear them all the time. And what do you mean I look great without glasses? Did I look awful with them?"

Jo's eyebrows shot up. "No of course not! I didn't mean it like that. I just meant you look great with contacts in." She saw Clare's face and realised she was joking around. "Oh stop it," she laughed. Then she said, "At least you haven't got any glasses to push along your nose; that was infuriating, it used to drive me mad."

"Well, I'm glad I don't annoy you any more! Right, I want to cash up quickly tonight, I'm seeing Dan."

"Is he meeting you here or somewhere else?"

"Well, we thought we'd have a cosy night in at my flat, maybe hire a DVD. We might even get a takeaway to save me cooking. So he's meeting me here."

Jo frowned then quickly replaced it with a smile. She still didn't feel comfortable about Clare's boyfriend, but could give no suitable reason why. She just felt uneasy and the "vision" she'd had a while ago didn't help either. But she tried to hide her feelings and be pleased for her friend. Clare really liked the guy. She'd fallen for him big time and it was the first relationship she'd had for a long while.

Dan had started waiting for Clare in the shop just before closing on Saturdays. Jo didn't like someone who wasn't staff hanging around while they cashed up, but luckily they always did it in the office, out of sight.

She wished he'd arrange to meet Clare in the pub or something, and decided that maybe she'd suggest that option, from a security point of view. But she didn't want to upset Clare. It was an awkward situation and Jo didn't know which approach to take.

She sighed. She always seemed to have something to worry about these days.

Chapter Twenty-Three

Mollie sat on Graham's boat waiting for him to come back from the pub with their drinks, and looked around her. It was so relaxing on the river watching other people on their boats, and the ducks quacking for any titbits that might be throw their way. Ah, this was indeed the life; one she could easily get used to. She closed her eyes then opened them as a shadow fell across her face and the boat swayed slightly.

"Here you are, one white wine spritzer. I ordered you a ploughman's, that okay?" Graham asked.

"Perfect, and afterwards we can have the cake I brought." Mollie raised her glass and said, "Cheers."

Graham clinked his glass against hers, and took a sip.

Mollie looked up into the face of the man she'd grown to love, and said, "When Victor died, I thought I'd never be happy again, but I am; wonderfully happy. Thank you."

Graham leaned over and kissed her softly. "And thank you too. You've brought something into my life that I never thought I'd have, so that makes us two happy people."

Mollie smiled then said, "I wouldn't have guessed when I first met you that you're a man of quite substantial substance. You're not the least bit showy."

Graham pursed his lips. "That's not my style, I don't believe in flashing my wealth around. I've worked hard for it, but it doesn't make me better than someone who isn't as well off."

"That's what I love about you; you're kind, and so natural and unpretentious."

"Ah, you said the 'L' word. Was it just a figure of speech?"

"No, it wasn't. I do love you. Oh, it's not that heady passionate love you get when you're a young person, like when Victor and I met all those years ago. I'm an old lady now and it's a different kind of love." She tutted then said, "I can't believe I'm sat on a boat, telling a man I love him."

"If you'd known about my affluence when we first met, would it have put you off me?" Graham asked.

"Not put me off you as such, but I may have viewed you differently and not agreed to go for that meal with you."

"Aha, you'd have thought I was trying to buy your company; get you into bed by flashing the cash." Graham made a lecherous face.

"Shh!" Mollie looked around to see if anyone was listening, then laughed, "Yes, something like that."

"I do too, you know."

Mollie looked at him puzzled. "You do too what?"

"Love you." Graham coughed, "Aherm, oh look, here's our lunch." He stood up and took the tray the young man held out to him, then turned back to Mollie. "Would you like to eat here on the boat, or get off and sit at one of the benches?"

Mollie tried to hide her amusement. She knew what he'd meant when he'd said "I do too", but she'd wanted to see if he would say the actual words. She should have known he would. Graham was a straight and honest man, and even if he got embarrassed at times, he did show his feelings.

"Here would be lovely, thanks. I still can't believe I'm on a boat," she said.

"So what do you think of her then?" Graham asked as he put the tray on the table.

"Why do people refer to boats in the feminine?"

"Not sure, something to do with tradition I believe. Well?"

"I love it. This is the sort of life I could very easily get used to." Mollie said as she buttered her roll ready to take a bite. "I'm not sure about the name though, Phantom Flyer."

"Well, the boat is a Fairline Phantom, so it's from that. It isn't the best name in the world, but I'm not too bothered about it."

"Can you change the name?"

"It's meant to be unlucky to do so, but you can if you do it properly. You have to get rid of everything with the old name on it, and once you've renamed it, you have to petition the Gods to accept the new name, or some such nonsense. It's to do with Greek or Roman mythology."

"Tsk, seems a lot of trouble to have to go to!" Mollie said.

"Exactly. By the way, I thought I'd invite our reading lot onboard for the day, like a group outing sort of thing. What do you think?"

Mollie finished her mouthful of bread. "I think it's a jolly good idea and I'm sure they'd enjoy it, especially Felicity. Even Michael might come along; he's a much happier lad now, isn't he? Wasn't it lovely of him to send me that beautiful bouquet, and the bottle of red wine for you? Bless him."

"Yes. He must have taken advice on the wine as it was a good one, and I don't think Michael would know a decent wine himself, but it was very thoughtful. What about Tessa, do you think she'd come?"

"She's got Amber, don't forget. She won't want to leave her all day with her grandparents," Mollie said.

"I suppose she can bring her along too, although I'm not used to children and it's meant to be a trip for adults." Graham frowned.

"Amber's a teenager so she knows how to behave. I'm sure Felicity will take her under her wing; she's good with children and probably teenagers too. Will we all fit?"

"Of course. Don't forget we have two decks, and inside the boat as well."

"Ooh what fun! Well, it'll have to be a weekend as the others work during the week. When were you thinking of?"

"I don't know, in a couple of weeks' time or something?" Graham suggested.

172

"Why don't you mention it at the next meeting, so that people can book a suitable day? I know Felicity has to work some Saturday mornings, so she can make sure she's got time off. Would you prefer a Saturday or Sunday?" Mollie asked.

"Makes no difference to me." Graham popped a pickled onion into his mouth then had a coughing fit. "Bloody hell! Sorry, Mollie, those onions are strong!"

"Good job I've eaten them too, else there'd be no kisses for you."

"Oh you reckon, do you?" Graham leaned forward, took Mollie's face in his hands and planted a kiss on her lips. Some people in a neighbouring boat cheered and Mollie flushed a deep red.

"Graham, not in public please!" But she laughed all the same. "I guess it depends how long we'll be out for. If it continues into the evening, then Saturday would be better, as they won't want to stay out too late on a Sunday, will they?"

"I have no idea how people behave nowadays. I always went to bed quite early on work nights; definitely by ten at any rate. But I was always up at five in the mornings. Mind you, I'm still up at six every morning now. I'm not the sort of person who can lie in bed," Graham said. He wiped his mouth on his napkin, sat back and turned his face up to the warm sun.

Mollie finished her meal and put her cutlery together on her plate. She moved to sit beside Graham. "I'm the same, I usually get up at half six. Well, why don't we just ask everyone which day they'd prefer? Thanks for lunch by the way, it was delicious. I do enjoy a good ploughman's, but I shouldn't really eat that much cheese. Right, how much do I owe you?"

"Mollie, please don't go on about money again, I thought we'd got over that..." Graham held his hand up as she started to protest. "It's my treat. Come on, it usually balances out, you can cook me dinner during the week."

"Just as long as you don't think I'm taking you for

granted," Mollie said.

"Okay, can we have an agreement? If we go out and I pay, just accept it. I'm the man, and that's how it should be. I can't be doing with all this equality nonsense. I have enough money to last for more than my lifetime, so I might as well have some fun spending it. And if I want to spend it on you, then allow me the privilege. Agreed?"

"But if you pay all the time, it makes me feel awful, like I'm using you."

"Mollie, I know you're not using me, you're hardly a gold-digger. And like I said, you can cook for me in return. So, agreed?"

"Is this our first disagreement?" Mollie asked.

"Stop changing the subject. I'll kiss you in front of everybody again."

"You jolly well won't!"

Graham turned towards her and Mollie quickly said, "Agreed."

They laughed and Mollie affectionately squeezed his arm.

"Okay, ready to go?" Graham asked. "If you're going to spend a lot of time on the boat, you need to learn about boat handling. Come here and I'll show you how to cast off."

"It sounds just like knitting, so shouldn't be too difficult," Mollie said with a grin.

***

The night of the summer solstice at Merrilies was a great success.

Not least because Jo was in extremely good spirits; she'd had her biopsy results and the lump was just a harmless cyst. She looked around at all the people enjoying themselves and offered a silent prayer of thanks that she was one of them.

"Jo, this lady would like a tarot reading." Clare gently pushed an older woman towards her.

"Okay, have you had your cards read before?"

"No I haven't. I've wanted to, but it's hard to find someone who isn't just doing it to make money. Some people charge a fortune."

"I know. Well, as it's a special evening tonight, I'm doing readings for £5, is that okay?"

"Oh yes," said the woman, and she followed Jo into the annexe.

Clare went to greet some people coming in the front door. "Tessa, glad you could make it. And who's this?"

"This is my daughter, Amber."

"Hi Amber, I've heard a lot about you, your mum talks about you all the time. Grab yourself a soft drink and piece of cake from that table over there. Tessa, have a wander around, there's lots going on. I don't know how long you're staying, but if you've got time, you can have a head massage. If you want one, go and see the lady as soon as you can as she's quite booked up already."

"Thanks, Clare. I'm writing a piece on the Summer Solstice for a magazine, would you mind if I mentioned the shop and the things going on here tonight?"

"Of course not, it's all publicity. How's Amber been behaving herself since the shoplifting?"

"She's been really good, well, almost. She still cheeks me at times, treats the house like a hotel and her bedroom's a tip, but she's not too bad. I think the police frightened the life out of her, so hopefully she's learnt her lesson. I'd love a head massage, so I'd better book it. I'll see you later."

"Okay, have fun."

Clare saw Mollie arrive and went to thank her for the buffet. "Mollie, thank you so much for the food, it's been a real hit. Your cheese straws have gone already, they were delicious."

"Jolly good. They usually disappear quite quickly. It's my special ingredient that does it," Mollie said.

"Oh, what's that?" Clare asked.

"I can't tell you, it's a secret recipe."

"That's not fair, I'll be wracking my brains now trying to think what it could be!"

Mollie laughed and said, "Only joking. I make three lots: plain ones, some with chilli and some with caraway."

Clare snapped her fingers. "Caraway. I knew I could taste something distinct, but I wasn't sure what it was. Oh, I didn't have any of the chilli ones, and I love chilli. You don't fancy making some for the café, do you? Say no if it's going to be too much for you." Clare looked at her hopefully.

"I don't mind making them now and then, but I don't have as much time as I used to; I spend a lot of my days with Graham as you know, but if I have any spare time on my baking days, I'll make some."

"Thanks, Mollie. I'm so pleased you and Graham got together, you make a lovely couple. Is it general knowledge now then?"

"Well, most people have guessed, especially as we turn up and leave together, so we're not hiding it any more."

"Where is he tonight?"

"He's going to pick me up later. He's not into things like this; he said it was women's stuff." Mollie rolled her eyes.

"Oh did he?" Clare raised her eyebrows. "I bet he wouldn't have said no to a nice relaxing head massage or reflexology?"

"He wouldn't have liked having a head massage in front of everyone, and he certainly wouldn't have got his feet out. Good gracious!" Mollie found the image of Graham sitting in Merrilies with his bare feet on show, outrageous.

Clare thought the idea of Graham with his feet out was hilarious. "Ha ha, that's so funny, bless him. I hear you're all going on a boat trip Saturday?"

"Yes, I think everyone's really looking forward to it. Right, I'm going to have a wander. See you later, or at the meeting tomorrow," Mollie said and walked purposefully towards the lady who was giving a talk about angels.

Jo came back with her client, who shook her head in amazement.

"Everything okay?" Clare asked.

"Oh yes," the woman answered, "Jo's marvellous. I don't know how she does it, but she knew things I've not discussed with anyone except my husband." She turned to Jo and said, "I'm going to tell all my friends about you. Thank you so much, my dear."

Jo smiled graciously. "You're very welcome, and you know where I am if you want me again, but leave at least six months between each reading."

"I'll definitely be back to see you again. Goodbye for now." The woman hurried out of the door.

Jo got herself and Clare a top-up of wine and they stood together watching the people wandering around.

"So, how's it all going?" Jo asked. "I thought we'd get a lot of people in, but I didn't expect this many, especially for a Wednesday. Isn't it great. Oh I can see Tessa, is that her daughter with her?"

"Yes that's Amber. Pretty, isn't she?"

"Yeah she is. Have any other members of the reading group been in?"

"Mollie's around somewhere but I haven't seen Michael or Flick. Graham wouldn't come, said it was women's stuff."

Jo laughed then turned around as someone tapped her back. "Annie! How are you, sweetie? What are you doing here at this time of night?"

"Mummy said I could come cuz I wanted to see all the things that were going on. We saw it in the paper. What's floxogy?"

Jo looked at Clare with a frown, then back at Annie. "I don't know what you mean, honey."

"It said there would be head massages and floxogy."

"Oh, you mean reflexology." Clare laughed and ruffled

Annie's hair.

"Yep that word."

"It's like a massage for your feet," Jo explained, trying not to laugh as well.

"Euck, that would tickle too much. I've got lots of money now for my trip to the dolphins, because the bank and a clothes shop are helping too. Mummy says there's nearly enough, so Daddy can book it soon, but we don't want to go when it's too hot, so Daddy will book it for later in the year. Maybe September."

"That's wonderful news, darling. Where are Mummy and Daddy?" Clare asked.

"Daddy's at home, he didn't want to come, but Mummy's talking to Tessa and her daughter."

"Okay," Clare told her, "don't leave the shop, will you? I tell you what, there's a storyteller in the children's section, do you want to go listen?"

"Yes please. Will you tell Mummy where I am?"

"Of course, come on then." Clare held Annie's hand and took her to the children's area, stopping on the way to tell Alice where she'd be.

At the end of the evening, Dan turned up to wait for Clare again. She'd taken the plates and glasses up to the staffroom, so Jo saw him first.

"Hi Jo."

"Dan."

"Good evening?"

"Yeah, very good thanks."

Jo didn't want to talk to him, so picked up a new book on the pretence of reading the blurb on the back.

"Clare hasn't gone already, has she?"

"No, she'll be down in a moment."

"Okay, I'll just wait here then." He sat on one of the reading group chairs.

"Dan…erm, maybe it'd be better if you wait outside the

shop." Jo said. Oh God, she thought, I've done it now. But she couldn't keep quiet any longer; she didn't like the man, and didn't want him in the shop. He made her feel uncomfortable.

"Why?"

Bloody hell, Jo thought, what am I going to say now? Then an idea struck her. "Because of the insurance. We're not insured to have you on the premises."

"That's ridiculous. What about all your customers?" He glared at her in a very unfriendly way.

"It's okay during trading hours, but not when we're closed. So if anything happened, we're not covered."

"If anything happened, like what?"

Uh-oh, now what do I say? Jo panicked.

She didn't have to say anything because Clare came downstairs. She saw Dan's angry face and Jo's embarrassed one. "What's going on?" she asked.

"Jo was just about to tell me why I couldn't wait for you in the shop," Dan said, a smug look on his face because he knew he'd dropped her in it.

Clare turned to Jo. "What are you on about?"

"I just said that maybe it would be better if he waited outside, as we're not covered by our insurance for him to be here after trading hours," Jo explained.

"He's not doing any harm. What do you think he's going to do?"

"I don't know, but just in case, maybe it would be safer if he waits for you elsewhere."

Dan stood up, kissed Clare and said, "It's okay, hun, I feel like a drink anyway. I'll be in the wine bar up the road, meet me there." He shot Jo a venomous look before leaving.

Clare turned to Jo, her face a combination of disappointment and anger. "Now look what you've done. What was that all about?"

"Nothing."

"Yes, it was, Jo. Tell me."

Jo put down the book she was holding, "I don't trust him, that's all."

"Don't trust him! What has he ever done to make you feel like that?"

Jo didn't reply.

"Well, I'm waiting for an answer," Clare said, trying to control her temper.

"He hasn't done anything in particular, it's just his whole manner, something about him."

"Jo, that's stupid, you don't even know him really. Are you jealous?" Clare asked.

"WHAT! NO. Okay, Clare, cards on the table yeah?"

"Yes. Go on then."

"Remember ages ago in my flat, you told me about Dan coming in the shop and picking up some books you'd dropped?"

"Yes."

"Well, do you remember that you said I looked like I'd had a shock or seen a ghost or something?"

"Yes, kind of. Oh, you said it was because you'd heard a noise."

"Yeah, but it wasn't. As you were talking about him, I got a vision of you lying in a hospital bed."

"Oh, you were probably imagining it," Clare said dismissively.

"Clare, you know my omens come true. I've never had one yet that didn't," Jo urged.

"Look, maybe you were mixed up and it was yourself you saw, having the biopsy. That would make sense, wouldn't it? Have you had any since?"

"No."

"Well then. If it really was to do with Dan, you'd have had more, wouldn't you? I've been seeing him for a while now, and he's come in the shop on several occasions."

"I suppose so. But I don't feel very comfortable with him

around. I'm only looking out for you, Clare; you're my best mate, I'd hate anything to happen to you." Jo fiddled with some leaflets. She felt really awkward.

Clare took a deep breath and exhaled. "Thanks for caring, but I'll be okay. Try to forget what you saw, you were probably confused. We had been drinking after all. And Dan's always been pleasant to you, hasn't he?"

"Yeah," Jo said grudgingly. She didn't want to mention the evil look he'd given her as he left. That look had spoken volumes. Jo just knew he was a dubious character.

"Well then. You do have a point about the insurance though. I'll tell him not to turn up early, so that he's only here for a couple of minutes whilst I get my bag and stuff, will that be better?"

"Yeah thanks. Sorry to be a pain. You won't tell him what I said about my omen will you. Please, Clare, I'd rather you didn't," Jo pleaded.

"Okay, I'll just say you were worried about the insurance, in case of fire or an accident. I'll tell him you're a bit of a health and safety nut."

Jo laughed and said, "Thanks. Why don't you go on? I can finish up here. I only have to switch off the lights and set the alarm. Don't keep Dan waiting."

"Okay, see you tomorrow. Bye."

"Yeah bye, Clare, have a nice evening."

When she'd gone, Jo sighed. Clare's reasoning hadn't changed her opinion. She knew how ill at ease she felt every time Dan was around. She'd just have to keep a close eye on him, because no matter what Clare said, Jo didn't trust him.

Chapter Twenty-Four

At the reading group meeting the following evening, Graham asked how many were going on the boat trip Saturday.

"I'm coming," Michael said.

"Me too, Pops," Felicity said.

"And me, but not Amber," Tessa said.

"Aw, why not?" Felicity asked.

"Well, she said it was nice of Graham to invite her, but she didn't want to spend the day with a bunch of old people."

"Oh that's charming. I'm only twenty-eight, well, nearly twenty-nine," Michael said.

"That's old to a thirteen-year-old. In fact, everyone over eighteen is old to Amber," Tessa laughed.

"Oh well," Graham said, "it'll be adults only then. We can get sloshed on wine now we don't have a child to set a good example to."

"Pops! Well, as long as it's nice cold Sauvignon Blanc, from New Zealand."

"But I like red wine," Michael grumbled.

"You didn't drink alcohol until you had one that night with us in the pub," Mollie reminded him.

"Don't worry; there'll be red wine, white wine and beer too, so everyone will be catered for. Felicity, if you're *that* particular, bring your own!" Graham said.

"I was going to bring a bottle anyway, I wouldn't dream of turning up empty-handed. So Tess, what's Amber going to do instead?"

"A friend's invited her out for the day, then back to hers for a sleepover. She had the choice of a wildlife park, or ice-skating, she chose skating. She's really looking forward to it."

"Ah, that's much better than spending it with a bunch of boring adults she doesn't really know," Felicity said with a smile.

"Talking about wildlife, how's the job going, Flick?" Michael asked.

Felicity turned to face him, her eyes shining. "Really well, thanks for asking, Mikey. I simply love it. You should see all the little kittens and doggies, how people can be so bloody cruel to a defenceless animal, I'll never know. Some of them are so cute, I want to take them home."

"I don't think your parents would be too pleased with a house full of unwanted animals," Mollie said pulling a face.

"Ha, Mummy would have an absolute fit. We never had pets when I was a child, even though I begged and begged. Mummy says they're just dirty smelly things. That's probably why I adore animals now, because I was deprived of them when I was young."

"That's a shame," Tessa said. "Animals can be very therapeutic. It's meant to relax you and lower your blood pressure if you own a pet and stroke it regularly."

"Bloody hell, I better tell Daddy. He comes home so stressed most days, it would be better for him to stroke an animal than hit the brandy."

"Felicity, your father has a high pressured job, there's nothing wrong with the odd drink of an evening," Graham said.

"What, every evening?" Felicity asked, as she pulled her ponytail out and held the band between her teeth while raking her fingers through her thick hair.

"Well, I have a glass of wine every evening, maybe two sometimes."

"So you're an alcoholic as well then, Pops," Felicity teased.

"Oh, and *you* don't drink, do you, Flick?" Michael said

with sarcasm.

"Yes, but not every evening, only every weekend." She re-did her ponytail and tied it up again.

"So how many do you have on a weekend night, young lady?" Graham asked.

"Erm a few."

"A few! You've been late for our Saturday meetings more than once because you've still been drunk from the night before, so I think it's more than a few," Michael said.

"Well, okay, quite a lot then." Felicity folded her arms in a defensive pose.

"How many?" Tessa asked.

They were all getting in on the act now; it wasn't often they could embarrass Felicity, and they were making the most of it.

"About ten a night maybe."

"Felicity!" Mollie gasped. "That's terrible, you'll damage your liver."

"You'd be better off having a drink every night like I do, not saving it up and drinking it all in one evening." Graham wagged his finger at her.

"Oh my God. So you go out Fridays, Saturdays and Sundays; ten a night; thirty alcoholic drinks in a weekend! Flick, that's binge drinking." Tessa was shocked.

Felicity squirmed. "You're making it sound awful and it's not that bad really. I don't have ten every night, and now I'm working I don't go out Sunday nights because I have to get up for work the next day. So, it's only Fridays and Saturdays. I may drink less than ten at times."

"Huh, and I bet you often drink more too." Michael gave her a stern look.

"Only if it's a really good night. Stop it! What is this, pick on Felicity evening? We're meant to be discussing books, aren't we?" She opened hers and slammed it down on the table.

"Yes come on, leave her alone, it's not fair. It's her life, and we were all young once." Mollie tried to stick up for her.

184

"Well, I'm young and I've never drank that much in my entire life," Michael said.

Felicity snorted, "Huh, that's because you don't know what a good night out is."

"What's that supposed to mean?"

"I don't mean to be rude, but you're hardly Mr Life and Soul, are you? Aw bloody hell, Mikey, don't look at me like that, you know what I mean. I'm a party girl and you're, well, a bit of a dork."

"A dork! What the hell..?"

Mollie rubbed her forehead and thought, oh jolly well done, Felicity!

"Erm children, children," Graham intervened, "can we call a truce now and get on with the reason why we're here? I think we've wasted enough time. Now, the next book we're reading is *The Time Traveler's Wife*. Read the back and see what you think."

Michael quickly scanned the back, then said in a huff, "It's a love story, do we have to read it?"

"Michael, if you read the back properly, you'll see it's about more than romance. It's also about a guy with a genetic problem who time travels. So, it's like a science fiction love story. You should enjoy it, you like science fiction," Graham said.

"Well, I think it looks fascinating, I'm happy to read it," Tessa said.

"Me too," Felicity added.

"Sorry, Michael, you're outnumbered four to one; don't knock it until you've read it. Now this is also the book I'm reviewing for the paper this month, so I'd appreciate your thoughts on it, and I may use them for the review," Mollie said.

"I thought you only reviewed new books, this one's been out for ages," Tessa said.

"Yes, but with the film version out on DVD, they want a

185

review of the book then the film to compare them both."

"Hey, you could do the book and I could ask if they'd like me to do the film," Tessa said. "Although they usually have their own people to do films and stuff."

"Good idea, you should phone them. Okay, who's going to read the first chapter, actually there's a prologue; who wants to read that out?" Mollie asked.

Felicity put her hand up. They all settled back and Felicity read the prologue out in her clear middle class accent.

As she finished, she looked up to see Annie standing by the table and gave her a big smile.

"You read nicely, Fecility, but I didn't understand what it was about really," Annie said.

"That's because it's an adult book. How are you, sweetie?"

"I'm okay. Can I sit on your lap?"

"Well, we're trying to have our meeting, darling. I thought you weren't coming in on Thursdays any longer?"

"Well, I don't uselly, but we were on our way home from my friend's house, so I asked Mummy if we could stop in cuz I wanted to tell you that I've nearly got enough money for my dolphin trip."

Felicity pulled the little girl onto her lap and hugged her. "That's brilliant, Annie!"

"That's jolly good news, darling," Mollie said.

"Well done, Annie," Tessa said.

"Yeah great," mumbled Michael, who wasn't interested in the least.

"That's the best news I've heard all day. When do you think you'll be going?" Graham asked.

"Well, Daddy said he'd book it for the end of September cuz it won't be so hot then. It'll still be hot, but not as hot as it would be now."

"September, that's only a couple of months away. Do you know how much more money you need?" Graham asked.

"Nope. Mummy and Daddy know though. Shall I get

Mummy and ask her?" Annie went to get off Felicity's lap.

Felicity held onto her and said, "No, that's okay, we have to carry on with the meeting, but we'll see you on Saturday. Oh no we won't, we're not here."

"Why not?" Annie asked.

Graham thought, oh no, she's going to ask if she can come on the boat too, and looked across at Mollie.

Mollie answered. "We're going on a reading group outing for the day."

"What, all of you? Where are you going?"

"Well, Graham's got a boat, and we're going out on that for the day," Mollie said.

"Just you five?"

"Yes, just us."

Annie thought about this for a few seconds, then said, "Okay, good job I came in tonight to tell you about nearly having enough money then. I've got to go now, but have a nice time on Graham's boat."

As Annie got off Felicity's lap, Mollie said, "Come here and have another cuddle."

Annie went and wrapped her little arms around Mollie's neck and hugged her tight.

"Very well done, darling," Mollie whispered into her hair. She held the child for a long time then released her.

Annie said, "Mm you smell nice, all clean like soap." Everyone laughed.

"We'll see you soon, Annie," Tessa told her.

"Yep, not this Saturday, but the Saturday after that, bye." She waved then went to find her mother.

"Huh, more time wasted, we haven't got much done today, have we? And we won't be talking books on Saturday," grumbled Michael.

"Don't be so hard; she's a little girl who's not very well, Michael. I don't begrudge her a few minutes with us," Felicity said.

"Me neither, and didn't we tell you we're still holding the meeting, on the boat?" Mollie said, shooting Graham a look.

"Oh yes, got to keep up the meetings, especially as this is a book Mollie's reviewing." Graham joined in the game.

"Oh, well, a fine day out that will be!" Michael said then he saw their faces. "Ha ha, very funny, erm, we're *not* having the meeting, are we?" he asked, still unsure whether they were joking or being serious.

"No, of course we're not. It's supposed to be a nice day out, relaxing with friends and having a few –and I mean a *few,* Felicity – drinks, so we won't be talking books," Graham said.

"Oi, Pops, I *can* have only a couple of drinks, you know. I don't always drink myself into a stupor. So don't worry, I'll be on my best behaviour. And I like what you said," she looked around the table, "about us being friends. We *are* all friends, aren't we? Good friends." She even included Michael in this despite their earlier spat, as she was feeling happy and generous.

The others nodded their agreement.

"If it wasn't for you lot, I don't know what I've have done at times," Michael said, looking down at the table.

"Yes, I agree. This group has been brilliant, it's certainly helped keep me sane and given me something to look forward to each week," Tessa said.

"Well, I for one am jolly glad I joined, because as well as friends, I've met someone very special too." Mollie reached out for Graham's hand. He held it and smiled into her eyes.

There was a few seconds silence, then Felicity broke it by saying, "Group hug, group hug. Only kidding." She laughed as she continued, "Well, seeing as it's almost eight anyway, why don't we end the group and go for a drink in the pub down the road? It's a lovely evening, we can sit outside. Anyone up for it?"

"Flick, you *are* an alcoholic, you know," Michael teased.

"I was thinking of a nice cold orange and lemonade

actually, who's going to join me?"

"Mollie and I are going for a bite to eat, but I suppose we can have one drink first. What do you think, Mollie?"Graham asked.

"Sounds like a good idea, why not? Tessa, you coming?"

"Okay, I won't stay for too long, but one would be nice."

They got their things together, said goodbye to Jo and Clare who were seeing customers out of the doors, then walked into the still warm sunshine.

There was some sort of commotion across the road with ducks quacking, and a little group of people gathered by the stream.

"What's going on over there, I wonder?" Tessa said.

"Don't know, but it doesn't sound too good," Michael answered.

"Let's have a look." Felicity waited for a gap in the traffic, and ran across the road.

The others followed her and joined the group.

A drake had hold of a duck and was pinning her head under the water, trying to drown her. The poor duck was desperately struggling, but she was obviously getting weaker by the minute.

"Oh no, someone do something, he's going to drown her!" Felicity cried.

No-one moved; they just stood around watching and pointing.

"Oh for God's sake!" Felicity yelled. Pulling up her trousers and kicking off her sandals, she jumped into the stream and grabbed the drake, who quacked furiously at being disturbed. The female, finding that she was free, scooted out of the water onto the pavement, shook herself and sat down to recover. Felicity put the flapping drake back in the water, shooed him away and climbed out of the stream to rapturous applause from the bystanders.

"It's a pity one of you didn't help instead of just standing there watching, isn't it?" she shouted at them.

They all looked away sheepishly, then one by one they drifted off.

"Jolly well done, Felicity." Mollie patted her on the back.

"Yeah nice one, Flick," Michael said.

"I've never seen a duck do that before," Tessa said in astonishment.

"I saw it once before. I didn't stay and watch it drown though," Graham added as Felicity glared at him. "Well done, young lady, that's your good deed for the day. You definitely deserve a drink now."

"I couldn't believe those bloody people stood watching and not one of them helped. If we hadn't come out, they'd have let her drown. How could they?" She shook her legs around to dry them off.

"I guess they didn't want to interfere with nature I suppose," Mollie said.

"Oh come on, Moll, so you'd have watched her die then?"

"Well, no. Graham and I were already trying to find a stick or something to push him off with. I wouldn't have jumped in the stream like you did though; I'm a bit too old to go doing things like that."

"But at least you were trying to do something," Felicity said. She turned to Tessa and Michael, "Would you have just watched her drown?"

"No I wouldn't, but I didn't know what to do to help, to be honest. I didn't think of getting in the stream," Tessa said.

"I was looking for something to throw at it," Michael said.

"See, you're all kind people. Even you, Mikey." Felicity pinched Michael's cheek and shook it from side to side.

"Flick, get off!" He pushed her hand away. "If we're going to the pub, you might want to put your trousers back down again."

Felicity looked at her legs and laughed. She rolled her trousers down. "Bloody good job the stream is only shallow.

That water's cold though. Mind you, if it *had* been deeper, I'd still have jumped in. There's no way I could have let her drown. Beastly creature. I've gone off drakes now. Why on earth do they do that?"

Graham shook his head. "I have no idea; maybe it's a mating thing. Okay let's get to the pub, and if you hurry, I'll get the drinks in."

"Nice one, Pops. Wait 'til I tell them all in work tomorrow. Hey maybe someone there will know why they do it. I'll find out if I can and let you know."

She linked her arm through Tessa's, and they walked to the pub.

Chapter Twenty-Five

The boat trip was a great success and everyone had a wonderful time. It was a warm sunny day with a gentle breeze, and they all relaxed, enjoying each other's company away from Merrilies.

They'd stopped for lunch at a pub on the river, then gently wended their way along, occasionally waving to the people in the other boats they met on the way.

Graham let Michael steer for a bit, which delighted the youngster. Tessa chatted with Mollie, and Felicity took photos of everyone then, to Michael's shock, stripped off to a bikini and went to sunbathe on the stern deck.

She caught Michael staring at her and removed her sunglasses to look at him.

"Michael, close your mouth, there's a love, and bring me a top-up of wine."

"Get it yourself, what did your last servant die of?"

"Answering me back! I thought you weren't interested in girls anyway. Aw please, Mikey, get me some more wine, I've just got settled. Pretty please," she wheedled, waving her glass at him.

With a sigh, he collected her empty glass, raised an eyebrow and tutted at her semi-naked body, refilled the glass with chilled white wine and took it back to her.

Graham laughed and whispered to Mollie, "That girl knows how to wrap men round her little finger, even gay ones! She's outrageous. Mind you, even an old man like me can appreciate what a good figure she has, and she's obviously proud of it too. If only I were forty years younger."

Mollie agreed. "Oh to be twenty again. Mind you, I wouldn't have lain around almost naked when I was Felicity's age."

"I bet you would! You were one of those flower power hippies, Moll, weren't you? All that free love and no brassiere lifestyle." He laughed at the look on her face.

"You know jolly well I wasn't like that. I was a respectable girl who worked as a legal secretary, thank you very much! Mind you, many of my friends were hippies, with those diaphanous see-through dresses and no bra underneath." Mollie's eyes widened at the memory. "The most risqué I got was to wear a miniskirt."

"And you've still got good legs now, old girl," Graham told her, giving her an affectionate squeeze.

They decided during the course of the day that Tessa would take over Mollie's share of the book reviews for the Herald. She *was* the writer of the group after all and, although she'd initially turned down the job, she'd organised herself into a manageable routine and was keen to do it. "It will look good on my writing CV; the more experience, the better," she'd said.

Mollie was quietly relieved. Since getting together with Graham she didn't have much time for anything else, so something had to go. She wouldn't give up baking – she loved it – and cooking for Merrilies brought her a bit of money too. But she didn't want to leave Graham to do the reviews by himself. Now Tessa had agreed to take over, Mollie could stop worrying. See, things always work out in the end, she thought to herself.

Because the boat trip was such a hit, they planned to do it once a month whilst the weather was good.

"We won't be able to go out in winter when it's cold and miserable, so why don't we make the most of it now?" Graham said.

He'd become fond of the little group, and because he and

Mollie were the oldies, he felt like a father figure to the three youngsters.

Michael was quite excited and asked Graham to teach him the ways of boating. "If I ever win the lottery, I'm going to buy a boat like this," he said.

Graham felt flattered; the boy obviously looked up to him. He was a strange lad and didn't appear to have many friends, but he was all right really. And since sorting out his trouble at work, he'd become more confident and even stood up for himself occasionally.

"I'll teach you as much as I can, so why don't we start with steering? Come and have a go," Graham had told him.

Surprisingly, Felicity had been quiet all day. She was content to sunbathe on the decks and join in with the occasional chat. She didn't even have much to drink. It was obvious to Graham that she was used to this sort of life; but then, with her background and lifestyle, she would be. Apparently, although her father didn't have a boat of his own, many of their friends had yachts and Felicity had got her sea legs when she was a young child.

So they'd all enjoyed themselves and looked forward to doing it again. The outing ended with them thanking Graham for a lovely day out, and saying they'd see each other at the next meeting.

"Well, that was a success. It was nice to see them outside of Merrilies for longer than a quick drink in the pub, wasn't it?" Mollie said as she and Graham walked to the car.

It was quite late in the evening by now. She'd helped Graham "put the boat to bed", as he'd called it. They'd turned things off, stowed everything away and put the covers over it.

"Yes it was. I'm glad everyone enjoyed themselves. I was a bit worried about Felicity getting drunk and being a handful, but she was actually the complete opposite. I was pleasantly surprised," Graham said.

"Hmm, I think maybe after the ribbing we gave her the

194

other day she was trying to prove she doesn't drink all the time."

"I think she was just chilling out and relaxing. Michael loved it. He's asked me to teach him how to look after and handle a boat."

"What on earth for? He'll never be able to buy a boat like yours." Mollie laughed.

"He said if he wins the lottery he'll buy one. Let the boy dream, it does no harm, and I quite like having someone take an interest. It's nice to show off my expertise."

"Nice to show off you mean!"

Graham raised his eyebrows at her.

"I'm just kidding; I know you're not like that." She patted his arm.

They got in Graham's car and Mollie stifled a yawn. "Well, I don't know about you, but all that fresh air's done me in. I'm about ready for my bed, can you drop me home? Thanks again for picking me up, by the way."

Graham didn't start the car, but turned to look at Mollie instead. "Do you want to stay over tonight? Actually I wanted to talk to you about that." He cleared his throat. "You and I have been seeing each other for a while now, and we often stay over at each other's house." He paused then said, "Why don't we make it a permanent arrangement?"

Mollie thought for a bit before answering. "I'm not quite sure what you're saying. Are you asking me to move in with you, or something more?"

"Oh dear, I'm not very good at this. Mollie, at our age we can't mess about, life's too short. Look, I've already told you I love you, and you love me, don't you?"

"Yes of course I do, but..."

Graham held a hand up to stop Mollie speaking. "Please let me continue otherwise I might not say it. I *was* going to ask you to move in with me, but with you now wondering if I meant more than that, well, yes, why not? Why don't we get married? Oh, I don't mean a big fancy wedding, just a small gathering. Oh heck, I hadn't planned this at all…'

"Well, that's a jolly good way to propose to a woman, Graham, no planning or anything."

"That's because I didn't mean to…"

"Oh, so you didn't mean to ask me to marry you!"

"No, that's not what I meant either…" He caught Mollie's amused face and stopped, then laughed. "Look, no, I hadn't planned on asking you to marry me yet. I would have at some point, but why not now? Neither of us know how long we've got left, I hope it's years but we don't know, do we? I *do* know how I feel about you however, and I think you feel the same way. I've got that big house. You could sell yours, move in with me and we can have a nice quiet wedding…"

"Stop! Graham, this is all rather sudden. Sorry, I do love you and enjoy being with you, but I need to think about things. It's not that I don't want to marry you, but that house has been my home for a long time; it has precious memories of Victor and… and other things. I need to have a jolly good think about this. Could you take me home please?" Graham started the car and they drove to her house in silence. Mollie kissed him, thanked him for a lovely day, said she'd call him soon and went indoors.

Graham watched her go, then turned the car around, wishing with all his heart he could rewind the last hour. What was he thinking of, expecting her to leave her home and move into his? How presumptuous of him!

"Graham, old boy," he said to himself as he drove home, "you've really gone and blown it."

He parked the car in the garage, let himself into his empty house and, with his heart like lead, took himself off to bed.

***

The weather had warmed up and it was the tourist season,

which was good for business. Merrilies buzzed with customers. The girls had permission from the council to put some tables and chairs outside so that people could sit with their coffees and books in the sunshine, and they'd extended their late night opening on Thursdays to nine, instead of eight.

Clare and Jo sat at a table enjoying a rare ten-minute break together.

"I don't know why we didn't think of this earlier," Jo said, as a customer sat down with a coffee and a book she'd just bought. "It's lovely for our customers to sit and enjoy the sun. I'm glad Fran was okay about it." She nodded towards the tea room across the road. "She's been pretty good about us having the café, but I thought this might be pushing things."

"A bit of healthy competition never hurt anyone. It's certainly better than sitting on that back step trying to catch some sun," Clare replied. "I like sitting here watching the world go by."

"Sam from the bank popped in earlier to empty the collection boxes. They've reached the target amount so we can stop collecting now. I bet Annie's excited because the trip's all booked. I'm glad they got enough money," Jo said.

"Me too. Did you know Graham put a cheque for five hundred pounds in the collection box? He tried to do it quickly, but he couldn't get it in the slot and I caught him folding it up. He asked me not to say anything." Clare took a sip of her orange juice.

"Really? Blimey, that was generous of him. I didn't think he was into kids," Jo said.

"Me neither, but he said he was doing it for Mollie, whatever that meant." Clare shrugged then asked, "When's the trip booked for, the third week in September?"

"Yeah only a couple of months now. I hope it does Annie the world of good. It might not help physically, but it'll give her such a boost emotionally."

"But isn't your emotional and physical health connected? I

want it to work because Alice has all her hopes pinned on this. I feel so sorry for her, sometimes she looks utterly exhausted. It must be hard work looking after Annie twenty-four seven." Clare got up to go back to work.

"Yeah, I don't think I could do it. Personally I'm not sure about this Dolphin Therapy, but if nothing else, it's a much needed holiday for them all," Jo said.

"Oh I'd have thought you'd be into all that, especially with you being a tarot card reader and your omens." Clare looked surprised.

"Ha, see, I don't believe in everything," Jo said and finished her drink.

"You just like being contrary. But it does work apparently; the ultrasound the dolphins emit has beneficial effects."

"Well, whatever, I hope Annie enjoys it. She hasn't been in today yet, has she?"

Clare looked at her watch, "Quarter-to-six, hmm, no she hasn't. The reading group will be here in a minute, I hope she doesn't come in when they're here. They do like to see her, but it holds up their meeting." She picked up Jo's glass with her own.

"No, she won't come now; Alice knows they don't like to be disturbed. I expect they'll be in tomorrow." Jo got up as well and they went back to work.

Chapter Twenty-Six

As usual, Felicity bought the drinks and cakes for the reading group. "They've run out of flapjacks, so I got us all one of Mollie's Bakewell tarts instead. I took the last five, so you better make some more, Moll."

"Thanks, Felicity. I'm making another batch tomorrow. It's much easier now that I'm not doing the book reviews. How are the reviews going, Tessa? I know you've only done the one so far, but do you think you'll like it?" Mollie asked.

"I'm sure I will. You know I spoke to them about the review of that film version of the book we read last month? Well, they asked to see some of my other work, liked it and asked if I'd review films for them on a regular basis. I won't get paid much, you know what local papers are like, but if I review a film or concert, they'll pay for my ticket." Tessa grinned, obviously pleased.

"Wow, that's good news, and you never know where it could lead. What about the magazine you did the crime serial for?" Felicity asked, joining the conversation.

"Oh I'm still writing stories for them. I have a six-part drama serial planned, which they're interested in."

"Jolly good. Remember, I want a signed copy of your first book," Mollie said with a smile.

"Me too, me too." Felicity bounced up and down in her seat. "Oh Mollie, I'm sorry!" Felicity knocked the table just as Mollie reached for her coffee and some of it spilt over her hand. Felicity rushed to wipe it off with a paper napkin.

Mollie was already dabbing her hand. "It's okay, Felicity, it wasn't too hot luckily."

"Phew! Sorry, Moll. Hey what's this?" Felicity asked as she spotted a ring shining on the third finger of Mollie's left hand. "I've not noticed this before, is it new?" Then the penny dropped and Felicity jumped up and down again. "Hey, is this what I think it is?"

Nobody spoke. Mollie looked at Graham then back at Felicity, a blush appearing on her mature cheeks.

"Well?" Felicity asked.

Tessa and Michael were looking at Mollie expectantly too.

Graham spoke. "Erm, yes it is, Felicity. I might as well tell you now the cat is out of the bag. A few weeks ago, I asked Mollie to be my wife. She kept me waiting for a while, and I thought I'd messed things up, but..."

"I kept you waiting because you didn't ask me properly the first time, and because I had a lot of thinking to do," Mollie said, taking a sip of her coffee.

Graham laughed. "Yes, she made me ask her properly so I went out bought the ring, asked again, and she said yes."

Felicity ran round the table and threw her arms around Graham. "Oh Pops, I'm delighted." She then kissed Mollie and had a proper look at the ring.

Tessa and Michael stood up and added their congratulations, Michael slapping Graham on the back.

"Hey, what's going on?" Jo asked as she passed the table.

"Pops and Mollie are getting married," Felicity told her.

"Really?" Jo said, her eyes wide with delight. "That's wonderful! Congratulations." She hugged first Mollie and then Graham. "Oh my God, I can't wait to tell Clare. Have you set a date?"

"No, not yet," Mollie said. "We only want a small quiet wedding. No point having anything big at our age."

"But," Graham added, "we'd be delighted if you'd all come. You and Clare too, Jo; if it wasn't for Merrilies, we wouldn't have met."

"We might as well tell you the rest," Mollie said. "Michael, I have no-one as such to give me away, and we'd like to get married in my local church. Would you do me the honour?"

Michael stared at her dumbstruck. After a few seconds he found his voice, "Me? You're asking *me* to give you away?"

"Yes, but if you don't want to..."

"No, no, I mean yes, I'd love to. Are you sure you want me?"

Everyone laughed.

"Yes, Michael," Mollie answered.

"So make sure you do a good job, Mikey," Felicity said, wagging her finger at him.

"Of course I'll do a good job, Flick. It'll be a privilege." Michael sat down in his chair, quite lost for words.

Mollie turned to Felicity and Tessa. "And I'd like you both to act as bridesmaids – well, not bridesmaids, you're a bit too old for that, but whatever older girls would do – Maids of Honour maybe?"

"Bloody hell, Moll, you haven't planned it all already? Gosh, I'd be delighted, thanks," Felicity said happily.

"Aw, Mollie, I'd love to," Tessa said with a big smile.

"Where will you live once you're married?" Felicity asked.

"Well, we've talked quite a bit about that, and I've decided I'm going to move in with Graham as soon as I can. His house is much bigger, and it has a huge kitchen."

"Ah, so the kitchen clinched it," Tessa laughed. "Are you okay about leaving your home?"

"I am now. I didn't know if I'd be able to leave my house with all its memories." Mollie looked at Graham. "But it's only a house, I can take my memories with me."

"Aw, Mollie." Felicity hugged her again.

"Well, I don't know about you lot, but I'll find it hard to concentrate on our books now. What say we go out for a meal and a drink instead? Do you mind if we don't hold the meeting tonight?" Graham asked, turning to Jo.

"Of course not, you've got something to celebrate. Have a drink for me and Clare too," Jo said.

"Oh I'm sorry, we'd love you to come, how about you both join us after you shut the shop? What time is it now?" Graham looked at his watch.

"Just gone half seven." Jo checked the clock on the wall. "We don't close until nine tonight remember. But if we cash up now, I can maybe get one of the staff to close up and Clare and I can leave at eight." She made a face. "You know what Clare's like about leaving the shop though, so if she won't come, I'll be there."

"That'll be great, we'll go to the Italian down the road. Is that okay with everyone?" Graham asked.

They all murmured their agreement and Jo said she'd do her best to get Clare to come too.

Clare was absolutely delighted for Mollie and Graham, and told Jo to join them straight away, but she didn't want to leave Merrilies without either her or Jo in charge. "Anyway, Dan's meeting me tonight," she said.

"Can't you put him off, say something's cropped up? It *is* a special occasion," Jo urged.

"No. I'm not leaving the shop without you or me here. You go off and have fun. Tell them I'm really pleased for them and I'll join them for a drink another time."

"Well, if you're sure. Thanks, see you tomorrow."

"Honestly, it's fine. Have a good time." Clare pushed Jo towards the stairs.

Jo collected her bag from the staffroom, and ran to catch up with the others.

Clare would have liked to join the rest of the gang for a drink, but didn't want to leave Merrilies. This was her business, her life; everything she had was tied up in it. She simply couldn't risk it, and didn't trust it to anyone except herself or Jo. Besides, she was looking forward to seeing Dan.

They'd been dating for months now, and Clare believed he was "The One". He was kind, attentive, funny, generous, and they both liked the same things. He liked poetry and loved cats; just as well, with Angus around. Before Dan had come into her life, she'd thought she'd be left on the shelf, but now she'd found her true love and couldn't be happier.

Her parents had met him briefly a couple of times and liked him too, which Clare took as another sign that things were good. Dan had even hinted recently about a more permanent arrangement, so perhaps they'd have two Merrilies weddings this year.

She hummed as she worked, looking forward to snuggling up on the sofa later with Dan beside her, Angus on her lap, a glass of wine and maybe some chocolates. What more could a girl want?

A quarter of an hour before closing time, Dan came in to wait for her. "Hi honey." He kissed her. Then, looking around, he asked, "Where's Jo, upstairs?"

He knew the girls usually worked it so that one of them was upstairs and one down.

"No, she's gone early. A couple from the reading group are getting married, so she's joined them for a drink."

"Oh, didn't they invite you?"

"As a matter of fact, they did, but I declined. I didn't want to leave the shop unmanaged, and besides, I want to spend the evening with you." Clare smiled at him.

"That's nice. So where are the staff?" Dan asked.

"Two have gone home and two are upstairs."

"Well, let them go home. I'm here, it's not as if you're on your own, is it?" he said.

"But there's still ten minutes to go, a customer might come in."

"I doubt it this late and if they do, you can serve them, can't you? Go on be a nice boss, tell them they can go now." He leaned across and tickled her under her chin.

Clare laughed then picked up the phone. "Hermione, you can both leave now if you like. Yes, I'll be fine, Dan's here with me. Can you bring the cash down and put it in the safe please?" She turned to Dan. "There, is that okay?"

"Perfect." He went around to her side of the counter, pulled her towards him and kissed her.

A few minutes later, the two staff members came downstairs. Clare said goodnight and asked them to drop the door catch on their way out.

"Right you, stay here, I just have to put the takings away," she told Dan.

"Aren't you going to cash up? I'll help; it'll be quicker that way," he offered.

"Thanks, but it can wait 'til the morning, Jo'll do it I expect. I'll just put the money in the safe, I won't be long."

Clare unlocked the till, took the drawer out and walked into the office at the back of the shop. She was just locking the safe when Dan appeared in the doorway making her jump. "God, you frightened me," she laughed, then froze at the look in his eyes. "Dan, what is it?"

"Give me the key."

"What?"

"You heard, give me the key."

"Dan, stop mucking about."

"I'm not mucking about, now give me the key," he said, moving into the room towards her.

"No. What do you want the key for?" Clare asked, a frightened edge to her voice.

"Because I want the money; why do you think, you stupid cow?"

"Don't talk like that, you're scaring me." Clare edged around the side of the desk, away from him.

Dan walked towards her and she edged back the other way.

"If this is some kind of stupid game, then please stop it." Clare's heart was hammering in her chest.

204

"It's not a game. Just give me the fucking key." Dan advanced towards her again.

"What's the matter with you? Why are you behaving like this? I thought you loved me," Clare said in a small voice.

"Love you? I don't love you! But I had to gain your trust somehow."

Clare gasped.

"Yeah that's right, it was all an act. I know how loaded you are, gotta be to own a business like this, so I played a little game." He sneered, "You don't think I'd seriously be interested in a boring little cow like you, do you? NOW GIVE ME THE FUCKING KEY!"

Dan grabbed at her and tried to drag her around the desk, but Clare kicked him hard in the shin and ran out into the shop, screaming at the top of her voice. She made for the cash desk and the panic button, which was located underneath the front of the counter.

As she reached for the button, she dropped the safe key, and Dan grabbed her hair, yanking her towards him and away from the counter. She turned her head and bit his arm, which made him yell and let her go. This gave her enough time to lean over and press the button. The shop alarm sounded and Clare prayed for help.

Dan panicked. Fuck it, he thought, no time to get the money now. He hadn't expected her to fight back; he thought it'd be easier than this.

Clare had nowhere to go. Trapped between him and the counter, she saw the fury in his eyes and screamed again, hoping desperately someone would hear and come to her aid.

"SHUT UP!" Dan grabbed her and threw her to the floor. She'd ruined everything he'd spent months preparing for. "Stupid fucking bitch!"

Clare looked up at Dan standing over her, then she curled up and tried to protect herself as he went wild and released a barrage of punches and kicks to her head and body.

Her screams died out as she fell into unconsciousness.

He aimed a final kick at her stomach before fleeing out the front door, leaving her lifeless on the floor.

Chapter Twenty-Seven

Laughing at something Felicity had said, Jo swore when her mobile phone rang.

"Sorry, everyone, I thought I'd turned it off." She looked at the display with a frown. "It's Fran from the tea room. She never calls me; I better answer it."

She stood up to walk away from the table but Graham said, "Take it here, Jo, we don't mind."

Jo answered and they saw a look of horror cross her face. She grabbed her bag and headed for the door. "I've got to go."

Graham caught her arm. "What's wrong?"

"It's Clare, she's been attacked."

"Oh my God! Right, I'm coming with you, you might need some help." Graham pulled his jacket from the back of his chair.

"Me too," Michael added, getting up.

"Well, I can't sit here worrying. You go on, Graham, I'll sort out the bill and catch up," Mollie said.

"Tess, help Mollie, and I'll go with Pops and Michael." Felicity rushed after the men.

Leaving Mollie and Tessa at the restaurant, the others raced as fast as they could up the road.

Jo heard an alarm sounding, and as she got closer she saw the police and ambulance and realised it was Merrilies' alarm. She approached a policeman and frantically asked what was going on.

They couldn't tell her much except that Clare was in a bad way. Jo climbed in the back of the ambulance and sobbed with shock as she saw her friend lying unconscious on a stretcher, her face unrecognisable.

The police needed Jo to check if anything was missing from the shop, but she wanted to go in the ambulance with Clare. "I don't care about the shop, I need to go with Clare," she cried.

"Jo, give me the keys. Don't worry, I'll sort it out. Tell me where things are and leave it to us." Graham wheezed with the effort of running up the road.

Jo gave him the shop keys, although she could see that the front door was already open, and quickly explained where the safe and tills were before getting back in the ambulance.

Mollie and Tessa appeared as it drove away, sirens blaring.

Felicity stood on the pavement outside the shop, close to tears and silent for once in her life. Mollie put her arm around her. "Come on, Clare'll be okay."

"Oh Moll, it doesn't look good. Jo came out of the ambulance in hysterics. Poor Clare's been beaten really badly. Who would have done such a thing?"

"I don't know, but I jolly well hope they catch whoever it is. Come on let's go in, see what we can do to help."

Graham and Michael were inside the shop with the police, who stopped the women from entering. "Sorry," said one policeman, "we can't have everyone in here, this is a crime scene."

"We're with Graham and Michael, can we do anything to help?" Tessa asked.

"No thanks, the best thing you can do is let us get on with our job."

A lady from the tea shop came over and asked if they wanted a cup of tea. Mollie said that would be a good idea and told the policeman where they'd be.

The "lady' was Fran, the tea shop owner who'd phoned Jo. She told the three women what she knew. "I was in the front of the shop, getting the tables ready for tomorrow, clean

208

tablecloths and napkins, when I heard screaming. It sounded like it came from across the road; then a few minutes later I heard an alarm, so I looked out and saw a man run out the door of Merrilies. I didn't want to go over in case there was still someone in there, so I called the police. But if I'd known poor Clare was lying injured on the floor, I'd have gone straight away. Oh my, what a terrible thing to happen in this lovely little street." She wiped her eyes with a tissue.

The others agreed; it was indeed a terrible thing to happen.

After drinking their tea, Mollie, Tessa and Felicity decided they'd better go home as they couldn't do anything to help. With the police, Graham and Michael across the road, and Jo at the hospital, they'd just have to wait for any news.

As they left, Graham and Michael came out of Merrilies and met them on the pavement.

"Everything seems in order. The tills are in the room with the safe and that's locked, nothing's been ransacked, it's a bit of a mystery. The police found the safe key on the floor behind the counter, but apart from that, there's no sign of a break-in or anything," Graham told them.

"The only person at the moment who knows what happened is Clare," Michael added, "But they've taken the CCTV tapes away to watch, maybe they'll find out what happened from them."

Graham glanced at Mollie, who looked a bit pale. "Come on, let's get you home. I suggest we all go home, there's nothing more we can do."

"If any of us hears anything, can we let the others know? It was good of you to help the police, Pops." Felicity kissed his cheek then turned and squeezed Michael's arm, "You too, Mikey. I feel a bit wobbly myself; must be the shock. I do hope they catch the bloody pig who did this, and I hope Clare will be okay."

Brought back down to earth by the horrific news, they each made their way home. Tessa wanted to see Amber as soon as possible, Felicity felt in need of some more alcohol, and Michael seethed with a rage he hadn't felt before; not even after those episodes with Spike at work. How could someone do that to an innocent person like Clare? She wouldn't harm a fly.

Mollie and Graham were just as baffled about what had gone on in Merrilies. Mollie prayed, as they all silently did, that poor Clare would survive.

***

Jo sat in the hospital waiting room and rubbed her hands over her face. Her eyes were red and swollen from crying and she was sick with worry. Clare's parents had arrived a couple of hours ago and Jo heard Clare's mother cry in anguish when she saw her daughter. Then nurses came running because Clare's father collapsed with an angina attack.

"I hope you rot in hell, Dan Sullivan, if that *is* your name," Jo muttered.

The police had questioned Jo about Dan. She'd said she didn't trust him, but she hadn't told them why. How could she say she'd had a premonition? They'd think she was mad. She'd just said that she always felt uneasy around him.

Jo was angry with herself. She'd known this was going to happen, but hadn't tried hard enough to stop it and now Clare was seriously injured. She burst into tears again. It was all her fault. But what more could she have done? She'd tried to warn Clare, but she'd dismissed it.

Jo sighed. Unfortunately, she hadn't been of much help to the police. She didn't know where Dan lived or worked, and the only person who did was lying unconscious.

"I dealt with it all wrong," she muttered aloud. "I should have found out everything I could about him, then maybe the police would have something to go on." She raked her hands through her hair, pulling it hard in anger.

The police had said that 'Dan Sullivan' might not even be his real name. If he'd been grooming Clare as they suspected, he would have covered his tracks well and used an alias, as well as a whole made-up life.

Even if Jo had known where he lived and worked, it might have been lies anyway. So either way, it seemed, she wouldn't have been much help.

Clare's father came out and sat beside Jo. "Clare's just woken up. She can't talk much and can hardly see, her poor face is so swollen, but the doctors think she'll be okay. It'll take her a while to get better, that bastard beat her good and proper. When she gets out of hospital, we're taking her home with us so we can look after her."

"Oh thank God, I've been so worried," Jo said between sobs. "I'm so sorry for leaving her on her own, Mr Stevens; I'll never forgive myself. Are you okay?" she asked.

It seemed to her that Clare's dad had aged about twenty years in the last couple of hours.

"I'm fine now, love. It was just the shock of seeing her like that. Don't blame yourself. You couldn't stay with her all the time."

"No but you don't understand, I knew this was going to happen," Jo blurted out. She had to tell someone, and the Stevens' knew about her omens. It was how she and Clare had first met.

"What are you on about?" Mr Stevens asked, and Jo told him about the premonition and the ensuing argument when she'd told Clare she didn't trust Dan.

"Oh Jo, love, you warned her and she didn't take any notice, there was nothing more you could have done. Please don't blame yourself. Now, do you want to come and see her? I've checked with the nurse and it's okay as long as you don't stay too long."

Jo nodded. She was thankful Clare was going to be okay, and relieved to have been told it wasn't her fault.

She hugged Mr Stevens and together they walked into the side ward where Clare was lying.

***

The next couple of weeks at work were strange without Clare. Jo tried to keep the shop running as smoothly as possible, but it wasn't the same. The reading group still held their meetings, and Annie came in with her mum. News of the attack had been in the local paper, so most people knew about it, but when Annie asked where Clare was Jo just said she was spending some time with her parents.

Jo visited Clare every night to keep her updated on Merrilies. She'd initially worried that Clare wouldn't want to come back to work, but her quiet friend could be remarkably strong at times. With help from friends and family, she'd pull through it; all she needed was time.

"If I let it stop me coming back to work, then he's won, hasn't he?" Clare said. She looked at Jo and her eyes filled with tears. "Do you know what hurts the most? Not the physical wounds, they'll heal, but I really thought he cared about me, Jo. I thought I'd finally found someone I could share my life with. I don't think I'll ever trust another man again." Clare bent her head and sobbed.

Jo put her arms around her and held her shaking body until the sobs subsided.

"Right," Clare said, wiping her face, "that's it. I'm not wasting any more tears or energy on that bastard." She gave a huge sigh. "Did I tell you the police came round earlier? I'm not the first woman he's attacked. He was violent to his previous girlfriend, although not like what he did to me. I got it bad because he couldn't get what he wanted, the shop takings."

She threw her sodden tissue down and got a fresh one. "He's committed burglary before too, so I hope he'll go to

212

prison for a long time. I don't need to go to court either. The medical records and photos show what he did to me, and backed up by the footage on the CCTV tapes, that's enough evidence to sentence him."

"Good. But prison isn't enough, he needs hanging. God, if I got my hands on him…"Jo threatened.

"He's not worth it, Jo. Now, when can I come back to work? I'm going mad with boredom here. Mum and Dad are great but I want to get back to normal; work, my own flat and Angus. Poor thing, he must hate it in that cattery."

They chatted for a while, and Clare decided she'd spend the rest of the week with her parents, move back home at the weekend and return to work the following Monday.

"But, if you don't feel up to it," Jo told her, "just say and you can go home. We managed perfectly well without you."

"Oh, did you? So you don't need me then?"

"Yeah of course we do. It's alright managing for a couple of weeks, but I wouldn't want to do it for longer. There are things you're better at than me, and I miss you like mad," Jo grinned.

"That's okay then. I've missed everything and everyone at work too."

"I'm so glad you're okay. We were all really worried about you, you know. I'd be devastated if anything happened to you. You're more than just my friend and boss…" Jo stopped as she saw Clare's face. Clare hated it when Jo called her the boss, even though she was. "Okay sorry, work colleague then, but you're more than that, I love you to bits."

"Steady on!" Clare laughed, then groaned because it hurt to laugh. "I know what you mean though. You're like a sister to me. Right, that's enough of the soppy stuff! I'll ask Mum to put some extra dinner in. You will stay, won't you? I'm able to drink again now so we can have a couple of glasses of wine."

"Huh, you're back to normal I see. You and alcohol aren't parted for long," Jo teased.

"You're a fine one to talk, you drink far more than I do, Jo

Davis. In fact, I hardly ever drank until I met you, so it's your fault I like a glass or two of wine," Clare said and stuck her tongue out.

"Bottle or two more like." Jo made a stupid face back.

For some reason this gave them the giggles and Clare shrieked, because laughing hurt her ribs and stomach, which made Jo laugh even more.

Mrs Stevens went in to see what the commotion was and found her daughter and best friend clutching each other, helpless with laughter. She returned to the kitchen and said to her husband, "I don't know what's got into those two, anyone would think they were a couple of kids, not fully grown women. But it's nice to see Clare laughing again. When I think of how she looked when we first got to the hospital…'

"There there, don't fret, love. It's over and done with and hopefully that animal will get what he deserves," said Mr Stevens. "Now, what's for dinner? I'm starving."

Chapter Twenty-Eight

Clare returned to work and, after being a bit anxious initially, she soon settled down and was almost like her old self again.

Almost, but not quite. Jo could sense the distance whenever Clare served men. She was polite and businesslike, but dealt with the sale as quickly as possible and avoided eye contact. Jo felt sad for her friend. One man's appalling behaviour had put Clare off all men. It would be a very long time, if ever, until she trusted one again.

***

As July gave way to August, a heatwave arrived.

"Phew," Jo panted, feeling all hot and bothered after unpacking boxes in the stock room, "I'm so glad we've got air conditioning. I know I shouldn't moan really, as it's better than rain, but I'd much rather be lying on a beach than working."

"I wouldn't, I can't stand the heat. Give me snow any time," Clare said. "Still it is good for business, people are coming in to buy their holiday and beach books. We've sold a lot of those special offer ones I put on the table yesterday."

"Oh good. Isn't it remarkable how people buy books at certain times of the year according to the colour of their covers? Those with the bright summer colours, yellows, reds, pinks and turquoise, are like the sun and Mediterranean seas. Very clever, those designers!" Jo said, pursing her lips.

Clare laughed. "Yes, then in the autumn, the books are rust, bronze and green colours. I agree, clever subliminal marketing. Look out, here comes the troop." Clare nodded towards Felicity, Graham and Mollie, who were making their way to the reading table. "Hi, you three. How's work, Flick?" Clare asked.

"Work's great, although the animals are really feeling this heat, poor things. Aw, someone brought in a box of kittens the other day. They are the cutest things you've ever seen. How someone could abandon them, I don't know. We now have to try to find homes for them all." Felicity made a sad face.

Tessa joined the table at that moment and half-heard what Felicity was saying. "Did you say you wanted to find homes for some kittens, Flick?"

"Yes, we have five new ones; really sweet little things. Three black and two tabbies."

"I'd like one, if I'm a suitable candidate. I promised Amber we'd get a kitten soon. I'm home a lot, so it wouldn't be on its own all the time."

Felicity clapped her hands with delight. "Yay, that's great, Tess. I'm sure you'll fulfil all our requirements. I'll recommend you. And we'll make sure the kittens are healthy before we give them to you."

"What do you mean *them?* I'm only having one."

"Oh, I don't suppose you'll take two, will you? It seems a shame to have just one. That way, they can play together and keep each other company when you're not there." She saw Tessa's frown and tried to persuade her. "Aw please, Tess, another one won't cost a lot more to feed. I'll see if I can get you some free samples of kitten food from our suppliers. Why don't you come up and see them tomorrow before you say no?"

Tessa agreed to take Amber, who was on school summer holidays, the following afternoon. She said she'd think about having two, but couldn't promise.

Felicity knew she would though once she'd seen them.

By now, Michael had arrived and Felicity and Tessa went

upstairs to get the usual coffees and cakes before they started the meeting.

When they came down and Felicity had given everyone their flapjacks, she said, "Tess was just telling me that the newspaper asked if she'd like to go and do a piece on Glastonbury Festival. I was going to go this year but couldn't really because of work. Have any of you ever been?"

"I played there once," Graham said, then quickly shut up, realising he'd spoken aloud.

Felicity pounced on this piece of information. "What do you mean you played there once?"

"Erm nothing. It doesn't matter. We should get on with the meeting," Graham replied.

But Felicity, being the tenacious person she was, wouldn't let the matter drop. Once she'd chanced upon an interesting snippet, she was like a dog with a bone. "Sorry, Pops, you can't do that. We're not having the meeting until you fess up. So come on, tell all."

Graham knew he wouldn't get away with it and sighed. "I was the bass player in a band and we played at Glastonbury many years ago, that's all. Now can we get on with the meeting?"

Felicity turned to Mollie. "Did you know about this, Moll?"

Mollie nodded. "Oh yes, he's told me all about his dark seedy past." She grinned at the look on Graham's face.

"It wasn't seedy; we were just a rock band, that's all."

"Yes, but you must have been pretty good to play at Glastonbury, Pops. What were you called?"

"Felicity, please, I don't think the others are remotely interested in what I got up to in my youth."

"Oh on the contrary, I bet they are. Mikey, you want to know, don't you?"

"Erm, well, if Graham wants to keep his business to himself that's up to... Yes I do," he quickly added as Felicity

217

kicked him under the table.

"What about you, Tess?"

"You bet! Sorry, Graham." She grinned at Felicity.

"Oh for heaven's sake, we were called Strange Affair, now can we get on with the meeting!"

"Okay," Felicity replied, but she determined to find out all she could about Graham's band days.

***

As luck would have it, Mollie and Graham were a bit late for Saturday's meeting because Graham's car had been in for a service, which took longer than expected. Mollie's house had sold quite quickly and she'd moved in with Graham, so they always turned up at the meetings together now.

Tessa, Michael and Felicity were already seated when the couple turned up.

All three looked up and grinned when Graham approached. As Mollie sat down, she stifled a gasp and looked across at Felicity, who was waiting for Graham to sit down too.

"What's going on here? Bloody hell!" he said as he saw a photo on the table in front of him. He looked around and, to his horror, saw that there was one in front of each person – like placemats on the table – and Felicity was looking very pleased with herself.

He couldn't believe it. There, for all to see, were pictures of him from his band days. With a beard and long shaggy hair, hippy clothes and what looked suspiciously like a joint in his hand, the young version in the photos was a complete contrast to the Graham that stood in front of them now.

"Oh my God, Felicity, where on earth did you find this?" he asked, trying to control his temper.

Mollie shot her a look as if to say, "You may have gone too far this time, young lady," and Felicity knew she'd done the

218

wrong thing.

Graham hardly ever shouted, and she could see by the twitch in his cheek that he was angry.

Oops, her little bit of fun might just have backfired on her. But she tried to brazen it out. "On the internet. There was loads of wicked stuff about your band. Did you really work with all those famous people?" She reeled off the names she'd read.

Graham saw the look of admiration on her face, the awe on Michael's and the interest in Tessa's, and realised he'd suddenly been elevated from "boring old duffer" to "seriously cool", and his anger evaporated. "Yes," he said, "but it was no big deal back then. I ran a recording studio in London and those people came and went as they used the studios. Then later I became a roadie for one of the groups, who introduced me to the lead singer of the band I eventually joined."

"Wow, that is so cool! You even made a few albums, and got a recording contract in America," Felicity said.

"Yes, and as I let slip last week, we played at Glastonbury, though not to as many people as go there now."

"And guess what?" Felicity said. "You can buy your CDs on the internet too."

"Can you really? Well, I never! I've got the original albums on vinyl, but didn't know they'd been produced onto CD." Graham shook his head in amazement.

"How fantastic, you're not such a boring old fart after all."

"Felicity!" Mollie said with a hint of irritation.

"Sorry, but who'd have thought our Pops was in a famous band? Wicked! I love the look too." She grinned at Graham.

"Yes, well, that's enough for today thank you, and get rid of these photos. I can't believe you did this. I'm not very happy with you, young lady," Graham admonished her.

Felicity said sorry again and pushed her bottom lip out like a little girl.

Graham couldn't stay mad at her. The girl is incorrigible,

he thought, but you can't help liking her. Graham *was* fond of Felicity; she was like a daughter to him.

They got on with the meeting. This time they discussed a book that had joined the new sub-genre termed "misery lit" or "misery memoirs". It was about twins who had suffered neglect by their adoptive parents.

Michael said he refused to read the rest and wondered how people could publish stories like that. Tessa said she didn't want to read any more either, because she found it too upsetting. Mollie said it was "Too jolly depressing for my liking," and Graham agreed. Only Felicity wanted to continue reading the book.

"I think it's good to read about things like this. It makes us realise what goes on behind some closed doors, and that not everyone has a wonderful home life," she said.

"Yes, but when I read it's for pleasure, not to be upset and depressed. I read to lose myself in another world, as a kind of escape from reality I suppose," Tessa said.

So they agreed to swap it for something else and Felicity would finish hers in between reading their next chosen book.

"Oh Tessa, did you go see the kittens yesterday?" Mollie asked.

"Aw, yes we did. Amber fell in love with all of them and wanted to take the lot home."

"And, are you having any?"

Tessa looked at Felicity and laughed. "Yes, we're taking two."

"See, I told you she'd have two, didn't I?" Felicity said gleefully.

"A little black one and a tabby one, both females. You should see them, Mollie, they're so cute. Amber's named them already – Fizzy and Fluffy."

"When can you have them?"

Felicity answered for Tessa. "Well, once all our checks are complete, she can come and collect them, so it should only be a couple of weeks or so."

"It'll be lovely to have a couple of boisterous kittens about. I bet Amber will enjoy playing with them," Mollie said.

"She can't wait, she's so excited; they're the first pets we've ever had."

"I've always had cats," Graham said. "Mine – ours,' he corrected, looking at Mollie, "are getting old now so are happy to stay in and sleep most of the time."

"Can we get on with the meeting please?" Michael asked, and Felicity tutted, muttered "Bloody grumpbox" and stuck her tongue out at him.

As the meeting ended and they were packing away their things, Mollie said, "We haven't seen Annie today. I must ask Jo if she's been in. I'm sure we would have known if she had, she always comes over to say hello."

"Perhaps they went out for the day. I wouldn't come in if we weren't holding the meeting. It's such lovely weather, I'd be lying on the beach by now," Felicity said.

"Or in a bar getting drunk," Michael answered.

"I so would not! You make me out to be an alcoholic and I'm not Michael. Just because I know how to have fun!"

"If getting drunk and making a prat of yourself can be called having fun."

"I do NOT make a prat of myself."

Michael snorted.

"Okay, Mister Know–it–all, when have you seen me drunk, and when have you seen me making a so-called prat of myself?" Felicity asked.

Michael didn't answer.

"I asked you a question... I'm waiting... Hah, you can't answer because you haven't seen it. So you bloody well take that back," Felicity fumed.

Still Michael didn't say anything, so Felicity leaned forward to prod him, but Graham put his hand out and stopped her.

"Felicity, sit back, please. Michael, apologise. There really

221

was no need for that."

Michael mumbled.

"Sorry, I can't hear you," Felicity said.

"I'm sorry okay!"

"I don't know why you even said that, Michael, what's the matter with you? Did I get drunk when we were on the boat? No I didn't. And besides, since I started work at the animal shelter, I hardly drink any more." Felicity looked very hurt and Michael felt a bit guilty.

"Look, I'm sorry, Flick, but you're always winding me up, so I was trying to get my own back." He stood up and shoved his book into a carrier bag.

Felicity huffed, her arms folded across her chest. Then she decided he wasn't worth getting worked up over, and he was probably right; she did tease him a lot. "Well, okay, but don't do it again," she said then stood up to leave and slung her bag over her shoulder.

Mollie, Graham and Tessa stood up too. Tessa looked at them both and raised her eyebrows as if to say, "Well, that nearly turned into a full blown row."

They said their goodbyes and left Merrilies, the query about little Annie forgotten.

Chapter Twenty-Nine

Alice sat beside the hospital bed, holding her daughter's hand. Annie had been admitted the day before, after suffering a severe asthma attack at a friend's house.

The friend had new guinea pigs, and the dust from their hay had brought on Annie's attack. She had used her inhaler, but it didn't help and the attack got worse. Her friend's mum called Alice, and once Alice got there and realised how bad it was, she'd called an ambulance.

Rubbing her hand wearily across her face, Alice wondered if things would always be like this, poor Annie in and out of hospital for the rest of her life. Watching her struggle for breath yesterday as the hospital tried to treat her, had terrified Alice; she'd felt so useless. Lord knows, it wasn't the first time they'd been in this situation, so why the hell didn't it get any easier?

She looked up as Annie moved and opened her eyes. "Hello sweetheart, you okay?"

Annie nodded and tried to speak.

"Shush, don't talk, honey, just lie there." Alice smoothed Annie's hair back from her sweaty forehead. "Do you want some water?"

The little girl's lips looked dry, so Alice held the beaker to her mouth for her to take a sip. Even the effort of half-sitting took its toll and Annie began to cough. A nurse came over to check on her.

"Do you want to sit up a bit, sweetie? Here you go. There, is that better?" The nurse lifted Annie into a sitting position and put another pillow behind her as the coughing ceased. "Give me a shout if you're worried or want anything," she said to Alice with a smile and went back to her duties.

Alice got out a book. "Shall I read to you, darling? Would you like that?"

Annie nodded, and Alice read her favourite story to her.

Earlier that morning, when the doctors had done their ward rounds, they'd been unhappy with Annie's apparent lack of improvement. Because of her weakened immune system, the asthma attack had left her quite poorly, so they wanted to keep her in for a few more days.

Annie had got upset and started crying, which made her cough again, and she complained of pains in her chest and that she couldn't breathe properly.

Alice knew that this time things were a bit more serious.

Late afternoon, hating to leave but knowing she had to have a break, Alice went home to collect some clean pyjamas for Annie, her teddy bear and some more books. She also packed some things for herself.

Thankfully, she was able to stay with Annie in the hospital. She sighed; it was going to be a long few days. At least Tom would visit in the evenings, giving her a bit of much needed support. But the one person Alice felt sorriest for in all of this was Annie. She should be out playing with her friends like other little girls were, not stuck in a hospital bed.

***

Two weeks later, Jo hung up the phone and went downstairs to see Clare.

"That's the third message I've left for Alice in the last couple of weeks. Maybe they've gone away?"

"Not with the trip to Florida next month surely, and they'd have told us before they went. Haven't we got Alice's mobile number?" Clare asked.

"No, only her home one. I don't know what else to do. I know Mollie's worried sick, she's got a real soft spot for that little girl, but what can we do if we can't get hold of them?" Jo asked.

"Not a lot. Let's see if she gets this message and calls us back."

"I don't like it, Clare, I have a feeling something's not right."

"A premonition?"

"No, they usually come as images in my mind. This is different, a kind of foreboding; whatever it is, it's not good."

When the reading group came in that evening for their meeting, they had to tell Mollie, sorry no news yet.

"Oh I wish I jolly well knew what was happening. Where is she?"

"Come on, Moll, don't get worked up," Graham soothed her. "Maybe they've gone on a little break."

"But that's hardly likely. Annie would have mentioned it the last time we saw her. You know what a chatterbox she is, she tells us everything. And why would they go away when they're going to Florida in just over four weeks' time?" Mollie asked.

"I don't know, but there's nothing we can do; we'll just have to wait until we hear something," Graham said.

"Yes, come on, Moll, let's get the coffees and cakes," Felicity said and linked her arm to go up to the café.

Mollie sighed and went upstairs with Felicity. She just hoped Annie was all right.

Jo answered a call late the following afternoon just as they were closing up, and Clare could tell by her voice and the look on her face that something was wrong.

"That was Alice," she said when she'd finished the call. "Annie's in hospital. She's been there for the last couple of weeks. I knew something wasn't right, didn't I?"

"Oh no. What's happened?"

"An ambulance rushed her in with a severe asthma attack, and she's now caught pneumonia."

Clare's hand flew to her mouth. "Oh my God, that's serious, isn't it?"

"Yes, unfortunately it is. I could tell Alice was trying not to cry on the phone. She apologised for not calling us sooner, but she doesn't know whether she's coming or going at the moment, and she's worried sick about Annie."

"Oh poor Annie; poor Alice. Oh God, I hope she'll be okay."

"Yeah so do I. I'd better ring Mollie and let her know."

Mollie put the phone back on its cradle, went into the lounge and sat on the sofa.

Graham looked up from the paper he was reading and saw the expression on her face asked. "What's wrong, love?"

Mollie looked at him, her eyes full of tears. "It's little Annie, she's in hospital with pneumonia."

"Ah poor little mite. But she's in the best place, Moll, and they'll be doing all they can, giving her antibiotics and stuff."

"Yes, but she's such a weak little thing with her immune system not working properly."

"But she's got youth on her side. Look, she'll be okay. Plenty of rest and antibiotics and she'll be as right as rain," Graham tried to console her.

Mollie's bottom lip trembled and she bit down to control it.

"Why don't you phone the hospital, see if she's allowed visitors? If so, I'll take you tomorrow."

"That's a good idea. I could make her some chocolate brownies, she loves them, doesn't she?"

As Mollie went off to look up the hospital number, Graham gazed out of the window and sighed, hoping Annie really would be okay.

226

***

The following afternoon, a nurse showed Mollie into Annie's side ward. They usually only allowed close relatives to visit someone as poorly as Annie, but Alice had pleaded with them, saying it might do her good to hear news of her friends from the bookshop. Reluctantly, the nurse in charge relented. "You can stay for ten minutes only though!" she warned as she left.

"Hello, Alice." Mollie gave the younger woman a hug. She looked thoroughly worn out, as if she hadn't slept for weeks, and Mollie understood why.

She went to the other side of Annie's bed, sat in the chair and took the little girl's hand. "Hi Annie, it's me, Mollie. I've brought you some of your favourite chocolate brownies. I made them just for you and they've got Smarties on top."

Annie drowsily opened her eyes and looked at her, so Mollie continued, "Felicity sends her love, and she said that when you get better, you can go up to the animal shelter and she'll show you around, so you can see all the little puppies and kittens. They've even got some horses in. She thought you'd like that."

Annie smiled a weak little smile, and Mollie squeezed her hand. "Graham says hi, and he'll take you out on the boat when you come out of hospital. He'll even let you have a go at driving it. Michael says to get better soon as well. Jo and Clare send their love, and they gave me this for you. He's called Dolphy. He's to keep you company and help make you well again."

She showed Annie a small grey toy dolphin. Annie tried to lift her hand to reach for it, so Mollie tucked it under her arm. "There you go, a special friend to look after you."

Annie closed her eyes again, so Mollie got up, leaned over, kissed the little girl's forehead and whispered in her ear, "Get better, darling. We all miss you." She kissed her once more and stood up.

"Thanks for coming, Mollie," Alice said. "Annie loves to come in the bookshop and see you all, so I'm sure your visit has helped. Thanks for the brownies; she's not eating at the moment, but I'll keep them for when she is. And thanks for Dolphy, she'll love him, you know what she's like about dolphins."

"He should be okay for her as he's been washed and was in the freezer last night."

Alice smiled. "Thank you."

"How's she doing, really?" Mollie asked.

"The doctors are optimistic; it looks like the antibiotics are working now they've started her on some stronger ones. Because she caught the pneumonia in here, it's a different form of bacteria to the other sort and she was resistant to the standard type of antibiotics. So all we can do now is wait, and pray."

"I'll be praying for you both in church this week. If there's anything I can do, or anything you need, please call me. Here's my mobile number. And take care of yourself as well; I know what you must be going through. Can I do anything? Take some clothes home to wash, or cook you a meal?"

"Thanks, Mollie, that's very kind but I'm okay. Tom does what he can. He visits lunchtimes and again in the evenings, so I manage to get a bit of a break," Alice said.

"Well, hopefully it won't be for much longer. If she's turned the corner, she'll soon be up and about. You know how quickly children recover, not like us old 'uns." Mollie smiled.

"Yes and Annie's a determined little madam, she won't want to be stuck in that bed for too long."

Mollie gave Alice a hug and, with one last look at Annie, she left the ward.

Chapter Thirty

Everyone arrived at more or less the same time for the following Thursday's meeting, and sat in their chairs.

Felicity usually got the coffees, but she was busy looking at her mobile phone and frowning.

"What's up, Flick?" Tessa asked.

"Hmm?" Felicity looked up at Tessa then back down at her phone. She put it away in her bag. "I've been getting these strange calls on my phone, but I don't know who it is, they withhold their number. I was just checking my call list to see if there were any numbers I didn't recognise."

"What sort of strange calls?"

"Well, when I answer, whoever it is doesn't speak. But I know someone's there, I can hear background noise."

Tessa tutted. "Probably just kids messing about. They phone random numbers to play pranks."

"Yes, I suppose, but it's the fifth one I've had now. Bloody annoying all the same."

"Serves you right for having such an expensive phone," Michael said.

"Michael! That's not nice, is it? What's having an expensive phone got to do with getting stupid calls?"

"Nothing, I was just joking."

"Just jealous more like. I can buy whatever I like with my money, I do work for it."

"Yeah, and get a generous allowance from Daddy!"

"I do not get an allowance from my father, especially now that I'm working. Yes, he paid for me to go to university, and gave me an allowance when I was out of work, but I make my own money now. Not that my financial situation has anything to bloody do with you anyway." Felicity's red face showed her anger.

"Hey, you two, time out! Can't you have a conversation without squabbling? You're like a couple of kids at times," Mollie told them.

"I didn't start it; he should learn to keep his mouth shut if he can't say anything nice."

"Yes he should. Michael, you are in the wrong again on this occasion, but the pair of you seem to take great delight in winding each other up." Mollie scolded him. "Can you call a truce and try being nice to each other for once? It's jolly unpleasant for the rest of us."

Michael looked sheepishly across at Felicity. "Sorry, Flick, it was uncalled for. I *was* only joking."

"Well, don't!" Felicity saw Mollie's raised eyebrow and went on, "Thanks for the apology, again." She turned to Tessa, "Coming to get the coffees with me?"

Tessa looked pointedly at Michael and followed Felicity upstairs. "God, he can be a pain at times, can't he?"

"He's a pain *most* of the time. He's a strange guy, I just don't get him. Yet on the odd occasion he can be okay, even pleasant. I don't dislike him, well, not much anyway, but he does my bloody head in," Felicity complained.

"But you do enjoy teasing him as well, Flick, you know you do."

"Only because he's so easy to wind up."

"Yes and that's probably why he does it to you. It makes him feel better, and it's getting his own back," Tessa pointed out.

"I suppose. But nobody else winds me up like he does; I'm usually quite laid back." Felicity sighed deeply.

"Anyway, about these calls, if you get any others you'll have to do something," Tessa said.

"Like what? The number's withheld, so it can't be traced, and whoever it is doesn't say anything. You're right, it's probably kids messing about. I'll leave it and see if I get any more. Right, what shall we have with the coffee, something different for a change?"

"I don't mind, I do like Mollie's flapjacks, but I like all her cakes."

"Me too. If I get something else, Michael will probably moan, but I don't care. Five Bakewell tarts please," Felicity told the girl serving.

When they'd got the drinks and cakes, they went back downstairs.

Clare was standing by the table talking to Mollie, Graham and Michael. Felicity heard Mollie saying, "That's jolly good news, Clare, it really is," and asked what was going on.

Clare turned to her and Tessa. "The guy who beat me up has got two years in prison."

"Oh Clare, that's brilliant news, although they should have given him ten years in my opinion. But at least he's behind bars. You must be so relieved," Tessa said.

"Yes I am. I'm glad I didn't have to go to court, and I was worried that he'd get away with it. Although I don't feel it's enough, it's better than community service or something." Her face clouded over for a moment, but then she smiled and said, "Well, I must get on, have a good meeting."

"Poor girl," Mollie said when she'd gone. "The physical scars may have healed, but I don't think she'll ever be quite the same again. She seems to have retreated into herself."

"Yes, and she'd really come out of her shell too. She was blossoming nicely until that monster ruined things," Graham added.

They were all silent for a moment, then Tessa handed the cakes around.

Michael looked at his. "Oh, didn't they have any flapjacks then?"

Tessa looked at Felicity and they both burst out laughing.

Michael looked bewildered, "What's so funny?"

"Nothing," Tessa replied.

"If you must know," Felicity told him, "I said you'd complain if we got something different to flapjacks. And I said that if you did, I would hit you over the head with yours."

Michael looked alarmed as Felicity stood up, then she laughed and sat down again. "Only joking, Mikey, but I did say you'd complain. I know you better than you think."

His only reply was, "Hmph." Michael was okay at making fun of other people, but not very good at taking it.

They were halfway through the meeting, discussing the latest book, an adult fairytale full of magic and mystical creatures, but with plenty of blood and gore too. They were all enjoying it, even Graham who usually read military history books, when Mollie's mobile phone rang. "Drat!' she said, searching through her bag to find it. "I thought I'd switched it off. Sorry, won't be a second." She frowned at the display. "Hmm, I don't recognise the number."

She answered the call and, as she listened to what whoever on the other end was saying, the colour drained out of her face. "Oh no, dear Lord no." She started to cry.

Graham took the phone, while Felicity, a worried look on her face, went to comfort Mollie.

Graham introduced himself, listened for a bit and then said, "I am truly sorry. Thank you for calling to let us know, it must be an awful time for you."

He put the phone down, ran his hand over his face, and put his arm around Mollie who was still weeping. The others looked at Graham, needing but not wanting to know what was going on.

"What the bloody hell's happened?" Felicity asked eventually.

Graham took a deep breath, and then said, his voice breaking, "That was Tom, Annie's dad. Sadly, Annie died yesterday morning."

Felicity gasped in shock then burst into tears, Tessa sat stunned, and Michael blinked rapidly then tried to put his arm around Felicity to comfort her. She pushed him away, but then turned into him and sobbed.

"Dear, dear, dear, I didn't expect this. How very sad." Graham gave Mollie a tissue to blow her nose.

"And she didn't even get to swim with the dolphins," Mollie said and wept even harder.

Jo had heard the commotion, so she finished dealing with her customer and rushed over to see what was wrong.

As Graham told her, her hand flew to her mouth and tears welled in her eyes.

"I can't imagine what poor Alice is going through right now," Tessa said.

"I can," Mollie murmured.

"Sorry, Mollie, no offence but losing a husband can't be the same as losing a child, so none of us really know how she feels," Michael said.

"But I *do* know," Mollie whispered and sobbed again.

"It's okay, love, come on. Let me take you home," Graham said.

"No, I don't want to go home yet," Mollie said through her tears.

Tessa stood up. "Let me get you another coffee or cup of tea, Mollie, shall I?"

"Yes please, dear. Tea, thank you."

"I'd better tell Clare," Jo said and called to Hermione to cover her at the till while she raced upstairs.

Felicity wiped her eyes and got up. "I'll help you, I think we all need one," she said to Tessa and they left the group.

"Oh that dear little girl, I can't believe it," Mollie wept. "I thought she was getting better. When I went to see her, they'd given her different antibiotics and they seemed to be working. Whatever can have happened?" Her blue eyes were awash with

233

tears.

Graham tried his best to comfort her, but knew there wasn't much he could say at a time like this, and Michael sat not knowing what to do or say. He was glad when the two girls got back with more cups of tea for them all.

"It's so sad, Jo and Clare are both crying upstairs," Tessa told them. She was having a hard job to keep from crying herself; she could only imagine how she'd feel if it was Amber, and that was bad enough.

Mollie waited for them to sit down before speaking. "I know how Alice and Tom must be feeling, because I had a little boy once."

Everyone looked at her. Graham held her hand and gave it a squeeze. "You don't have to do this, Moll," he told her.

"But I want to." She continued, "I had a son, Johnny. A gorgeous little boy with chestnut hair and the bluest eyes. He used to be friends with the boy across the street.

"They'd play on the pavement outside our houses. They never wandered off like some of the kiddies did, but always stayed where we could see them. Such a sweet little boy he was."

She used another tissue to wipe the tears that were falling down her face then went on, "One day, he was playing outside his friend's house while I cooked his tea; sausages, his favourite. They were almost done, so I opened the front door and called him to say they were ready. I watched him get up, but then heard the sausages spitting so went back in to take them off the heat. That's when I heard the bang – a terrible noise that has stayed with me all these years."

She stopped and took a gulp of tea. The group around the table watched her, listening intently, dreading what was about to come.

Mollie looked down at her lap while she talked. "I heard the bang and ran outside to see what it was, and there was my little boy lying in the road, not moving. A car had smashed into another one parked further down the road and there were people everywhere, but I ran to my Johnny, and knew when I saw him that he was dead. I held his little body and wiped the blood away from his nose and mouth. I just lay there in the road, holding him. Someone told me later I'd been screaming hysterically, but I don't remember that. I just remember holding my boy and thinking life would never be the same again."

Felicity and Tessa were now both sobbing uncontrollably, and Michael kept gulping because of the lump in his throat. "What had happened?" he asked.

"He'd been killed by a drunk driver who'd taken a wrong turn. The driver tried to escape the scene, but he smashed into a parked car. Apparently he got out and tried to run, but some men stopped him. They gave him a good beating too."

"Oh Mollie, I am so sorry. We didn't have a clue; you've never talked about him," Felicity choked out.

"No. Something died in me that day along with my little boy, and I blamed myself."

"But it wasn't your fault!" Tessa cried.

"It jolly well was! If I had stayed to watch him across the road instead of going in to tend the sausages, he wouldn't have been killed. I was a bad mother for letting him cross the road on his own. He was only five years old," Mollie said.

"Come on love, you can't blame yourself, it was only a small road in the middle of the streets of houses, and wasn't busy. You told me hardly any traffic came down it, except for people that lived there," Graham gently reminded her.

"Yes, but I still should have watched him across. I will always feel guilty. It was the worst day of my life, apart from the funeral. I let my little boy down." She shook her head sadly.

"Oh Mollie, I'm sure Johnny wouldn't blame you. Why didn't you talk to someone about it? You shouldn't have kept it to yourself all these years, you know," Tessa said through her sobs.

"I may not have spoken about it, but I've never forgotten him. I say a prayer to him every night, and can still see his beautiful little face with those blue eyes."

"And now with Annie dying, it must have brought it all back. Oh Mollie. Oh poor little Annie." Felicity hiccoughed on a sob.

They sat there, the women crying, the two men not really knowing what to do, until Graham said, "Well, we're not going to continue with the meeting, are we? Do you all want to go home?"

"I don't think I want to go home yet, I could jolly well do with a drink though, and after that I'd like to go to church and light a couple of candles. One for Annie, and one for my Johnny."

"Do you think it's okay to go for a drink after hearing about Annie?" Tessa asked with a frown.

"Well, I think we could all do with one, and we can raise a glass to her, wherever she may be," Felicity said, making the women cry again.

They got their belongings together and Graham stopped to tell Jo – now back downstairs behind the till – that they couldn't continue the meeting after the bad news, so were going for a drink.

"I'm going to phone Tom tomorrow to find out about the funeral arrangements as Clare and I both want to go, and to see if I can offer any help or advice," she said.

"Oh yes, you worked in the business before the bookshop, didn't you? We'll go as well, I expect. Just a thought, Jo, what about the fundraising money? Could we give that to them to help pay for it?"

"They won't need it, a child's funeral is usually free, but we'll give them the money anyway; it was for Annie after all. I just can't believe it, Graham; can't believe we'll never see her happy little face again," Jo said sadly.

"I know. She was certainly a ray of sunshine and a happy child even though she was ill. We'll miss her visits. Mollie's taken it very badly. She was so fond of Annie and it's brought back memories of her own child."

Jo gasped. "I didn't know Mollie had a child!"

"Yes, a long time ago, but he was killed," Graham said.

"Oh my God, poor Mollie. How awful." She pointed a book out to a customer, then turned back to Graham. "I'll let you know about the funeral and pass on all your condolences."

"Yes, please do, Jo. Well, I'll see you Saturday afternoon maybe. I'm not sure if we'll be having the meeting now, with what's happened. We should do though, life goes on, doesn't it?"

"Yes it does unfortunately, or fortunately, whichever way you look at it. Okay, tell Mollie I'm thinking of her too," Jo added.

"Will do, bye." Graham hurried to catch up the others who were waiting outside for him.

Chapter Thirty-One

Everyone attended the funeral the following week. The crematorium chapel where the service was held was packed to the brim, with people even standing outside. Annie had been a local celebrity because of the fundraising, and the Herald had reported her death, so nearly the whole community turned out to see her off.

Mollie was touched but saddened to see Dolphy sitting on top of the little white coffin, and it brought back painful memories of her son's funeral.

Alice was inconsolable and sobbed the whole way through. It was a very sad affair, except for the ending, which was movingly beautiful. Once outside, the mourners each wrote a message on a little tag, which they attached to a lilac balloon, and when everyone was ready, they released their balloons in one go and watched them soar into the sky.

"Night night, darling. Sleep well and be happy," Mollie whispered, and Graham tightened his arm around her.

Tom, Annie's dad, shook Jo's hand and thanked her for all her help. She'd advised them on the funeral procedure and answered the many questions they'd had. Alice had decided she wanted her daughter cremated so that she could keep her ashes; she couldn't face going to visit a grave, and felt that having Annie's ashes would keep her close.

Tom invited everyone back to the house for a drink and food, but Jo and Clare had to go back to Merrilies and Mollie really couldn't face it. It had been a difficult day for her and she just wanted to go home. Tessa, Felicity, and Michael, who'd surprised them all by turning up, declined too. It was best to let the family grieve alone now.

Tom and Alice had talked it over and they didn't want the fundraising money. Instead, they asked Jo to give it to a worthwhile charity. With everyone's agreement, she was going to give it to a charity conducting research into childhood diseases.

***

Graham had been quite worried about Mollie, he'd never seen her so down. She was usually such a cheerful outgoing woman, but in the last couple of weeks she seemed to have lost all her *joie de vivre*. He knew it was because of little Annie's death and the memories it had brought to the surface of her own son, but he felt so useless. He couldn't do anything to make it better. He even asked if she wanted him to get the doctor for her, but she'd shaken her head and said she'd be okay.

They hadn't held the reading group meeting since the night Mollie had received the bad news. Nobody felt like attending, but now two weeks later, Mollie appeared in the lounge with her hair freshly brushed and a touch of lipstick on. "Well, are we going to Merrilies tonight then?" she asked.

Graham put down the book he was reading. "If you think you're up to it, my dear."

"Of course I'm up to it! I'm sorry, love, I know I've been a misery these last couple of weeks, but it was something I had to work through myself."

She sat on the edge of Graham's chair and he took her hand.

"It upset me deeply Annie dying like that and it took me right back to my Johnny's death. But I'm okay now; well, I'll jolly well make sure I am. Neither of them would want me to be unhappy forever." She smiled weakly.

Graham wasn't convinced as she still looked sad.

"It's not right, you know," Mollie continued, "children dying, while we reach old age. But if it's the Lord's decision to take them early, He must have done it for a reason."

Graham didn't feel the same about religion as Mollie did, but he didn't say anything. He just held her hand and let her talk, hoping it helped.

"I'll never forget either of them. I can still see Annie's lovely face, the way it lit up when she spoke about dolphins, and how funny she was when she got words wrong. I can picture my Johnny's face too, even after all these years. I don't think I'll ever forget it."

She was quiet for a moment, then pulled herself together. "Right, I'll go and phone Felicity and Tessa, and send a text to Michael; he's always so monosyllabic on the phone, it's easier to text him."

Graham laughed. "I can't get the hang of this texting business, it takes me too long. I can have a conversation much quicker and easier. Okay, that means I better go make myself presentable then."

Mollie wrapped her arms around him. "You're always presentable. I'm sorry I've been so sad lately. I'm jolly glad I've got you, you know. Weren't we lucky to find each other?"

"We were indeed. I just wish we'd found each other sooner," Graham said.

"But it may not have worked then. It's right when it's right, all in God's plan," Mollie said.

"Well, that may be true, but I don't have your faith. I wish I did sometimes, and other times – like when Annie died – I don't understand it."

"If I didn't have my faith, I would have gone to pieces when Johnny was killed, and again when Victor died. It was my belief that helped me, because I know I'll see them again one day."

Graham had a look of consternation on his face. "Well, if

240

that's the case, there'll be a fight when we all get to heaven, because Victor will want you, but I'll want you too. I might have to challenge him to a duel."

Mollie laughed. "I don't know how things work, Graham, but I *have* to hang onto my faith, it helps me keep going."

Graham patted her hand. "I know, love, now off you go and make those phone calls, while I get changed out of these old trousers."

He watched her go, pleased that she was more like her old self again and grateful that she had a faith, even if he didn't believe in it all. He felt so sorry for Annie's parents. Seeing how upset Mollie was, it must have been a hundred times worse for them. He wondered if they had a faith and thought how angry they must be at a God who allowed a small child, their only child, to die.

He went into the bedroom to find a clean pair of trousers. It'd be good to get back to the reading group meetings. Although they'd spoken on the phone, he missed the others. He was fond of them all and he enjoyed the social aspect of it; they often went for a drink or grabbed something to eat after. Because they were all kids – well, they were to him and Mollie – it helped keep him young. They were like the children, or almost grandchildren in Felicity's case, he'd never had.

The reading group was a bit subdued that evening but they were all glad to be back on track. Felicity, as usual, went up to get the drinks and cakes, and Michael went to help, which was most unusual.

"Anything wrong, Mikey?"

"No not at all, why?"

"Let's face it, you don't usually help me, do you? That's Tessa's job. You just sit and wait for the drinks to be brought to you."

Michael looked hurt, then as usual, retaliated. "So do Graham and Mollie!"

"Pops and Mollie are in their sixties, I don't expect them to

241

go up and down stairs carrying trays, but you're only in your thirties," Felicity told him.

"Twenty-nine, if you don't mind!"

"Well, you look older'.

"Thanks a lot!"

"You're welcome. Now did you want something or were you really just being helpful?"

"No, I don't want something. Just thought I'd help you for a change. I...um..."

Felicity interrupted him, "Spit it out, Mikey, stop stuttering!"

"I was going to say, after Annie dying like that it made me think how short life is, and that we should all be nicer to the people we care about. That's all." Michael looked embarrassed.

"Bloody hell, that's deep for you," Felicity said. "Are you trying to hit on me? I thought you batted for the other side."

Michael was about to respond when he saw Felicity's grin and realised she was joking.

"Mikey, it's nice of you to care and, just for the record, even though I find you bloody annoying most of the time, I care about you too. And Tess and Pops and Mollie. And yes, it's made us all think a lot. Now take this." Felicity handed the tray over to him, whilst she paid for their drinks and flapjacks.

Michael carried the tray downstairs to the others and Felicity followed.

"Come on, you two, we've been waiting. Tessa has some news for us all," Mollie said.

Felicity and Michael sat down and looked at Tessa expectantly.

"Well..." Tessa started.

"Stand up, Tess," Graham told her.

Tessa blushed and stood up. "Well, you know how I got that agent who asked me to send in the synopsis and sample chapters of the book I've finished writing? Well, a publisher is interested in offering me a book deal. I have to meet him for a chat, when we can arrange a suitable date."

Felicity squealed, then ran round and gave Tessa a hug. Mollie hugged her too, Graham kissed her cheek and said how delighted he was, and Michael shook her hand and said well done.

"That's jolly good news. I don't know how you've managed to write a book as well as do the book reviews, your crime series, work in the doctors' surgery *and* look after Amber. And you still find time to come to these meetings, you must be Wonder Woman," Mollie told her.

"It wears me out just thinking about it!" Felicity said.

Tessa grinned, pleased with all the attention. "I'm going to see if I can give up the book reviews; that will help a lot actually. I can concentrate more on my writing then. I'll almost surely have to produce another book or two in the next couple of years."

"Really?" Felicity asked.

"Yes. If a publisher takes you on, they want to know that you can produce further books, so they usually offer a two or three book deal."

"And do you have any ideas for more books?" Graham asked.

"Luckily yes, I've got an idea for an historical romance, so I can start on that soon. Oh God, I'm so nervous about meeting this publisher, I just know I'll be all tongue-tied and won't be able to speak," Tessa said with a grimace.

"Hey, he's just a guy. Try imagining him without his clothes on, that'll make it easier. Oh, second thoughts, if he's a hunk that'll make it more difficult. Oh just try to relax, I'm sure you'll be fine," Felicity said.

"Erm thanks, Flick." Tessa laughed. "Graham, it means leaving you to do the reviews by yourself. Sorry, do you mind?"

"Not at all, it gives me something to do. Don't worry about it."

Michael excused himself to go to the toilet. Merrilies didn't have customer toilets, but Clare allowed the reading group to use their staff loo. A few minutes later, Felicity's phone vibrated.

"Sorry, my phone's just gone off." She answered it, then hung up and threw it on the table with a huff.

"What's wrong?" Graham asked.

"Nothing, Pops, just another bloody silent phone call!"

"What, again?" Tessa said.

"Yes. Remember I mentioned the nuisance phone calls, well, I'm still getting them. When I answer, nobody speaks. I know there's someone there because I can often hear breathing and I sometimes hear other noises – a TV, or road noise or something."

"Have you got their number?" Graham asked.

"No, it's always withheld."

Mollie looked worried. "Maybe you ought to contact the police if you've been getting them for a while now."

"They won't take any notice. No crime's being committed and whoever it is doesn't say anything or threaten me. Hopefully they'll get fed up and stop soon."

Michael came back and asked what was going on. Mollie told him.

"You're still getting them? Why don't you change your number?" he said.

"Why should I? I like this phone, and it would be too much hassle telling everyone my new number. It'll be okay! Now can we get on with the meeting please?"

They ate their flapjacks and drank their coffee while discussing the good and bad points of the latest crime thriller they'd been reading. Tessa loved it and said she hoped to write a crime thriller one day. Michael liked it too. Felicity didn't like the main character, and confessed that she'd skipped ahead to see what happened, so had missed a huge chunk of it.

"Oh Flick! Honestly, what are you like? You should have

stayed with it and you'd probably have liked him in the end," Tessa said.

"What's the point being in a reading group if you don't read the entire book?" Graham shook his head in exasperation.

"Well, you can go back and read the bits you've skipped, young lady," Mollie told her sternly.

The meeting finished, and they voted on the next book to read. They chose one that promised to be 'a humorous tale of life as a village veterinary surgeon, which will have you laughing out loud'.

"You should like this one, Flick, seeing as you work with animals," Michael said.

"Would you like a book about poofs, seeing as you are one?" Felicity asked unkindly.

"Oh here we go again. Felicity, that was out of order. I also thought you might enjoy it because you work with animals. And the word nowadays is gay, not poof, as you jolly well know!" Mollie said, shocked at Felicity's sudden vindictiveness.

"Sorry, Mikey." Felicity had the grace to look as if she meant it. She didn't mean to take her bad mood out on anyone, but she was wound up by the phone call.

With so much tension in the air, Graham didn't suggest an after-meeting drink as he usually did. He wasn't in the mood for playing referee to the kids tonight, and Mollie didn't need it either, so they both said goodnight to the others and left.

Felicity wanted a drink, so she headed for the wine bar up the road. God, she needed a glass of wine. These phone calls were really getting on her nerves, and she hadn't told the whole truth. The call earlier *was* silent, but she'd had one yesterday as she was leaving work, and the caller had said they liked her pink scarf. That had really spooked her because she *had* been wearing a pink scarf. But then she'd decided it was just a lucky guess. Lots of people wore scarves, especially now it was mid-October and the weather had turned colder. Being a girl, the chances were high that her scarf would be pink.

"Stupid kids," she muttered now. "If I bloody get hold of you, you're in big trouble!"

She ended up drinking more than she should and had to get a taxi home instead of the bus, which resulted in her father moaning at her for being drunk, and for the money she wasted on taxis.

"Those driving lessons I bought you for your eighteenth were a total waste of money. You passed your test and haven't driven since! Isn't it about time you got yourself a car? Think of the money you'd save, and it's *your* hard-earned cash now. Thank God it's not coming out of my pocket!"

The mood she was in, her father shouting at her was all she needed. "Oh bloody hell, Daddy, why do you always go on at me?" she shouted back, but she knew there was some truth in what her father said. She did waste a lot of money on taxis to and from work, if she got up too late to get the bus, and home after a night out.

It's not really my fault though, she thought. Mummy's always caught taxis because she doesn't drive, so I've grown up doing the same. Maybe I will get a car. If I'm driving, I won't be able to drink, and that'll please Daddy too.

She stomped upstairs to her room without saying good night to her parents, and her father poured himself another brandy.

Chapter Thirty-Two

Mollie had been thinking about the wedding. Since announcing it to the reading group a few months ago, they hadn't really talked about it much and she didn't quite know how to broach the subject with Graham. He hadn't mentioned it recently, and Mollie was a bit afraid he'd decided he didn't want to get married after all.

So she cooked one of his favourite meals – beef stew and dumplings, followed by warm chocolate sponge and custard – and decided to pluck up the courage and ask him outright.

"Graham, love, are we still going to get married?"

Graham almost spluttered on his red wine. "Of course we are, woman, what makes you think we aren't?

"Because, since we got engaged, we haven't spoken about the wedding at all really. I thought maybe you'd changed your mind and didn't know how to tell me."

"Mollie, you daft thing! I thought you weren't in any hurry. I was leaving it to you to let me know when you were ready."

"Tsk, typical man, I suppose." She laughed. "So when would you like to get married?"

"Oh I don't know, my love, whenever you'd like."

"What sort of answer is that? Well, as soon as possible then. We aren't getting any younger are we, and who knows what's around the corner?" She sighed, as the comment reminded her of Annie dying so young. "It will take a bit of planning. We have to speak to the vicar and everything, so we need a bit of time."

"How about Christmas?" Graham suggested.

"That would be lovely, but we can't get married in church on Christmas Day, and it's an awkward time for people attending. How about New Year?"

"New Year? Yes, why not? That'd be nice – a new year, a new life as husband and wife."

"Really, are you sure about this?" Mollie asked with a frown.

"Positive. You know me well enough now to know that I don't say or do things I don't mean, and when I asked you to marry me, I meant it; just as I mean it'd be wonderful to get married in the New Year." He saw Mollie's happy face and her love for him shining in her eyes. "Go get the calendar and let's choose the nearest weekend to New Year's Day."

She got up and went into the kitchen for the calendar.

Poor Mollie, Graham thought, she needs something to look forward to, to help her get over Annie, and planning a wedding would be the perfect distraction.

He was annoyed with himself for not thinking about the wedding more, but he'd been content with things as they were. A typical man, he needed reminding about such matters. It didn't mean he didn't want to marry Mollie – he did, very much – but if he was honest, he'd rather the two of them just went and did it without any fuss. But he knew Mollie was looking forward to doing it all properly, and was happy to go along with what she wanted.

***

Several weeks later, as the reading group were coming to the end of their Saturday afternoon meeting, Felicity asked, "Can I give anyone a lift home?"

Michael sneered. "No it's okay, we don't all get taxis everywhere, some of us use our legs or buses."

"I meant in my car actually."

"Oh you have a car, do you, Flick? I didn't even know you

could drive. What is it? How long have you had it?" Tessa asked all the right questions.

Felicity grinned, pleased at the interest. "Yes, I thought it was about time I stopped shelling out for taxis, and got myself a run around."

"Bought it yourself, did you?" Michael asked.

Felicity looked a bit sheepish. "Well, no, Daddy bought it for me. I got it a couple of days ago. I've been able to drive since I was eighteen, but never needed a car really."

"No, Daddy paid for taxis everywhere."

"Michael, I've been paying for my own taxis, thank you, which is why I've now got a car to save money."

"That'll put paid to the socialising, Felicity. You can't drink and drive," Graham told her.

"Actually, that was what brought about the car. I got horribly drunk a couple of weeks ago, and Daddy shouted at me for drinking too much and wasting money on taxis. So I thought if I had a car, I couldn't drink because I'd be driving."

"Jolly well done, sounds like you're finally growing up. And I mean that nicely."

Felicity laughed, "Thanks, Moll."

"So," Graham asked, "what is it?"

"It's a BMW, three series, metallic blue cabriolet."

"Very nice, Felicity. Just the right car for the girl about town. Bet the insurance was steep though."

"Erm yes, but–"

"Don't tell us, Daddy paid for it," Michael interrupted.

"Yes he did, it came as part of the present."

"Blimey, how the other half live. Wish I had someone to buy me presents like that." Michael raised his eyebrows and folded his arms with a huff.

"It's for my birthday, Michael, so shut up."

Tessa frowned. "I didn't realise it was your birthday already, have we missed it?"

"No, Tess, it's next month but Daddy said he got a deal on

the car by buying it early."

"Phew, I didn't think we'd missed it, but you had me thinking then," Tessa said.

"Well, thanks for the offer, Felicity, but as you know Graham always drives us," Mollie said.

"That's okay, Moll. Tess, have you got your car tonight?"

"Yep, but thanks for offering."

Felicity turned to Michael. "I'm not giving you a lift if you can't be civil to me."

"I wouldn't get in the car with you anyway. You haven't driven since you were eighteen? No thanks, I'd rather walk."

"Oh for heaven's sake, you two! Can't we have one week when you aren't at each other's throats. It's jolly tiresome!" Mollie snapped.

"Sorry, Mollie, he just winds me up."

"Yeah sorry, but she deserves it."

Tessa couldn't help it, she had to speak up. "No, Michael, sometimes she doesn't but you can't help having a go. It's pure jealousy. Sometimes people have more than we do, that's life. It may not be fair, but life isn't always fair. Get used to it."

Everyone turned to look at Tessa. It was most unlike her to speak out like that. She blushed under their scrutiny.

Felicity clapped. "Go Tessa! Bloody hell, I never knew you had it in you. Where did that come from? And well said, by the way." She glared across at Michael who was sulking.

"Thanks." Tessa looked round the table. "Sorry for the outburst. Amber's become a right handful recently, she talks to me as if I'm pond life most of the time and I'm fed up with it. I come here for a break and a bit of sanity, then I get you two arguing like five-year-olds. I guess I've just had enough."

"Haven't we all?" Graham said.

Mollie decided to say something too. "Can you both please try to get on and not bicker all the time? It's jolly unpleasant for the rest of us. I thought you'd got over that a while back and were getting on well."

"So did I, but then he opens his bloody mouth again." Felicity turned to Michael. "So much for life's too short, let's be nicer to the people we care about. That didn't last long, did it?" she said with a pointed look.

"It's not always me."

"To be fair, Michael, you do usually start it by making some snide comment, which Flick can't help responding to, so can you try to keep your mouth shut?" Tessa asked.

"Right, Felicity, how about you give Michael a lift home?" Mollie said.

Felicity was about to say no way, and Michael was going to say he wouldn't be seen dead in a car with her, but they both saw Mollie's face. Instead, Felicity said, "Okay if I must." And Michael muttered, "Right okay, thanks."

Satisfied, Mollie addressed the three younger members, "Right, now that's sorted, would you like to come for lunch tomorrow and hear about our wedding plans, or do you have things to do? If you can behave that is," she added.

Both Michael and Felicity could make it, but Tessa had to check Amber's plans. After a quick phone call, and finding out her daughter would be going to her friend's for the day, Tessa said thank you, she'd love to go.

"Ooh, we get to see where you live at last," Felicity teased Graham. She smiled and winked at him, to show she wasn't serious.

But Michael looked forward to having a nose round the house Graham now shared with Mollie.

On the way home Graham asked, "Are we sure about this lunch, Moll? You know what I'm like about my privacy. Is it a good idea to let them see where we live?"

"Well, we can't not invite people to visit, love. Goodness knows how you socialised before you met me."

"That was mostly business or family. I never had time for proper friends. And I usually took people out for dinner, not to my home."

"Well, I enjoy socialising so it's something you'll have to get used to. You've got me to help." Mollie gave his arm a squeeze.

"In that case, I can do anything." Graham smiled, still keeping his eyes on the road. "Do you want to get any shopping?"

"Yes please. What shall I cook – roast lamb, pork or beef?"

"Beef please, because I love your Yorkshires that go with it."

"You know jolly well I do Yorkshire puddings with whatever meat we have, so if you'd prefer lamb we'll have that, as it's your favourite."

"No, stick to beef, most people like roast beef unless they're vegetarian and none of them are, I don't think." Graham had a sudden moment's worry as he tried to remember what he'd seen them eating whenever they went for a meal. "They're not, are they?"

"Not now. I know Felicity was for a while, but she gave up because she couldn't have bacon sandwiches," Mollie said.

Graham laughed. "That girl is a treasure, isn't she? I like her best of all; she's got such character."

"She's my favourite too. She makes me laugh. But I like Tess as well. She works so hard and her persistence with her writing is admirable. Most people would have given up after the first few rejections. She's good too, that crime serial she wrote was brilliant."

"Yes, it was. She has such determination, doesn't she? I do like Michael when he's being himself and not rubbing Felicity up the wrong way. I don't know why he does it. Well, I do, because he feels inferior to her, and Tess was right when she said he was jealous."

"I agree, but I do feel sorry for him. It's not been easy for the poor lad. All that rotten business at his work, keeping his secret to himself, not having many friends and knowing he doesn't really fit in anywhere. He is a bit of a nerd, as Felicity said, but if only he could stop trying so hard to be liked. He's

252

quite pleasant when he lets his guard down," Mollie said.

"The trouble is, he thinks he's being amusing when he makes snide comments, but he can't see that nobody else finds it funny. He tries to copy Felicity's wit, but it doesn't work. Then when we chastise him, he feels even more inferior. Oh I don't know, maybe this lunch tomorrow isn't such a good idea after all, they'll be constantly bickering."

"No they won't, because when they arrive I shall say I want us all to have a pleasant lunch so they can behave themselves. They're okay when they come out on the boat for the day."

"True, but Felicity spends most of the time sunbathing and Michael stays with me asking questions."

"There you go then, they'll be ok because they'll be in our home, so they'll be on their best behaviour." Mollie searched in her handbag for a pen and piece of paper to write a quick shopping list.

"Hmph! They'd better be." Graham turned into the supermarket car park.

While Mollie browsed the aisles getting what she needed for the roast lunch, Graham pushed the trolley, hoping the day wouldn't be a disaster.

***

"What's your address?" Felicity asked Michael once they were in the car.

"Oh, I need to get some stuff in town, so can you just drop me by McDonalds on the corner by the furniture shop?"

"Are you sure? It's no problem to take you home."

"I'm sure, Flick. McDonalds will do, thanks."

"Okay, up to you," she said and drove on in silence.

They didn't really say much else to each other throughout the whole journey. Felicity felt a bit awkward alone with Michael. She just couldn't figure him out. Because they'd been in the reading group together for so long, she cared about what happened to him, but he seemed to bring out the worst in her. And when he made his snide comments, she could happily throttle him. But other times he could be quite nice.

She pulled in at the corner and Michael got out. "Thanks, Flick, great little car and your driving's not that bad," he said with a grin.

"Thanks, Mikey. How are you getting to Mollie and Graham's tomorrow?"

"Dunno, bus I suppose."

"I can pick you up if you like and drop you home after?" Felicity offered.

Michael thought for a moment, it would save him having to get two buses. There wasn't a bus direct from his street to where Graham lived, but…

"That'd be great, Flick, thanks. Can you pick me up from the new supermarket that's just opened on the edge of the Faraday industrial estate though? I'll get some flowers to take to them first."

"Oh Mikey, that's thoughtful of you. Okay, I'll be there about eleven, look out for me."

"Right, thanks, see you tomorrow. Bye."

"Yeah, bye," Felicity said.

And with a quick wave, Michael walked off.

See, thought Felicity, we can actually be civil to each other if we try.

Michael walked around the corner and made his way to the bus stops. Damn it, he'd have to get the bus all the way back to his flat now. He didn't really need anything in town, but he couldn't bear to let Flick see the grotty little street his flat was in, not when she lived in one of the smartest places in Bewford. He was glad he'd thought up the idea of getting some flowers from the supermarket, but he'd have to find another excuse when she dropped him off later in the afternoon.

Chapter Thirty-Three

Lunch the next day was a complete success.

When they first arrived, Tessa made Graham give her a tour of his house, which he hated doing, but she said how much she liked it and that he had good taste, which pleased him.

Felicity stayed to help Mollie in the kitchen because, despite what she'd said at the reading group meeting, it wasn't really of interest to her; a house was a house. She was used to luxury and took it for granted.

Michael trailed around after Graham and Tessa. He was very impressed. Coming from quite a poor background – his parents had a simply furnished house without elaborate ornaments or pieces of art – Graham's house was in a different league.

It wasn't showy or ostentatious, but was the home of someone who had money and good taste. It was quite minimalist, but the few pieces he did have were obviously expensive.

"Wow, you must have earned a fortune to have a house like this," Michael said unashamedly.

"As I've told you before, I was well paid for the job I did," Graham said.

"Yes, but *how* did you get to be so well paid?"

Tessa glared at Michael and gave a little shake of her head to try and let him know he shouldn't be asking questions like that.

Graham sighed inwardly and tried to have some patience.

"I don't really like to discuss my financial matters, Michael, but hard work, and a little luck along the way."

"What, winning the lottery?"

"No, but someone I knew years ago offered me a job because he trusted me, and from that, over the next twenty odd years, I became the managing director and built the company up into a very profitable business."

"Huh, it's alright for some!"

"I got a lucky break, but as I've told you before, it wasn't much fun. I sometimes didn't finish work until eleven at night, and had to go away a lot. It was damned hard work," Graham explained.

"But worth it," Michael said grudgingly.

"Of course. I'm comfortably off now, but my personal life suffered. Money isn't the be all."

"No, but it's nice to have enough to buy what you want."

Tessa stepped in to change the subject. "Let's go see what Mollie and Flick are getting up to, shall we?" she said and headed downstairs.

Graham held Michael back. "Michael, it's no good being jealous of what other people have all the time. If you want those things, you've got to work for them."

"Yeah, but no-one's going to give me a job and make me a managing director, are they?"

Graham had to agree. "Probably not. But you could go to evening classes and train for new skills to get a better job. If you want something badly enough, you have to work for it. But as I said, money isn't everything. I'm lucky I've finally met Mollie, but I'm almost sixty-five years old and getting married for the first time. I just didn't have time for a wife and family when I was younger, and I regret that. If I could change things, maybe I'd go for the family, not the money. So think about what I've said, ok?"

"Okay, thanks, I will."

They joined the others downstairs. Mollie gave Graham a

questioning look, but he shook his head then smiled at her.

While they waited for lunch to finish cooking, they had a glass of wine each and played cards. Michael was delighted because he won three games out of five, and decided that maybe *his* luck was changing for the better.

They all thought lunch was delicious. Felicity said Mollie's homemade Yorkshires were the nicest she'd ever tasted. Michael liked the potatoes because they were crunchy on the outside and fluffy inside. "As good as my mum's and hers are the best," he said.

The beef was cooked to everyone's liking, and Tessa enjoyed it all, even the mashed swede and carrot, which she didn't often do. Mollie said it was her secret ingredient that made it so tasty – curry powder.

"You've put curry powder in the swede and carrot?" Tessa asked incredulously.

"Yes. I can't remember where I got the tip from now, but it works, doesn't it?"

"It certainly does. I'm going to do it like that from now on; I might even get Amber to eat it."

"And I'm going to tell Mrs Harris about it too. Great lunch, Mollie." Felicity then asked, "Did you ever think of cooking for a living, Moll?"

"Yes I did, years ago. I dreamt of running my own tea room. One of those old-fashioned Victorian-style ones. I'd have been in my element baking cakes all day long."

"Why didn't you, then?" Tessa asked.

"It just never happened. I got a job straight from college, met Victor, then had Johnny and... Well, you know what happened, then I threw myself into work. Victor had his job and we carried on like that. I've always loved baking, but it just stayed a dream."

"Well, if you did have a tea room, I'd come in every day for your cakes. You're a great cook," Felicity said.

Mollie laughed. "Thanks, Felicity, it's nice to be

appreciated. But you wouldn't buy cakes every day, you're always watching your weight. Now, guess what?"

"What?" Felicity, Michael and Tessa said in unison.

"Do you want to tell them, or shall I?" Mollie asked Graham.

"You can tell them." Graham smiled. He went to put a pot of coffee on.

All three faces looked at Mollie expectantly.

"Graham and I are getting married on Saturday, the third of January next year."

Felicity and Tessa both screamed then laughed delightedly, and Michael said it was great news.

Then came question after question. Have you spoken to the vicar? What about the reception? Are we still invited?

"Of course you jolly well are. More than that, I still want your help. Michael to give me away, and you girls as maids of honour."

"Are you sure you want me to give you away, Mollie? You must have someone else who can do it, family or something?" Michael asked.

Mollie turned to look at him. "Don't you want to do it?"

"Of course I do, but I don't want to be stepping on anyone's toes."

"Don't worry, you're not. My brother lives a long way away and isn't in the best of health, so I don't expect him to come to the wedding. I have nieces but no nephews, and I lost touch with most of my friends after Victor died. I have my church friends of course, but I'd like someone young and up to the job, like you."

Michael blushed with pleasure and said he'd be delighted.

Graham carried a tray of coffees into the room.

The two girls were chatting about what colour dresses they'd wear. "Are you going to wear white, Moll?"

"No I think I'm a bit too old for that, Felicity; I thought maybe a nice cream, or pale blue suit of some sort. I'll have to

258

go shopping."

Graham groaned and the girls laughed.

"Hey," Tessa said, "if you like, we could make a day of it; we three women go shopping together. Flick and I can help you choose your outfit, what do you think?"

"I think that's a jolly good idea, but we might need more than one day, maybe we should make a weekend of it. Is that alright with you, love?" Mollie turned to Graham.

"Of course it is."

"I'll need to sort out something with Amber though," Tessa said and took a sip of her coffee.

"If you can't find a sitter, bring her along. Little girls love that sort of thing, don't they?" Mollie asked.

"Not Amber any more. All she's interested in is hanging around the mall with her friends, chatting up boys."

Felicity was shocked. "At her age! But she's only thirteen."

"Nearly fourteen, going on twenty. I expect she'll go to my parents for the weekend, she doesn't mind spending time with them for some reason," Tessa said.

"Probably because they spoil her rotten. What about you, Felicity?" Mollie asked.

"I'll need to get a weekend off work. I'll check tomorrow, see when I've got a clear weekend and let you know. I can't wait, it'll be great fun." Felicity clapped her hands excitedly.

"Erm, I'll need to wear a suit, won't I? I only have one, my interview suit, and it's not very good," Michael said with a worried frown.

"You'll need a new one then. I'll pay for your suit, Michael. Girls, the dresses are on me. I'm taking care of the wedding costs so just go shopping and have a great time," Graham said.

"Does that mean you're coming with me to choose my suit?"

Felicity laughed aloud at Michael's horrified face.

Graham laughed too. "No, Michael, don't worry. You can either buy yourself a suit, give me the receipt and I'll give you the money back, or I'll give you some money upfront and you can get one with that."

"Oh, okay, thanks very much."

The rest of the afternoon passed very pleasantly as they talked about the wedding and the reading group. Tessa wondered if Mollie and Graham would still attend after they were married.

"Of course we will, we love our group. We might go on honeymoon for a week, but after that it'll be back to normal."

Graham agreed with Mollie and assured them they'd continue with the meetings.

After offering to help tidy up – an offer Mollie adamantly refused – Felicity said it was time she left and thanked Mollie again for a wonderful lunch. Tessa said she'd also better get going as she still had some writing to do, and Michael got up as well because Felicity was giving him a lift.

They all said their goodbyes with kisses and hugs, and left.

"Right, Mikey," Felicity said, "where am I dropping you?"

Michael wasn't prepared with a destination. "Oh, err, umm."

"Come on, you can't have forgotten where you live."

"No, but I don't want you to take me home, I want to go to..."

Felicity turned to look at him. "Why don't you want me to take you home? What's wrong?"

Michael sighed and decided to come clean. "Because I don't want you to see where I live, okay!"

"Oh, Michael. You have to stop this. I don't care where you live. I just want to get you home, so give me the bloody address."

He reluctantly told her the address and she drove there in silence. Once outside his flat, she asked, "Do you live here on your own or with someone?"

"On my own."

"Well, what the hell are you ashamed of then? You're better

260

than me; I still live with my parents, for God's sake. At least you're standing on your own two feet."

"Yeah, but look at it, it's grotty compared to where you live."

"Michael, it's home. Okay it's not as posh as where my folks live, but it's your flat, you live here all on your own and you manage. I think that's great."

"Really?" Michael looked as if he didn't believe her.

"Yes. Look at me, living off Daddy for the whole of my life so far. It's only been this last year that I've got myself a job and earned my own money. Daddy even bought my car, as you pointed out."

"Yeah but at least you've got one," Michael said.

"If my dad hadn't bought it, I wouldn't have. It would take me ages to save up for a car of my own. I spend all my money as soon as I've earned it, I bet you don't."

"Well, no, I do have quite a bit saved up."

"There you go then. You're more grown-up than me in many ways. But you have to stop this jealous bitching, and let people see the real you. If friends are worth being friends, they'll accept you completely for what you are, not what you've got or where you live. It shouldn't matter whether you live in a castle or a cardboard box." She ran her hands through her hair. "God, you are infuriating at times. Right, can we stop all this nonsense and be a bit nicer to each other from now on? I know you can do it, look at the other day when you came and helped me get the drinks and stuff. Remember what you said?"

"Yeah." Michael looked anywhere but at Felicity.

"Well, remember that when you're about to say something mean, will you?"

"I'm sorry, Flick, I just feel so inferior compared to you and Graham." Michael stared out of the window.

"Why, for heaven's sake? You have no need to. Look what Graham did when he helped you with that bully at work. He's a good guy is Pops."

"I know he is, you all are, I wonder what I'm doing there sometimes, you're all so much better than me."

"Who says?"

"What?"

"Who said we were better than you?" Felicity asked.

"Well, err, no-one, but..."

"Exactly, no-one. It's all in your head, Michael, and the sooner you stop feeling like that the better it'll be. You're making yourself miserable as well as us, you know."

Michael shifted in his seat, his head down.

Felicity sighed. "Sorry for the lecture, but now that's out of the way, can we see you being yourself? You're not inferior; you have as much to offer as the rest of us, okay?"

"Okay. Thanks, Flick."

"You're welcome. Now scram, see you at Thursday's meeting."

"Yeah, see ya. Bye."

He got out of the car, and Felicity watched as he let himself into his flat, then she drove away. I'm in the wrong job, she thought, I should be a bloody counsellor!

Chapter Thirty-Four

The following evening Felicity left work quite late. She occasionally worked until eight, and when she got to the car park, there were only a few cars left belonging to the staff who were still in the building.

She was about to get in the car when she spotted a note under her windscreen wiper. Tutting, she got out, removed it, and tossed it onto the back seat along with her work folder.

She arrived home, collected her things from the car and went into the house. "Hi Mummy," she called.

"Hi darling, had a good day?"

"Yes, thanks. We managed to re-home those puppies I told you about, so that was good. I'm starving, what's for dinner?"

"Mrs Harris has made a moussaka. Why don't you have a shower while I warm it up?"

Her mother said this every night in case Felicity stank of animals.

"Mm, I will in a mo', just need to look over my notes." Felicity sat at the table and got out her folder. As she did so, the piece of paper that had been on her windscreen fell on the table. She opened it up and stared at the words written there. She gasped, closed it, and opened it again.

YOU LOOKED NICE TODAY. I LIKE YOU IN GREEN.

Felicity's heart thumped like crazy in her chest, and the colour drained from her face as she looked down at her jade shirt. Oh my God!

She realised that things had become more serious. It

obviously wasn't kids messing about, but who could it be? Whoever it was, they must be watching her to know she was wearing green.

Her mind raced as she thought back to where she'd been that day.

Lunchtime she'd gone to the supermarket to get a sandwich and a magazine, was it someone there? She was a regular customer. But how could they have got hold of her phone number? Okay, who knew her number? Her friends and family, Jo and Clare from Merrilies, and Mollie, Graham and Tess from the reading group. Had she given it out when browsing online websites? But even if she had, they couldn't have put the note on her windscreen.

Her mother walked back into the kitchen and saw Felicity's pale face.

"Anything wrong, darling? Are you feeling okay? You look a bit peaky."

"I'm fine, Mummy, just tired; we're quite busy at work at the moment." Felicity hid the note under the table.

"Well, why don't you go up and have that shower, then come and eat your dinner in the sitting room with Daddy and me?"

"Okay."

Felicity put the piece of paper into her folder and took it upstairs to her room. It had freaked her out quite a bit. Phone calls were one thing, but this had moved up a scale. What should she do – phone the police, or wait and see what else happened? She couldn't tell her parents. Bloody hell, Daddy would go berserk and march straight down to the police station! She loved her father, but he could be rather bombastic at times.

Mummy would just panic and worry herself stupid, and her friends would think it was funny, especially Celia. She'd want her own stalker too. Felicity grinned at that thought, but soon sobered again and tried to think clearly.

Graham and Mollie, that's who she'd ask for advice. Pops would know what to do, and Moll would be all motherly and sympathetic. They'd been a great help to Michael that time when he was being blackmailed.

Feeling relieved at her decision, she went into her en-suite and decided to have a bath rather than a shower. She switched on the tap and added a huge capful of relaxing lavender and camomile oil.

***

Wednesday evening, Mollie answered the knock at the front door. "Felicity, my dear, how are you?"

"Bloody cold. Hasn't it got chilly recently?" Felicity said, stamping her feet and then removing her shoes.

"It has, we've turned the heating up. Poor Graham really feels the cold. I usually don't, but I must admit to being a tad chilly. Come on in and sit yourself down, would you like a glass of wine?"

"Just a small one, Moll, please. I'm driving."

"Okay, you can have a slice of cake as well, that'll help soak it up." Mollie went into the kitchen and left Felicity sitting with Graham in the lounge, making small talk.

When Mollie came back, Graham said, "So, young lady, what's bothering you? Mollie knew there was something wrong, she could tell by your voice when you phoned yesterday."

Felicity took a deep breath, then said in a wavering voice, "You know those phone calls I've been getting, well, something else has happened now. Monday night I got this, and today I got this."

Felicity gave the first note to Graham, then gave Mollie another note, which said,

I PREFER YOUR HAIR DOWN, IT'S SEXIER.

Mollie swapped notes with Graham, then looked up at

Felicity. "Oh my goodness, Felicity, you poor girl. Come here, lovey."

Felicity went and sat beside Mollie, who gave her a cuddle and kissed the top of her head.

"You must be terrified," Mollie said.

"I am a bit scared. Well, more than a bit now, but I'm also bloody angry that some sicko is doing this. The phone calls were one thing, but this is ridiculous."

"Have you told your parents?" Graham asked, giving her back the notes.

"No, Daddy would have an absolute fit and start raging about when he gets hold of whoever is responsible, blah blah blah. You're the first people I've told."

"Right, you need to think, Felicity. Think hard about everyone who's got your phone number."

"I have, and apart from you and the girls at Merrilies, my family and friends and HR at work, no-one else has it." Felicity put the notes back in her bag.

"Where were you when the notes were left?" Mollie asked.

"The first one on Monday was in the car park at work, and the second one I found when I came out of the supermarket at lunchtime."

"So, could it be a colleague?" Graham said.

"No. Nobody has my number except my boss and HR, and it wouldn't be them."

"Well, it's got to be somebody. Do you think it's time to contact the police?" Mollie asked.

Felicity ran her hands through her hair. "Oh I don't know. No not yet. I haven't been attacked or anything and the notes aren't sinister as such, so they probably won't take any action anyway."

"Right then, here's what I suggest you do," Graham said. "Write down the time of any phone calls, and what's said if anything, and keep all the notes you receive. Then, if in a month you are still being hassled, go to the police and show them the evidence. I'll come with you if you want."

"Thanks, Pops. That sounds like the best thing. Hopefully whoever's doing this will soon get fed up with their stupid games and pack it in."

"But they might not, Felicity, it could get worse. So if anything more sinister happens, you jolly well go to the police. Please don't put yourself at risk. And keep us up to date with what's happening, it'll help if someone else can corroborate your story," Mollie said.

"I will. Thanks, you two. I don't know what I'd do without you. I'm sure that goes for Tess and Michael too, you've helped us all out at some point, it's much appreciated." Felicity finished her cake and drank the rest of her wine.

Mollie tutted. "It's no problem; we're very fond of you all. We like to think of you as family, the children we didn't have. Don't we, love?"

Graham nodded his agreement.

"Now, tell us about your job, are you still enjoying it?"

"Oh Moll, it's the best job I've ever had; well, the only one so far, but you know what I mean." As Felicity enthusiastically told them what she'd done at work, her recent problems were put to the back of her mind for a while.

***

The next evening at Merrilies, Jo waited until all the members of the reading group were present then approached their table.

"Hi everyone, I've got something to show you. Come with me a minute."

They followed her to the left of the shop near the stairs, where the children's area was, and looked up at the newly-erected sign she pointed to.

Tears sprang to Mollie's eyes as she saw the lilac sign with "Annie's Corner" written on it. Underneath in smaller writing

267

it said, "In Memory of a Special Little Girl Annie Matthews, Forever in Our Hearts."

Tessa was the first to speak. "Oh Jo, that's lovely, it really is. Do her parents know?"

"Yeah, I asked their permission when I first got the idea, and they said Annie would have loved it. She was a big part of the shop after all."

"Yes, she was. She came in everyday, didn't she?" Tessa asked.

"More or less, apart from the times when she was poorly. So it seemed only right to name the children's area after her," Jo said.

Even Graham felt choked up, but he managed to say, "That's a wonderful gesture, Jo. I'm sure Annie would approve."

Felicity put her arm around Mollie as they went back to their table. "You okay, Moll?"

"Yes I'm fine thanks, love. It just upset me a bit, although it's a lovely thing to do. I still miss seeing her little face."

"I think of her sometimes too. Remember how she used to say my name?"

Mollie laughed. "Yes, Fecility. She was so funny, bless her."

"She was. Now we'll always remember her, and other people will see the sign and wonder about her too."

"I'd never forget her anyway, sign or no sign. Lots of things make me think of her, like when I see dolphins on the TV for instance. Such a shame she never got to swim with them, she was so looking forward to it." Mollie sniffed and searched her pocket for a tissue.

"Well, maybe one day one of us can do it for her. Right, I'm going up to get the drinks, Tess, you coming to help me?"

Tessa went with Felicity for the usual drinks and flapjacks while the others sat down and got their books out, ready to get the meeting underway.

Chapter Thirty-Five

A couple of weeks later, Felicity got a taxi to Merrilies because she was going to meet some friends in the wine bar after the reading group meeting. She hadn't had a decent night out for ages, so had left the car at home so she could drink.

She was still receiving silent phone calls, and she'd had one where somebody did speak. But she didn't recognise the disguised voice of the person who'd whispered huskily down the phone, "How are you today, sexy?"

What worried her most, though, was that she'd had a note delivered to her home. There wasn't a stamp on it, so it'd been hand-delivered. That meant someone had either obtained her address from somewhere or, even more scarily, followed her home to see where she lived.

She'd told Graham and Mollie, and Mollie thought she should go to the police immediately. Graham said to hold off a bit longer and see what else happened. Luckily, as it was addressed to Felicity, her mother hadn't opened the note, and when she'd enquired about it Felicity told her it was from Clare at Merrilies, to do with the reading group. Eleanor had accepted this without question.

After a fun meeting where everyone seemed to be in good spirits – even Michael – Felicity said her goodbyes and set off for the wine bar. She buttoned up her coat and pulled her scarf around her ears to ward off the chilly winter evening air.

She stopped walking because she thought she heard a noise behind her, and looked round, but there was no-one there, so she carried on.

Then she heard it again; definite footsteps, hurrying up behind her. Felicity was so scared she felt sick and got the high pitched sound in her ears that signified she was going to faint. She took a few deep breaths, then anger overtook her. No-one has the right to try to frighten me like this, she thought, so she decided to confront her pursuer.

She stopped abruptly and swung round, coming face-to-face with...Michael.

"YOU!" she screamed and launched herself at him, pummelling his chest.

Michael, taken by surprise, tried to grab hold of her arms to stop her hitting him, but that only made her worse and she kicked out at him as well.

"OW! Flick, for God's sake, what's got into you?"

"It was you all along. How could you do that to me? You bastard!" she yelled at him.

Michael managed to grab her, and he threw her away from him, then bent down and rubbed his shin where she'd kicked him.

"Flick!" He held his hands up to ward her off as she came at him again. "I have no idea what you're ranting about, what the hell's wrong with you?"

"It's you who's been stalking me," Felicity said, her breath coming in sharp gasps.

"WHAT!" Michael was incredulous. "I have NOT!"

"Why were you following me then?"

"I wasn't following you! I decided to go for a quick drink at the wine bar, saw you in front of me, and tried to catch you up. Didn't you hear me call you?" he asked, still rubbing his leg.

"No. I thought I heard something, but when I looked, there was no-one there. Then I heard someone running up behind me." Felicity didn't know what to believe.

"Yes, me. I dropped my scarf and bent down to pick it up, then had to run to catch you up, you idiot."

Felicity saw the look on his face and knew he was telling the truth. She started crying, with relief that he wasn't the stalker, but with fear that someone was still out there. She tried to pull herself together because she didn't want to turn up at the wine bar with her make-up all smudged.

Michael offered her a tissue, saying, "It's clean. Flick, what on earth's going on? Why did you attack me like that?"

"Can we get to the wine bar please? I need a drink," Felicity said, blowing her nose. "I'll tell you on the way."

Michael limped and stopped to rub his leg. He flexed it then continued walking.

Felicity felt bad about kicking him. "I'm really sorry if I hurt you, Mikey. I didn't mean to, well, I did, but I thought you were someone else."

As they walked, she told him about the notes and phone calls.

Michael couldn't believe it. "You mean the calls are still happening, and you're getting notes as well? Flick, you really must go to the police. What if this person really does follow you one night?"

"Pops said to hang on a bit longer, but after tonight I think I will tell the police. I know it was only you, but you're right, what if it *had* been the stalker? I've got Monday afternoon off. I'll phone Pops later and see if he'll come with me."

When they got to the wine bar, Felicity tidied herself up in the ladies loo, then had a drink with Michael while waiting for her friends to turn up. When Celia arrived, she teased them both, asking if Michael was Flick's new boyfriend. She soon shut up when Michael said, "Actually, although Flick's a lovely girl, I don't fancy her. I'm gay."

Felicity was amazed at how open he was about it, and was glad he'd found the confidence not to hide who he was any more.

Michael left soon after, but Felicity stayed all evening. And probably because of the events earlier in the evening and

271

because she hadn't gone on a binge for ages, she drank far more than she'd intended.

**

The following day, Graham nipped into town to look at iPads. He was introducing Mollie to the wonders of the internet, and wanted to get her an iPad so she didn't have to share his. He'd left her at home, happily baking.

He stopped for lunch at the tea room opposite Merrilies for a warming bowl of soup. As he paid, he said to Fran the owner, "If you ever think of selling, let me know."

"Well, it's funny you should say that," Fran whispered, and invited Graham into the sitting room at the back of the shop for a chat.

An hour later, Graham entered Merrilies and walked around looking for Jo. He found her serving in the café. "Jo, can I have a quick word in private please?"

Wondering what he wanted to talk about, she asked Hermione to take over, and led him to the staff room.

"Now remember," Graham said as they came out again, "not a word to anyone, it's still early days. I just wanted you to know what was going on."

Jo grinned and on an impulse hugged him. "My lips are sealed."

When Graham got home, Mollie told him Felicity had phoned, and relayed details of the previous night's incident. Graham laughed then said, "I know it's not a laughing matter, but the image of Felicity's wrath being taken out on poor Michael is very funny. That poor girl. I guess it's about time we took action. I'll call her back tonight when she's finished work."

Chapter Thirty-Six

Monday afternoon, Felicity arrived at Graham and Mollie's later than arranged, and rang the doorbell several times.

"Okay, okay, I'm coming," Mollie shouted.

She opened the door and said, "Felicity, what's all the noise about?"

"Oh Moll, you'll never believe it!" Felicity flew in and dropped her bag on the sofa in the lounge.

Graham looked at her flushed face and asked, "Where've you been, young lady? I was expecting you two hours ago. I thought we were meant to be going to the police station?"

"No need now, it's all done and sorted out," Felicity said.

"What? Okay, have a seat and start at the beginning. Mollie, would you put the kettle on, love?"

"I will, but don't start without me. I want to hear this. Come and help me, Felicity."

Once they'd made the tea and were sitting down again, Felicity explained that as she'd been leaving work earlier than her usual lunch hour time, she'd caught someone putting a note on her windscreen.

Mollie's hand flew to her mouth. "Oh you didn't! What happened? Who was it?"

"It was Neil; a guy who'd asked me out ages ago when I first started working there. I turned him down because he isn't my type. He's a bit, well, a bit intense."

"And was it him making the phone calls too? How did he get your details? Why did he do it?" There were dozens of questions Mollie wanted answering.

273

Graham just sat and listened.

"When I saw him, I tried to grab him, but he ran off so I shouted for help. A couple of the men came out to see what was going on, and they ran after him and caught him." She took a sip of tea then continued, "They took Neil back inside and, once I'd explained what'd been happening, my boss called the police."

"Oh Felicity, thank God he's been caught! But how did he get hold of your phone number?" Mollie asked.

"Really bloody easily, actually! He just waited until I was out in the kennels with the animals, took my phone out of my bag and got the number."

"But don't you have a pin code on it to stop someone getting into your phone?" Graham asked.

Felicity looked embarrassed. "No I didn't. My phone is usually with me, except occasionally at work. I even take my bag to the loo, but I don't take it when I'm out with the animals obviously."

"Oh Felicity, you silly girl! Isn't your bag in a locker or hidden away?" Mollie said.

"No, I just put it under my desk. I thought it was okay there. No members of the public come into the office area, and you think you can trust your work colleagues, don't you? I've pin-locked my phone now though." She smiled sheepishly.

"So, what happened?" Graham asked.

"The police came and really told him off. They've put it on record, but because it's his first ever offence and no real harm came to me, I agreed not to pursue it. The police said that if I *did* want to take it further, he'd go to court, and the court could issue a restraining order against him. And because of the anti-stalking laws, he could go to prison for six months. But I don't want to take it further; he's going to lose his job, that's enough."

"So he should. Serves him right! Thank heavens it's all over, you must be so relieved," Mollie said.

"I am. I'm glad he was caught because I'd have been terrified when I'd read the latest note." Felicity finished her tea and put the cup on the coffee table.

"What did it say?" Graham asked.

"I like your silky pyjamas."

"Oh my God, Felicity, does that mean he's been watching you at home?" Mollie was horrified.

"Must have been. I know he's been to the house once before, because he put a note through the door. But to know what I wear at night, he must have stood outside, watching me through the windows." She shuddered.

"You should have jolly well taken it further, Felicity."

"No. I wanted to initially, but after I'd calmed down, I felt a bit sorry for him really. He's just a sad pathetic creep. He looked so scared when the police came and he won't get a reference, so finding another job will prove difficult."

Graham put his arm around her and gave her a quick hug. "Well done, you, I agree that he's probably been punished enough. Sounds like the police put the fear of God into him."

Felicity laughed. "They did. I've never seen someone so frightened. He kept saying, 'I've never been in trouble before.' Even one of the policemen felt sorry for him in the end, and offered him a lift home, but he refused, saying he couldn't turn up at home in a police car."

"Is that an end to it now then?" Mollie asked. She cleared their empty cups onto the tea tray.

"I think so. One of the policemen, Greg, has taken my phone number and said he'll call me tonight to make sure I'm okay." She blushed as she said this and it wasn't lost on Mollie.

"Ah, Greg, was it? First name terms." Mollie smiled. "I suspect he's phoning for another reason too. So did you like him?"

"Yes I did actually. I'm hoping he'll ask me out for a drink. God, he was lovely, Moll, a real..."

Graham interrupted. "What did you call someone once?

275

Ah, a stud muffin. That's it?"

Felicity laughed out loud. "Yes, Pops, he was a stud muffin. Ooh, he was bloody gorgeous. Tall, with dark hair and green eyes and very fit."

Mollie laughed too. "Well, I hope he does ask you out and that it's the start of something wonderful. You deserve it."

"Steady on, Moll, I'm not getting serious about anyone yet, not until I'm at least thirty! But if he doesn't ask me out, I'll ask him."

"He may be married, young lady, have you thought about that?" Graham said.

"He wasn't wearing a ring, so I don't think so. I'll let you know if he phones me tonight. I'll text you."

"I wonder what your father's going to say about all this," Graham said.

"Oh bloody hell, I'd forgotten about him! He'll be livid and tell me to take it further. You know what he's like. Well, you don't, but I've told you about him often enough. I'm going to *have* to tell him, because he'll find out from his friends in the police force, and then I'll be in trouble for not telling him. Bugger it!" Felicity stamped her foot.

"How are you going to tackle him?" Mollie asked, thinking, rather you than me.

"Don't know. I'll make sure his brandy and newspaper are ready when he arrives home, wait until he's relaxed, and then tell him I suppose. I better get going. Oh hell, wish me luck," Felicity said with a grimace.

They both wished her luck, kissed her, and Mollie saw her to the door.

"Poor Felicity," she said as she came back into the lounge. "I wouldn't want to deal with her father. He won't be relaxed once she's told him her news, that's for certain."

"Oh I'm sure Felicity can handle her father. She can wrap most men round her little finger. I bet that policeman *will* ask her out," Graham said.

"I bet he will too. She's an attractive young girl."

"And she has a lovely personality."

"Yes she's really bubbly. I'm jolly glad that awful man was caught. There are some strange people in this world, aren't there? Right, how about a game of cards?" Mollie suggested.

"Why not? Another cup of tea would be nice, and a slice of cake?" Graham asked hopefully.

Mollie tutted at him. "You'll spoil your dinner."

"Not if we have it a bit later, and I'll just have a small slice of cake. You shouldn't be such a good cook, then I wouldn't want to eat all the time."

Mollie laughed and went into the kitchen.

***

Clare was back to her old self and, despite her adamant statement that she'd never trust another man, she'd started dating again. But she was being very cautious, and hadn't told him she was the owner of Merrilies. She didn't want him going near the shop; she couldn't risk that again. Maybe in time if it developed into something more permanent, she'd open up.

She and Jo were getting ready for Christmas. It was one of their favourite times of year. They loved decorating the shop and seeing their customers excited about the coming festivities.

They were going to have late night shopping evenings, and offer mince pies and glasses of mulled wine, as well as non-alcoholic drinks for people who were driving. They were also inviting a local author along to sign copies of his first novel. They'd made Tessa promise that when her book came out, she'd do a signing evening too.

"As long as you prominently display my book for me. I want it everywhere; face out on the shelves and on the tables too," she'd said laughing.

"Of course we will, and we'll ask Rob at the paper to do a

piece on you," Jo said.

Clare came downstairs with a pile of books for the New Releases table and smiled across at Jo who was behind the till. "Any idea how Mollie and Graham's wedding preparations are coming along?" she asked.

"Everything's going well, apparently. The church and reception are booked and the women are going shopping for their outfits soon."

"I bet it'll be a lovely wedding. I'm still not sure about leaving the shop whilst we attend though."

"It'll be fine. Our employees have worked here for ages now and all of them are trustworthy. Stella and Hermione are brilliant. Besides, we can't *not* go. If it wasn't for us starting the reading group, Mollie and Graham would never have met, so we have to attend. I'm looking forward to it, it'll be a wonderful day," Jo said.

"Yes, I'm looking forward to it too; I'm just worried about the shop." Clare stacked books on the table.

"I know, but it's only one day. We could close, but we'd lose too much business. I know we've never left it with neither of us here before, but we've never had a situation where we both wanted to attend something. Stop fussing, Clare, it'll be fine."

"You're right, sorry for being an old fusspot. Okay, as a wedding present, I was thinking of getting them a silver photo frame from us both. They can put a wedding photo in it, what do you think?"

"That's a great idea. I couldn't think what to get them. At their age, they have everything already. Yeah, we can have a look around for a really nice one. I'll look in the jewellers down the road on my next day off," Jo said as she looked up a book title on the computer.

"I can't wait to see what Mollie, Tess and Flick are going to wear," Clare said.

"Me neither. Bet they'll look lovely. Wonder if they'll mind the newspaper doing a piece on them. Something along the lines of, '*Couple Find Love at Reading Group Meeting*' or '*Merrilies Wedding*'."

"Oh I don't know, Jo, they may not like the fuss. You know how upset Graham got when Flick did those photo placemats of him from his band days." Clare moved a few books around on the table as she talked.

Jo laughed out loud. "That was hilarious! He was okay about it after a while."

"Yes, but I think he's quite a private person."

"But they're getting married, that's not private, is it? I'll ask them. If he says no, I won't do it. But it'll be good publicity."

"You should have been in PR, do you know that?" Clare laughed.

"Hmm, that's an idea."

"Don't you dare leave. I don't know what I'd do without you. This shop wouldn't be half as good if you weren't here."

"Thanks. We've come a long way, and a lot's happened, hasn't it?" Jo said thoughtfully.

"Yep and I wouldn't change a thing." Clare then looked sad for a moment, and added, "Well, I would. I wish Annie was still alive, and that business with Dan hadn't happened."

Jo put her arm around her best friend. "I miss Annie too. We'll never forget her. But come on, we've got a whole future ahead of us, starting with Christmas and a New Year wedding!"

"Yes, you're right," Clare said. "We've got a lot to be thankful for, and a lot to look forward to. Now, where do you think we should put the Christmas tree?"

Chapter Thirty-Seven

The three female members of the reading group were having a great time shopping.

They'd scoured the stores, had a slap-up lunch in a nearby hotel restaurant, and were now in a dress shop where Mollie was trying on outfits.

"This is the one, Moll," Felicity said, as Mollie stood looking at herself in the full- length mirror.

"Do you think?"

"Oh yes, Mollie, you look wonderful," Tessa told her.

She had on a champagne-coloured suit, which fitted her perfectly. The skirt was the right length, just below the knee, and the jacket, with its fabric covered ball buttons, was beautifully cut. It showed off her waist, even though Mollie was quite a generously-sized lady, and the colour complimented her white hair and blue eyes.

The shop assistant brought her a hair fascinator to complete the look, but Mollie felt she was too old to wear something like that, and the girls tactfully suggested that maybe a hat would look better. The assistant found a small sinamay hat, with an upturned brim and flower and feather detail. Mollie usually hated wearing hats, especially ones that came down over her face, but she quite liked this one and it matched the suit well.

"Okay, I'll take it, thank you," Mollie told the assistant, and the woman took the items to the counter to wrap them.

"Right, that's me almost sorted, I just need shoes. We need to get you girls something." Mollie opened her bag to find her purse.

"What about that department store over there, shall we have a look?" Tessa asked, pointing across the road.

"A department store? I'm not sure they'll have anything, but we can look if you like." Felicity shrugged.

So Mollie paid for her purchases and they marched across the road.

The ground floor had women's clothes – ordinary items like trousers, skirts blouses and cardigans – but there was a sign stating "Bridal and Evening Wear on First Floor" so they took the escalator up.

Tessa gasped as she saw the racks of beautiful dresses. There were glittery dresses, sequined dresses, silky dresses and satin dresses. "Ooh look at these! Come on, let's have a rummage," she said and disappeared into the nearest rack.

Two hours later, after a lot of trying on, Felicity and Tessa had their outfits. They'd chosen long strapless ballgowns in a pale blue colour, with fluffy faux-fur bolero-style shrugs in a deeper blue. They'd even found shoes as well, gorgeous silver diamante strapped sandals, and they were going to wear little silver tiaras to complete the look.

Mollie had also found some shoes to match her suit and hat.

They stopped in the department store's café for a much needed cup of tea and piece of cake, which they agreed wasn't half as good as Mollie's.

"I can't believe we got everything we wanted in this one shop. I would never have thought of looking somewhere like this," Felicity said.

"Designer shops more your style, eh?" Tessa teased.

"Yes, usually Tess, but I tell you what, this has changed my mind. I'll be looking in places like this from now on, how bloody marvellous!"

"Oh girls, you are going to look beautiful, really beautiful." Mollie had tears in her eyes.

Felicity smiled at her. "We are *all* going to look beautiful, you as well, Moll. Hell, I hope Pops doesn't have a fit when he sees the bank statement! We've had rather an indulgent day."

"No he jolly well won't! He told me we could spend as much as we wanted and not to worry about the cost. He gave Michael two hundred and fifty pounds to buy a suit with, and your outfits were a bit less than that each, so he can't complain."

"Well, tell him thank you from me, he's very generous," Tessa said.

"I will. But he wanted to pay for the whole wedding. He won't even let me pay for anything out of my savings. He's had years of not spending his money on anyone or anything much, so I think it's nice for him to be able to treat people for once."

"Aw he's such a sweetie," Felicity said with affection.

Mollie said, "I never knew how well off he was when we first met. Just as well, I'd have run a mile and thought I wasn't good enough for him."

"Oh Moll, you're good enough for anyone, you're lovely. Now, let's get you home, you look done in." Felicity took Mollie's purchases from her.

"I am rather worn out, to tell the truth. I haven't shopped like that for years. I did enjoy it, but I couldn't do it again in a hurry. I need a lie down." Mollie surrendered the bags quite willingly.

They left the café, and back in the store, Tessa asked a woman behind one of the tills if she could order a taxi for them.

Graham had told them not to drive in. "You'll have to find somewhere to park, then walk back to the car park with all the shopping; much better to get a taxi," he'd said.

Good old Pops, Felicity thought now as they waited for the taxi. She loved Mollie and Graham to bits; they were both very dear to her.

They dropped Mollie at home and helped her in with the

shopping.

"Thanks, Pops, we've had a wonderful day," Felicity said, her eyes shining.

"Yes thanks, Graham, you've been more than generous," Tessa added.

"You mean you've done it all in one day? I expected it to take a couple of days of hard shopping at least," he joked.

"No, we got the lot today, so no peeking. You can't see it until the day of the wedding. Which reminds me, what are you doing the night before the wedding, Moll? You can't stay in the same house together. Pops can't see you in your outfit before you get married."

"Tsk, we're not worried about superstition like that," Mollie said.

"Oh, but you have to do it properly. Tess, tell them."

"Well, yes, it is tradition for the man not to see the bride beforehand," Tessa agreed.

"Mummy said you could stay with us, if you like. You too, Tess, and Amber. We could help each other get ready. I could get the hairdresser to come and do our hair for us, and we could have our make-up done too. Go on, say you will, it'd be lovely." Felicity looked at them excitedly.

"I don't mind if that's what you'd like to do," Graham said.

"Tell your mother thank you, and I'll think about it. Now scoot, that taxi's still waiting, and thanks for a lovely time. I'm tired, but it was a really nice day."

"Okay, let me know, Moll, because I'll need to book the hairdresser and make-up girls in advance. Thanks again for a super day. Thanks, Pops."

The girls got back in the taxi, and, after waving goodbye, Mollie went into the lounge and flopped down on the sofa. "I've had a wonderful day, they are such fun those two, but I am thoroughly worn out. Think I'll have a bit of supper and an early night with my book, if you don't mind."

Graham kissed her. "Of course I don't mind. You sit there

and I'll make supper."

Mollie ate her meal, then retired to bed with her book, but she'd only read a few pages when she fell asleep.

A couple of hours later, when Graham went up to get ready for bed, he found Mollie sleeping soundly. He gently took the book out from under her arm and looked down at his soon-to-be wife. He couldn't believe how lucky he was to have found her this late in life. He loved her dearly, and genuinely looked forward to their wedding day.

Chapter Thirty-Eight

The Christmas period passed in a haze of activity with everyone busy in one way or another.

Merrilies was busy with shoppers looking for presents for those "hard to buy for" relatives and friends. Books were always a good choice.

Clare and Jo were working harder than ever. There might be a recession, but people were still buying plenty of books.

Mollie and Graham were going through last minute details for their forthcoming wedding. Mollie had made their wedding cake herself, even though Graham protested loudly at this.

"But I want to do it. It'll keep me busy, stop me fretting about the event. Besides, it's quite unusual for the bride to make her own cake, it'll make our wedding extra special," she said.

Graham had kissed her and said, "If that's what you want, my love, then you do it."

They'd had a rehearsal, dressed in their ordinary clothes, and everyone knew what their roles were. Although it was a small church with only a handful of people attending, Mollie still wanted things done properly.

Apart from Graham's sister and brother-in-law, no other relatives were attending. Most of their relations were too old, too unwell, or too far away to make the journey, but they'd already received a couple of thoughtful cards wishing them well.

As well as Graham's sister and her husband, also going were

Jo and Clare from Merrilies; Tessa, Felicity and Michael; Tessa's daughter, Amber; Annie's parents, Alice and Tom – Mollie had been delighted when they said they'd love to attend – Fran from the tea shop; a couple of boating people Graham and Mollie had become friends with; and a few women Mollie knew well from church and coffee morning.

Despite Felicity saying she didn't want to get serious about anyone until she was in her thirties, she'd been seeing a lot of her policeman boyfriend, Greg. So Mollie invited him too. She wanted to meet the man who seemed to have tamed young Felicity.

***

Graham smiled with joy when he saw Mollie walking down the aisle towards him. He shouldn't have turned to look, but he couldn't help it. She looked delightful. The two girls looked beautiful in their ball gowns, and Michael... Well, Graham had never seen the lad look so smart. They all did him proud and he honestly felt it was the best day of his life so far.

He stood up in the small private room of the restaurant where they were having their reception, and tapped the side of his champagne glass to get everyone's attention.

"I'd like to thank you all for coming and making it a wonderful day, but most of all I'd like to thank Mollie for agreeing to become my wife." He smiled down at her, his eyes full of love. "I'd also like to thank Jo and Clare for opening Merrilies and starting the reading group. Without them, I'd still be living on my own with two cats for company."

Everyone laughed then said, "Ah!"

"I'd like to thank Michael for doing a splendid job of giving Mollie away, and I'd like to say how beautiful Tessa and Felicity look. If only I was forty years younger."

Again, everyone laughed, and Mollie agreed that the girls looked beautiful.

Felicity's boyfriend smiled at her, pulled her close and whispered something in her ear.

"And now," Graham turned to Mollie, "for a little, well-kept surprise." He fished in the inside pocket of his jacket and removed a set of keys which he presented to Mollie. "This, my love, is your dream come true."

Mollie looked blankly at Graham, then at the keys in her hand, then back at Graham.

He laughed at her puzzled face. "You – we – are now the proud owners of a tea room."

Mollie gasped and held her hand against her chest. "You're having me on. Really? I don't believe it. Where?"

"Across the road from Merrilies. Isn't that right, Fran?"

Fran smiled and nodded her confirmation.

"Your tea shop, Fran? No!"

Graham explained. "A couple of months ago, I jokingly told Fran if she ever thought about selling the tea room, to let me know. Well, she *had* been thinking about it, and in the weeks since, we've sorted it all out. You now own Mollie's Olde Tea Shoppe, or whatever you'd like to call it."

"But Fran still works there," Mollie said, looking confused.

"Yes, she agreed to stay on and manage it until we can sort out how we're going to run it, and to help keep the secret."

"Oh Fran, I don't know what to say. Thank you. Thank you so much." Mollie wiped away the tears that streamed down her face.

"I couldn't think of better people to sell it to," Fran said.

Mollie wanted to know who else had been in on the secret.

"Only Jo, and the solicitors handling the sale. Because she lives in the flat above the tea room, Fran and I had to let Jo know what was going on, and that she wouldn't lose her home. But she's done a good job of keeping quiet. Well done, Jo."

Jo smiled across at Mollie and said, "I did let Clare in on it, but swore her to secrecy."

"Well, you both did a good job of staying tight-lipped," Graham said.

Mollie couldn't quite believe it. "I don't know what to say. I must be the happiest person in the world right now. I've married a wonderful man, and my dream of owning a tea room has come true. Thank you all so much for sharing this day with us, and thank you, Graham, for being the kindest, most generous man I know."

As Graham sat down, she gave him a hug.

There were more "Ahs" from everyone.

Then Michael stood up and said, "I'd like to propose a toast."

"Good old Michael!" Felicity shouted.

"Thanks, Flick. I'd like to propose a toast. Everyone hold up your glasses and drink to Mollie, Graham and the new tea shop."

The shout went up, "Mollie, Graham and the new tea shop!"

The small room filled with the sound of happy people chattering, and Mollie looked round the table at all the people she cared about, then at her wonderful new husband – the man who'd made her dreams come true. And, with a contented sigh, she sipped her champagne and looked forward to all that the future held.

The End

Fantastic Books
Great Authors

Meet our authors and discover our
exciting range of books:

- Gripping Thrillers
- Cosy Mysteries
- Romantic Chick-Lit
- Fascinating Historicals
- Exciting Fantasy
- Young Adult and Children's
  Adventures

Visit us at:
www.crookedcatpublishing.com

Join us on facebook:
www.facebook.com/crookedcatpublishing

4111089R00165

Printed in Great Britain
by Amazon.co.uk, Ltd.,
Marston Gate.